THE LEGEND OF POPE JOAN

By Rachel Dax

PART 2. ATHENS

For Jay, Teddy & Muffin

CHAPTER 1

The Seminary Of St Joseph, situated at the foot of Mount Lycabettus, was large and imposing. Yet in spite of its vastness, it was dwarfed by the magnitude and majesty of the Parthenon on the Acropolis that dominated the Athens' skyline.

As soon as Joan entered this scholarly sanctuary, she knew she was home. It was like walking into paradise. The main building contained a library twice as large as her beloved one back in Fulda. Within it were housed books and scrolls, not only of the Christian faith, but also of the great Greek philosophers and even some texts from lands far to the East. In addition to this giant library, there were two great halls—one for public lectures and one for dining, along with several large classrooms where the young seminarians were taught.

Annexed to either side of the main structure were two blocks of sleeping quarters for seminarians, staff, and visiting theologians from across Christendom. Standing on its own to the side of the main building was the seminary chapel which, although humble looking on the outside, was overflowing with colourful iconography within. Beyond the chapel and its small graveyard were various outbuildings, but Father Savas, the man giving them a rudimentary tour, did not take them that far or elaborate upon their purpose.

Joan and Michael had arrived at the seminary late into the teaching day. Michael had been expected—

his father having arranged his attendance with the head of the seminary in Mainz, in order to get him away from home after he had made the 'mistake' with the monk. When they'd arrived, they'd explained to Father Savas that 'John' was a friend from a nearby village who had decided to join him.

Once Father Savas had completed their brief tour, he took them to the largest classroom to meet Father Nikolis who was preparing to teach the last lesson of the day. On seeing them enter, the tall, middle-aged and black-bearded Head of Seminary smiled warmly. "Are you boys from Frankia? I was expecting one, not two!"

Father Savas briefly explained who 'John' was and Father Nikolis smiled warmly. "So you would like to join your friend and train to be a priest?"

Joan nodded shyly. He seemed like a pleasant man but there was no guarantee that he would accept her just because that was her desire.

"Father Helmut from Mainz informed me that young Michael here could read and write in Frankish tongue and also understood rudimentary Greek and Latin. How about you? Have you studied before? Do you even understand me?" the seminary head asked, with a raised eyebrow.

Joan replied in her best Greek, "I am nearly fluent, Father Nikolis. I can read almost anything but my conversation needs a little more practice. I have been taught thoroughly though..."

Father Nikolis started smiling as she spoke, realising just how proficient she was. "And what about you?" he turned to Michael. "Do you understand me as he does or are you just a beginner?"

"Yes, I understand both of you well," Michael stated flatly, with eyes downcast.

Father Nikolis looked at him kindly before turning his attention back to Joan. "What makes you wish to train to be a priest?"

"I adore the scriptures and I love discussing the nature of God. All I want to do is immerse myself in learning. I hope one day to be like you—a scholarly priest who teaches theology."

Father Nikolis smiled at this but had not yet finished asking questions. "And what made you leave Frankia, given that you had such good teaching there?"

Joan panicked for a moment and had to work hard to think of what to say. Then she remembered Amadeus Reichenbach's advice—that in cases where she might have to lie, tell a related truth instead that partially answers the question. In this way she would have no trouble remembering her explanation and also would not sin. "Where we lived in Frankia was a holy area, but parts of it are overrun by barbarians and recently their raids on our villages have become more frequent. Even many of the convents and monasteries have been attacked and in some cases all were slaughtered."

Father Nikolis was sufficiently disturbed by what she had said not to need any more detail and instead put his arm around her shoulder. "Well, you'll be quite safe here, young man. We have had no trouble in over a decade so let this be a sanctuary for you both.

You are more than welcome to join us. We always have room for another intelligent and devoted young man!"

"Thank you," replied Joan, beaming up at him gratefully.

"You may as well sit with us for this lesson and then I'll show you to your cell. You'll have to share. I hope you don't mind?"

"Not at all, Father," she said, desperately trying to disguise her relief.

Michael smiled weakly, and Father Nikolis looked at him with compassionate brown eyes. "Do not worry, young man. I know it is hard leaving home but we are a family here too, and we will look after you in every way we can."

Michael just nodded politely and they moved towards the desks at the front where Father Nikolis indicated they should sit. Joan was brimming with excitement at the thought of starting lessons straight away but Michael could barely contain his distress. Her friend's heart was full of sorrow at parting from his love, and the fact that Joan had been welcomed with open arms meant little to him. Joan was deeply sorry for him and felt another pang of guilt, knowing that she was in part responsible for him being in this condition. But the seminary was already far more than she could have hoped for, so it was hard not to smile in spite of both her guilt and his misery.

Within moments of Joan and Michael sitting down, a flood of young men, aged roughly between fourteen and sixteen, poured into the classroom. The students all carried scrolls and quills which they organised on their desks in keen anticipation of Father Nikolis' lesson. Joan was fascinated to see so many young men just like her wishing to serve the Lord and eager to develop a scholarly mind. As the lesson began, she was instantly absorbed, forgetting all about Michael still in so much anguish beside her.

Father Nikolis was lecturing on the 'Augustinian Theodicy', which was an attempt by the sainted scholar to make sense of why there is evil and suffering in the world. Joan felt extremely fortunate to have had a father who'd taught her so well during their time together. She was already familiar with Augustine's argument and had often discussed its strengths and weaknesses in heated debate—but hearing it afresh now from Father Nikolis was like a gift. He was passionate in his exegesis, and Joan discovered new aspects to the theodicy of which she had previously been ignorant. As Father Nikolis spoke, his warm brown eyes met hers several times and she knew already that she would come to love him dearly and enjoy every moment of his teaching. This made Joan sad for a moment, for the absolute completion of her happiness right now would be if her father were sitting next to her, listening to the scholar lecture and waiting with bated breath to discuss. But as her father was not there, Joan sent a mental thank you to him and a silent prayer of thanks to God for giving him to her. For unbeknownst to him, her father had prepared her to fit in here perfectly.

As she looked around at her classmates, Joan noticed that all of them were fully engaged in the lecture and some even took notes. At the front, on the opposite side of the centre aisle sat a very serious looking young man, perhaps a year older than herself. His hair was slightly lighter than the other boys—dark-brown, rather than black—and his features, although not unpleasant, were sharper than most. He was taking copious notes and seemed to hang on Father Nikolis' every word. Joan wished that she, like him, had a quill and scroll. She had never studied in this way, but instantly saw the value of it; for after the lecture, she could take away her notations and think more about the questions that had arisen. As she was observing him, the boy must have sensed her curiosity and looked up. Their eyes met and Joan was instantly taken aback. Instead of returning her smile, the young man glared at her as though annoyed. Embarrassed, Joan quickly turned her attention back towards the lecturer, trying to catch up with what she had missed through distraction.

"So St. Augustine concluded that because we were all seminally present in Adam, we therefore must all be born corrupted by his sin. What consequence does this have for us as human beings?" asked Father Nikolis.

The brown-haired boy's arm immediately shot up in the air and Father Nikolis nodded for him to answer.

"All of us are guilty and deserve to be punished."

"That is correct, Benedict. And what form does this punishment take?"

"Disease, pestilence and great acts of wrath such as earthquakes and floods. Then for women, who are doubly evil, bleeding and childbirth."

"And why did Augustine argue that women are doubly evil?"

"Because it was Eve who gave into the Devil's temptation and ate the forbidden fruit from the tree of knowledge. Therefore, women *deserve* even greater punishment."

Joan felt herself squirm from both Benedict's words and Father Nikolis' passive acceptance of them. Suddenly she found her own hand darting up to refute what had been said. "But that's not the only interpretation," she argued nervously, feeling self-conscious at the sound of her own voice. "To say that we are all born evil and guilty because Adam and Eve sinned thousands of years ago makes our Lord sound like a monster. Surely Irenaeus was correct in thinking that evil is present in the world to help us grow into wise and responsible beings, capable of having a genuine relationship with God—not as a punishment for other people's wrongs."

Father Nikolis looked at Joan and raised an eyebrow but did not reply, allowing Benedict to refute the challenge instead. "But, 'new boy', Rome has rejected that view in favour of Augustine's position because Irenaeus suggested that God is partly responsible for evil which, as He is completely good, He clearly cannot be."

"I disagree," retorted Joan, now becoming excited and feeling empowered by the intellectual engagement. "I think Augustine makes our loving Lord sound vengeful and cruel, whereas Irenaeus reveals there is ultimate purpose in our sufferings for the spiritual and mental growth of all—both men and women alike. Why would an omnibenevolent and loving God create a world containing so much pain, if this did not to lead to a greater good?"

Benedict tried to find an answer but had obviously been challenged too far and responded with a string of 'buts' and 'erms' that eventually ended in embarrassed silence.

"It seems you have some competition, young Benedict," interjected Father Nikolis, seeing his pupil lost for words. "We will continue this debate tomorrow for there is much more to be said from both standpoints. All of you come prepared to discuss John's question. I want to hear everyone's thoughts. Class dismissed."

Benedict glared at Joan fiercely, before picking up his belongings and marching out of the classroom, alone. She was saddened by this, for he was clearly an intelligent student, and she had enjoyed debating with him even though she'd disagreed with his views.

Whilst they waited quietly for Father Nikolis to gather his scrolls and texts, Joan noticed that although she herself was elated by their first lecture, Michael was no happier than before. Joan felt guilty again then. Her dream had come true just as his had been shattered. It seemed so unfair. She hoped desperately that over time his heart would heal and he would come to like it here as much as she did already.

"So," asked Father Nikolis, indicating they should walk next to him. "Who taught you to argue like that?"

"My father. He loved debating theology more than anything else. He was originally going to be a teacher like you, Father, but then he met my mother and decided to marry and become a missionary priest instead," Joan answered honestly.

Father Nikolis smiled. "He must be very proud that his son has followed in his footsteps. What a shame that your lands are overrun with barbarians. I'm sure he will miss watching you grow up to be just like him."

"I will miss him too, but it is much safer for both Michael and I to be here rather than there," Joan answered, touching Michael's arm briefly as she spoke.

Michael forced a polite smile but still could not engage. Father Nikolis, however, continued to be unfazed by Michael's sorrowful demeanour, probably having dealt with many a new boy overwhelmed by leaving home for the first time and not seeing it as anything out of the ordinary.

When they reached their allotted cell, Joan's happiness could not have been greater. The small stone room had two beds, a high window and a solid wooden door with a lock and key. She would have absolute privacy to continue with her guise as a boy. What's more, there was even a small hole in one corner which led to a channel that carried waste water straight to the river. According to Father Nikolis, this was called a 'sewer'—a thing that she had never seen in Austrasia or anywhere along their journey through Frankia, but apparently had been used in Greece for over a thousand years.

The seminarians were given a bucket for washing and a bucket for urination and the 'sewer' was where they would empty them as necessary. Joan was filled with relief, for it meant that when she bled each month she would be able to wash both herself and her rags, disposing of the evidence immediately. The only place where she would have to be careful was in the communal defecation area that Father Nikolis had briefly pointed to on the way to their cell. This was a roofless four-sided building, edged with a low stone shelf that had a series of holes cut out of it. Thankfully though, she would be wearing her robes when she used it and so long as she was not careless, her body would remain hidden.

Having shown Joan and Michael their cell, Father Nikolis left them to settle in, explaining that a bell would ring when dinner was ready. Then after that, they would be expected to attend evening Mass in the Chapel. The rest of the seminarians were doing their work duty until dinnertime, but Joan and Michael were allowed to rest from their journey and their jobs would be discussed tomorrow.

Once the door to their cell was shut and Father Nikolis' footsteps could no longer be heard, Joan let out a whoop of joy and ran to hug Michael. God had led her to the perfect place. There had been nothing, so far, that was cause for alarm or posed a threat, and she was full to the brim with happiness.

Michael, however, was unable to celebrate and although he returned the hug, it was stiff and awkward.

As soon as they moved apart, he lay down on the bed, facing the wall and pulled his hood over his head.

"I'm so sorry, Michael," Joan whispered softly, realising once more the depth of his pain.

"I just need to sleep for a while," her friend replied.

But as Joan moved across to her own bed, she could tell from the gentle shuddering of Michael's body that he was silently weeping for his lost love and her own heart became heavy again.

*

Joan and Michael were the only students from Frankia currently studying at the Seminary Of St Joseph, and they made sure that during their first communal meal, they sat together at the far end of the long table nearest the back wall. They were polite to their fellow diners but did not attempt to make friends. Joan had been advised by Amadeus to keep a 'friendly distance' from students and teachers alike. Getting to know anyone too well would lead to questions being asked about her past, which might cause her difficulties. She let Michael do most of the talking, and when they addressed one another they did so in Frankish tongue, to reinforce their separateness. Michael seemed just as happy with this strategy as she was, for he had his own secrets to keep.

Later, they adopted a similar approach during Mass by sitting at the far end of the back pew. Father Nikolis, now dressed in robes of white rather than black, led the service. In the candlelight, the faces of the saints in the icons and mosaics covering the walls seemed ablaze. This small chapel was so much more lavish than her village church in Frankia where only simple images of Jesus, Mary and the disciples were painted on lime-washed walls. Even compared to the Cathedrals of Mainz and Fulda, this was more decorative and ornate. Joan loved it though. The chapel design seemed only to enhance the notion of a sanctuary dedicated to glorifying the magnificence of God, and as the chorus of holy voices resounded from the walls, Joan felt uplifted by the colourful environment. Participating in the Blessed Sacrament and feeling the Holy Spirit so viscerally as she sipped the blood of Christ, sealed Joan's belief that the Deity Himself had a special purpose in allowing her to join these men in His service.

After Mass, Michael too seemed lighter in spirits so Joan suggested that before returning to their cell for the night, they take a walk by the river Eridanos, which created a natural boundary along one side of the seminary grounds. As they strolled in the setting sun, everything glowed with burnished oranges and reds and the air was perfectly still. It was by no means warm, but the early winter temperature was not unpleasant and Joan felt anointed through all of her senses. On reaching the trees, they stopped and looked back, taking in the magnitude of the city. The Parthenon, now turned pink from the sunset, crowned Athens in all of its glory. Whilst they stood there together, overwhelmed by the breathtaking sight, Joan put her arm around Michael's waist and leant her head on his shoulder. Michael was stiff for a moment but then relaxed and let his head rest on hers.

"He would love it here," he whispered.

CHAPTER 2

Joan slept deeply that first night and was bleary eyed when the bell rang to wake the seminarians the next morning. She hauled herself out of bed and dunked her face in the water bowl that lay on the stand in the corner of the cell, before turning her attention to Michael. Like yesterday afternoon, her friend was lying facing the wall with his hood over his head.

"Come on, Michael," she pleaded in a low voice, knowing he was awake but did not want to get up.

"I'll be with you in a minute," he replied gruffly, pulling the blanket more tightly around his shoulders.

Joan stared down at her friend, not knowing quite what to do. Part of her wanted to climb onto the bed and hold him, but she suspected that, rather than giving comfort, this might exacerbate Michael's feeling of not being with the person he loved. So instead, she offered up a silent prayer that God would mend his heart soon. Then she returned to the water bowl and finished washing, ready for the day ahead.

Once she was done, Joan went off for her first visit to the communal latrines. It made her nervous having to go there but, equally, shitting in the tiny hole in their cell, which was only intended for pouring away water, would be both impractical and undignified. Such a thing would test even Michael's tolerance of her situation. So she really had no choice.

On reaching the latrines, Joan saw that three other young men and one of the priests were already defecating. No one made eye contact; rather, they stared at the ground just ahead of them as they went about their business. Joan noticed that each held a stick with a piece of rounded cloth at one end. Looking around, she spotted a small heap of sticks, all with the same strange-looking cloth attached. She knew what these were for, however. Once one had relieved oneself, the material on the end of the stick was used to clean one's private parts. Joan noticed one of the students dipping his stick into a thin channel of water that ran in front of the latrines and instantly saw the cleverness of the design. Rather than having to use several pieces of cloth, one could clean off a single piece in the water as many times as necessary.

Joan collected one of the pre-prepared sticks and noticed that the unfamiliar material stuck on the end was disconcertingly hard and rough. On choosing a corner latrine, she looked around anxiously and then put one hand under her robe and managed to pull down her braies, whilst using the other hand to make sure that the outer garment did not rise too high. At the same time, she said a mental 'thank you' to Amadeus for creating a harness for her phallus, which remained securely in place rather than falling to the ground. Then she sat and evacuated.

Afterwards, Joan pointed the end of her stick towards the channel at her feet and watched, incredulous, as the unfamiliar material expanded twofold, sucking up water through countless tiny holes.

To her surprise, when she touched the rounded mass, it was now as soft as silk. It took her several moments to work out how she was going to apply the said object without pulling up her robe to reveal all. Eventually, she concluded that if she put one foot up on the edge of the latrine nearest the corner wall and quickly shoved up the stick, she would be all right. She glanced around again to check if she was being watched but no one was paying her any attention, so she went ahead with the plan. Joan managed one wipe before the strange cloth fell into the latrine and was lost forever. Thankfully, it did not feel like she needed more. *Lord help me if I ever have an upset stomach,* she said to herself, whilst mentally assessing the odds of discovery if she went into the trees for this purpose and used leaves to clean herself, just as she had during her journey through Frankia.

When she returned to her cell, Michael was up and nearly ready. "Did you use that strange cloth when you went to the latrines last night?" she asked.

"Yes," he replied. "I asked one of the boys what it was. It's called 'sponge' apparently and it grows like a plant in the sea."

"Oh...how odd!"

As Michael finished washing, the bell rang again and they made their way across to the dining hall for breakfast where they were given bread, honey and goat milk. They sat again at the furthest end of the room, responding politely when people wished them 'good morning', but not engaging in direct conversation.

Morning Mass was taken by a young priest named Father Pavlos. It was a shorter service than the night before, concentrating on the sacrament itself, with just one hymn sung at the very end. Nonetheless, it was a beautiful experience, and once again Joan felt the presence of God enveloping her as she participated.

In the short break after Mass, before the day's lessons commenced, Joan and Michael met with Father Nikolis to determine which classes would be appropriate for them to join. He explained that class one consisted of boys aged twelve to thirteen, along with some older students who were just beginning their theological studies. The fourteen to fifteen year olds and students with a rudimentary understanding of theology were in class two; and class three contained sixteen to eighteen year olds and those ready for advanced learning.

On realising they might be separated, Joan looked at her friend in panic. Michael, however, smiled at her reassuringly, before quietly addressing Father Nikolis on their behalf. "I am only just sixteen and John is fourteen," he said, stretching the truth about their ages. "So could we both be in that intermediate class we saw yesterday, please?"

The seminary head was thoughtful in his response. "Hmm. I can see that you don't feel confident enough for the older class yet, Michael. But are *you* ready, John, to join the intermediate class?" he asked, turning his attention to her.

"Although John is younger,' Michael interjected, "he's had far more education than me because his father is a priest. So, I think we are at about the same level."

Father Nikolis spoke directly to Joan again. "You are clearly well-schooled in theology, but are you as advanced in the many other subjects we study here, in order to participate fully in those?" he asked.

"Yes, very much so," she replied, eagerly.

"Then, so long as you both thrive, that's the class you'll be in."

The curriculum was vast and included Theology, Biblical Exegesis, Pastoral Studies, Ethics, Canon Law, Philosophy of Religion, Philosophy of the Ancients, Literature, History and Mathematics. Joan looked forward to all of these except the latter, which she dreaded. For no matter how hard she'd tried when being taught by her father, apart from the basics, she'd found the art of numbers beyond her scope.

In addition to their formal studies, students were also expected to learn an art or craft and take on a particular job to help the seminary sustain itself and learn the value of work. And these were to be decided upon by the end of the day.

*

"Are you sure you want to learn calligraphy, young man?" asked Father Amos, an elderly priest with a curve in his back from years of bending over parchments.

"Yes," replied Joan, nervously, glancing down at her pathetic looking attempt at illuminating the letter 'J'.

"I can see straight away that you have absolutely no natural aptitude for this art form. It will take you a year to get to the stage a talented beginner could reach in a week."

Joan glared at the older man, annoyed by his swift and negative judgement of her. She had to struggle to be polite. "I have always excelled at everything I have done. I see no reason why one day, with plenty of hard work and practice, I could not also reach excellence in this as well, Father Amos," she replied gruffly.

The old man rolled his eyes in despair. "Very well, boy. It's up to you, but don't expect your work to be distributed to the monasteries any time soon..."

Joan had to resist the urge to yank the priest's long grey beard in response to this insult and instead pressed her hands to her knees. Thankfully, her derogator moved swiftly on to another student, but for a while after he left her, Joan just sat there feeling cross and humiliated. She was not used to such criticism and it hurt.

During her first Biblical Exegesis class earlier that day, she had impressed Father Theophilus with her extensive knowledge of the Book of Ecclesiastes and her analysis of its myriad messages. Like Father Nikolis, he could see she had been taught well prior to joining them. Then, in Father Nikolis' lesson, as promised, the discussion from the day before had continued. Each of the fifteen young men in her class, including Michael, had given their views on Saint Augustine's attempt to resolve the problem of evil and suffering, and Joan had fiercely debated with each one of them, revelling in every moment. The only student who had displayed negativity towards her was Benedict whom she had defeated the day before. He had scowled at her throughout the entire lesson. But it didn't bother her. What mattered to Joan was that she had impressed Father Nikolis again and this is what she intended to do for the rest of her time there.

Now as she sat there in Father Amos' studio, having failed to impress, she did not know what to do with herself. It was hard not to feel instant dislike towards the man for having pointed out her inadequacies so brutally. What's more, Michael was not there to sympathise with her because he had chosen to learn the lute for his artistic lesson instead. Joan looked around the room. Most of the young men were deep in concentration and no one spoke except when addressed by Father Amos. She then looked back to the parchment before her. *If I can learn in less than a week to convince the world I am a boy when really I am a girl, then I can learn how to make my writing look pretty and to draw and colour in fancy big letters!*

And so she started again. This time twice as carefully.

*

After classes finished at three o'clock, Joan was excited to investigate every inch of the Seminary Of St Joseph. Michael, although still quiet, was willing to explore with her, and together they discovered several new parts of the complex, each serving a different purpose.

At the far end of the grounds, next to the river, was the area where the washerwoman did her work. Copious lines of white, black and light brown robes swayed together in the gentle breeze along with braies and camisia. Joan and Michael had been told to sew their initials into all of their garments so that the washerwoman, Mrs Andropolous, would know who to give them back to each time she was done.

The elderly woman, dressed in the attire of a widow, was on her knees by the river scrubbing a white robe with soap when Joan and Michael introduced themselves. She was polite but distant, so they did not linger in her presence, realising it was not fitting for them to converse with her at any length. Her cottage lay at the furthest point from the seminary building, not far from the edge of the woods, and its windows and door faced the river rather than the grounds, delineating her as the only woman at the institution, separate from everyone else.

Joan and Michael received an entirely different reception when they entered the medicine kitchen, run by a grey-haired priest with a kindly face, by the name of Father Takis. He welcomed them warmly, showing them an array of homegrown herbs hanging from the rafters and explaining their medicinal usage. At the far end of the giant kitchen were half a dozen beds, which Father Takis explained were for treating the sick in emergencies and during outbreaks of disease. There were also several private cells behind the kitchen where people with long-term afflictions could stay so they were nearby the older priest and his assistant, Father Stefanos. As they were talking, a small white cat appeared and began rubbing itself against Michael's leg. For the first time since being in the mountains with Amadeus, Joan saw Michael's smile reach his eyes.

"He likes you, Michael," said Father Takis. "You are honoured. Normally he snubs my guests. Would you like to give him a saucer of goat milk?"

"Yes, please," replied Michael, bending down and petting the cat, who purred at him appreciatively. The priest went to the table and removed the lid from a terracotta jug. He poured the white liquid into a small dish and handed it to Michael, who knelt down on the floor, stroking the cat's back as it drank.

Father Takis looked at Michael fondly. "Do you like being around animals?" he asked.

"Yes, very much. My parents were farmers and we raised animals for both work and food."

"And do you know about growing vegetables and herbs too?"

"Yes. We all worked on the farm from infancy."

"Well, if you would like to work here, we desperately need another pair of hands. Father Stefanos and I cannot cope with the demand of looking after all of the animals and growing enough food for everyone to eat, on top of preparing medicines for those who fall sick. And the boys who work in the food kitchen do not have enough time to work in here as well. We used to have proper help on the farm from a layman, Mr.

Andropolous, who did all the building maintenance for the seminary, but since he passed away six years ago, they've not replaced him, and it has been left for us to do all the work, even fixing the fences. The last seminarian working in here was ordained a few months back and given a church of his own. Since then we have found no one to help us. Everyone is too busy with other work. We would welcome a young man with your background in farming. Would you be interested in joining us here?"

Michael looked around again at the herbs, hanging from the kitchen ceiling and then back at the cat who had nearly finished its milk. "Yes. I think I would like to join you very much," he replied, looking pleased.

Joan felt a huge weight slip from her shoulders. Since her arrival at this holiest of places, she had been deeply concerned for the well-being of her friend. Now she knew that he would be all right. It would take a long time for his heart to recover, but Michael could flourish here and one day heal.

"What about you?" Father Takis asked her hopefully. "Would you also like to work here, John?"

Joan considered his offer for a moment. It was tempting. She thought back to Sister Hildegund who had treated Amadeus so expertly when he was in peril. She had been so impressed by the woman and her skill that she had almost been tempted to abandon her guise as a boy just so she could live in the nun's presence. But learning the herbs was still not as inviting as the possibility of a job in the library, where she knew they also needed help, so politely Joan declined.

Father Takis then showed them around the farm, now paying special attention to Michael who had agreed to start work there the following afternoon. As well as rows of vegetables and herbs of every kind, there was an ample herd of goats in a small enclosed field and a flock of chickens in a large wooden coop. Further along from there, was an orchard where olives, dates, figs, lemons and oranges grew. To the side of the orchard were several beehives, which Father Takis explained were tended by another priest and his seminarian assistant. They produced propolis and honey for medicines and food, in addition to brewing mead for everyone to drink and making all the candles. The seminary was, according to Takis, almost self-sustaining. The only thing they did not grow themselves was grain, which they bought at market.

Michael looked at home on the farm before he'd even started. Joan knew that learning the herbs would also appeal to him because it was something Amadeus had done when he too had been shattered inside from losing his first true love. In doing so, Michael would feel closer to him. This was also why, she suspected, he had chosen to learn a musical instrument as his artistic pursuit. He wanted to feel Amadeus' presence in everything he did and not lose his memory of the incredible man whom he had loved so very much.

*

The next day, Joan had her first lesson in Mathematics. So far, she had excelled in all aspects of her academic work, only receiving criticism for her failings in the art of Calligraphy and Illumination.

She was nervous even as she entered the classroom. When Father Philon, a man approximately fifteen years older than herself, announced that today they would be studying the geometry of Euclid, Joan's heart sank. She could manage adding, subtracting, dividing and multiplying. With much effort, she had eventually mastered Pythagoras' Theorem that the square on the hypotenuse of a triangle is equal to the sum of the square of the other two sides. Euclid, however, took the whole notion of geometry much further and Joan dreaded what was to come.

By the time Father Philon had drawn his third triangle on the large rectangular slate at the front of the classroom, Joan's mind was completely blurred. His words were floating around her head like pollen in a breeze and she felt lost.

"So," Father Philon asked the class. "How do we remember the 'parallel postulate'?"

Joan watched as every boy in the class, except for her, raised his hand, and she was immediately overcome with shame at her ineptitude. To make matters worse, as soon as this feeling of inadequacy arose, Father Philon homed in on it. He looked at her sternly as he spoke. "New boy, remind me of your name."

"John, Father..." Joan almost whispered, sensing everyone's eyes upon her.

"Ah, yes, John of Frankia. Well, John, your friend sitting next to you has his hand in the air along with the rest of the class. So why don't you?"

Unable to make words, Joan stared down at the parchment where her badly drawn copy of the last meaningless triangle was scratched. But soon she realised she had made a mistake by not answering, for the priest came over and slammed his hand so hard on the desk that the vibration echoed around the room several times. The man looked at her fiercely. "Is this how they behave in Frankia? How dare you ignore a question asked you by your teacher!" he boomed.

Joan's shame multiplied thrice over as she tried unsuccessfully to form an apology. She was mortified and did not know what to do with herself. She would have run from the classroom but Michael, seeing her distress, quickly intervened. "Sorry, Father Philon, but we do not learn this subject back in Frankia. John here is an expert in Theology and Philosophy, but has never studied Mathematics other than adding up and subtracting. I only know about Euclid's Elements because a monk I knew had a special interest and taught me."

This, of course, was a barefaced lie but the priest seemed to believe him. "Ah, yes," said Father Philon, turning to the class with a mocking smile. "You come from a land of uneducated barbarians. I had forgotten. It is a wonder that either of you can read and write."

At this, the class erupted with laughter. Joan was so furious at the insult that she was about to explode. But once again, Michael saved the day by pinching her hard on the leg and shaking his head for her not to respond. So instead, Joan returned her gaze to the parchment and gripped the sides of the desk to contain her anger.

Father Philon then pointed at Benedict who, Joan noticed, now had a look of deep satisfaction on his face. "Benedict, you are not from Athens either. Did they teach you Mathematics in the Lombard Kingdom or are you from a nation of half-wits as well?"

Benedict blushed slightly, but smiled. "I do indeed understand Mathematics, Father Philon. I had an excellent education in the Lombard Kingdom and, of course, from Father Alexios for two years before joining this class."

"So perhaps you might like to enlighten our young barbarian here as to the somewhat simple axiom that Euclid devised which we refer to as the 'parallel postulate'."

Benedict was smug and made sure he smirked at Joan as he spoke, "Euclid said, 'That, if a straight line falling on two straight lines make the interior angles on the same side less than two right angles, the two straight lines, if produced indefinitely, meet on that side on which are the angles less than the two right angles.'"

"Thank you, Benedict. I am glad that we have only one ignoramus amongst us!"

Joan was beside herself with rage. It was only because Michael's hand was pressed firmly on her leg that she did not get up and storm out. Thankfully though, Father Philon returned to his lecture and left her alone. The rest of the lesson seemed to go on for all eternity as Joan sat in an angry fog, willing the torment to end.

But it was not over yet, for when the session finished, Father Philon ordered both Joan and Michael to stay behind.

"I cannot have you in my class if you are ignorant. You will need to join the twelve year olds taught by Father Alexios," he stated, looking at her with disdain.

Then he addressed Michael. "Do you know enough to keep up or should I put you in the infant class as well?"

Michael, Joan saw, took a deep breath before answering. "I understood the lesson perfectly today, Father Philon, so I hope to manage well."

With a flick of his hand, the priest indicated they should leave, and Joan found herself being firmly ushered out of the classroom by Michael, who knew she was about to lose her decorum.

Once they were outside, instead of joining their classmates who were making the most of the short break between lessons, Joan marched off in the direction of the woods.

"Calm down, John!" Michael urged as he matched her pace. "You'll draw too much attention to yourself if you show your anger publicly."

"That's why I'm going to the woods, stupid!" she snapped, almost breaking into a run.

Michael did not speak again for a few minutes until they were under the tree cover and Joan had begun violently kicking a trunk. "You'll break a toe, Pickle," he stated flatly.

"I don't care!" she shouted.

"The tree might, though," her friend replied.

Instantly guilty about the tree, Joan stopped kicking and turned to face him angrily.

"I want to go back to Frankia!" she declared.

"No, you don't! You're being ridiculous."

"I do. I'm a failure and everyone thinks I'm a dunce…"

"Heavens above! So you can't draw pretty letters and you might have to work hard to understand Geometry. It's not the end of the world, Pickle."

"But they all think I'm a half-wit now. How can I possibly study here when people perceive me as such?"

"People do not think you are a half-wit. It is obvious to everyone that you are as sharp as a knife. Look at how you out-manoeuvred each of your classmates in Father Nikolis' session yesterday and how insightful you were in each of your other lessons. You can't expect to be brilliant at everything."

"Yes, I can! And that Father Philon is a bastard! I want to go home. This whole thing has been a dreadful mistake!"

"Now you are being a child, Pickle, *and* you are making me cross. I did not bring you all this way and leave behind the love of my life for you to run off at the first sign of difficulty. You insult me by taking such an attitude! No one excels at everything. Think about all the other students here. Would you believe them unintelligent if they were good at everything except one academic subject and an artistic pursuit?"

Joan, finally seeing reason, shook her head.

"Well, there you have it. You are outstanding at everything except Mathematics and Calligraphy. Is that really grounds to go home?"

Joan shook her head again.

"If Amadeus were here, he'd give you a slap for being so silly," Michael stated.

"No, he would not!" she replied. "But I concede that he would have told me off much worse than you have."

She found herself smiling a little then. Amadeus would probably have given her some task to perform that demonstrated why she needed to learn her lesson and not have let up until he was sure she had.

"I'm sorry, Michael. I did not mean to upset you...but...do you think Father Philon hates me?" she asked.

"Of course not! Why would he hate you? He doesn't even know you. He is probably mean to many a student who doesn't understand. Not everyone has the patience of your father or the kindliness of Father Nikolis. Anyway, it looks like you won't be taught by him for a while, now you're moving to the other class."

"It's so embarrassing..." she grumbled.

"Well, at least I made up a good excuse. People will think that it's because you have never learned it before and not because you're actually useless at it!" Michael laughed.

Insulted, Joan gave him a shove which made him laugh all the more until finally she saw the funny side of it too, and joined in. Then he turned serious again. "Come on, we'll be late for next lesson if we stay here any longer."

CHAPTER 3

Joan did not miss being a girl. In fact she loved living as a boy in an all male environment. She had never enjoyed the company of the other girls in her village and had always been a misfit, but here at the seminary she felt like she belonged. The only thing she missed from her life in Frankia was her father. That she really might never see him again did cause her sadness. Joan thought of him, particularly when she learned something new and wanted to know his opinion. She felt bereft that she would never actually hear it.

However, Joan barely thought of her mother at all, or her brothers and sisters. She wished them well but she had never felt connected to them in the way she had her father. The thought of returning home to live amongst them and then marrying and bearing infants of her own still filled her with horror. It would be a life without study, a life without scripture. Nothing but drudgery, childbirth and misery.

Although she had only spent a few short months with Amadeus Reichenbach, Joan felt his absence more keenly than that of her own family. Unlike Michael, she had not been in love with Amadeus. However, the man had changed her life and taught her the skills she needed in order to survive in this masculine environment undetected. Without his training, Joan would have given herself away a thousand times by now. He had saved her from an existence that she could not bear and had provided the means necessary to embrace the life she wanted above all else. And, she loved him for it.

It was hard seeing Michael still in so much pain. At first, Joan had wanted to talk about Amadeus all of the time, but had soon realised that this only made things worse. It was a good thing that she'd had no idea what it meant for two people in love to be separated from one another before actually witnessing this level of emotional agony. Had she known what it would do to her friend, she would never have let him leave. Joan also knew that even Michael had not realised the magnitude of his future devastation and that if he could do it all over again, he would not have left either.

One evening, three weeks after they had arrived at the scholarly institution, Joan had come back to their cell to find Michael weeping uncontrollably. Overwhelmed with sorrow and guilt, she had told him she could manage there alone if he wanted to go back to join his love. If all had gone to plan, Amadeus would still be a winter guest at the Hospice run by the Sisters Of The Virgin Mother, on the mountain in Bavaria.

"But you won't manage," Michael had replied. "You survive now because I am like a shield. I do most of the talking and interacting on our behalves. Without me, you'd struggle to maintain a friendly distance. Besides, you'd have to share a cell with someone else and that would be a living nightmare. The only way we can guarantee your safety, is if I stay here too."

"But I cannot bear to see you in such pain," she had countered.

"It's not your fault. You tried to find solutions that would enable us to be together. It was Amadeus who refused to see the possibility in them."

"He didn't want you to come to harm. He loved you too much to endanger you," Joan had reminded him.

"I know. But did he know that *this* would kill me too?"

At that, Michael had started weeping again and this time she'd wrapped her arms around him and rocked him deep into the night.

*

It had not taken Joan long to recover from her first two glimpses of failure with Mathematics and Calligraphy, and she soon came to accept that she could not be top of the class for everything. Joining Father Alexios' class for Mathematics had actually been a good thing because the subject was taught at a level and in a manner that suited her, and eventually she began to understand concepts that she had struggled with back in Frankia, as well as embrace those that were new to her. What's more, Father Alexios was gentle and kind with his students; so on the occasions where she faltered, she did not feel shame in asking for more clarity.

Her Calligraphy and Illumination lessons were another matter. She really was untalented. Nonetheless, Joan was determined not to give up. She had no desire to learn a musical instrument for her artistic pursuit, and her drawing and painting skills were far worse than her Calligraphy. Some of the young seminarians learned to perform tales of the saints and stories from scripture, just like Amadeus Reichenbach had in Frankia. Joan would have loved this but on discussing it with Michael, they'd agreed it would be far too dangerous. She might reveal her female physicality when taking on different characters, so she decided to stick with the Calligraphy instead. Even though she was very unskilled at the art, she did get some enjoyment out of copying scripture. As she laboured over each letter, she thought deeply about its meaning for herself and the world. Father Amos remained critical of everything she produced but although this wounded her deeply at first, she gradually got used to it and came to expect nothing less.

In addition to her studies, she had been given her desired job in the library and loved it. Joan took great pleasure from organising and maintaining the books, scrolls, and parchments. The Head of Library, Father Dimitrios was a quiet and studious man, just past the prime of life. He taught her how to handle and store each document not just with care, but also with love. He was delighted to have an assistant with the same degree of passion and reverence for the texts as himself. Within a few weeks, Joan knew every nook and cranny of the great library and felt it was the very heart of her home. Most days, once her librarian duties were complete, instead of socialising with the other boys or returning to her cell, Joan would sit in her favourite corner and read there until the bell rang for dinner.

Michael had thrown himself into his job on the farm, working many more hours than required. Joan knew that tending the animals, growing herbs and learning how to make medicines was her friend's way of keeping himself occupied so he would not go insane from loss. She was glad that he had this distraction, as witnessing him suffer relentlessly without anything to assuage the pain would have been too overwhelming.

Joan was not perturbed by the fact that they now spent a significant portion of each day apart from one another. For the activities she had chosen that were separate from Michael's did not require her to talk much or make friends. The library was a silent area and calligraphy was such a delicate affair, that the members of her class barely breathed unless they dared ask assistance from Father Amos.

She also spent more time in the chapel than Michael did. As well as the twice daily Mass, almost all of the seminarians would go there for personal prayer. However, Joan, still concerned that she might have committed a grave sin by continuing with her deception as a boy, ensured that she made an extra effort. After Evening Mass, she would remain behind, giving prayers of thanks and asking the Holy Spirit to enfold her. Without fail, on each request she would be filled to the brim with love as she had whilst travelling through the mountains of Frankia. So long as this kept happening, she would trust that God was blessing her and giving His permission to carry on.

Her theological and philosophical learning grew exponentially, and Joan became increasingly confident in debate—much to the annoyance of Benedict who fiercely challenged her every word. At first, Joan thought this antipathy towards her was merely academic, but after a few days of being at the seminary, she realised it was deeper than that. On several occasions, whilst caught up in a crowd, she'd been pinched or pushed more aggressively than expected from everyday student hustle and bustle. Each time she had looked around to see Benedict nearby and in spite of his innocent demeanour, she knew it was he who had assaulted her. Joan refrained from telling Michael, for she did not want to alarm him when he was still in such a fragile state. But as a result of these physical attacks, Joan avoided Benedict at all costs, apart from in the classroom where she continued to engage with him in fearless intellectual battles. Thankfully, Benedict's cell was in the block on the other side of the main complex; he did not do Calligraphy and Illumination and when she saw him in the library, there was little he could say or do without drawing attention to himself.

Joan returned to her cell late each evening, excited and vital from the day's pursuits and climbing into bed, she would be overwhelmed with a burning need for physical release. She had become so addicted to it during her time alone in the back of Amadeus' wagon whilst travelling to Venice that she literally ached for it again now. At first she had not dared touch herself, fearing that Michael might hear and be disgusted by her doing it in his presence. But soon her need was so great that she was fit to burst. One night, after several long weeks of abstinence, when Michael had fallen asleep, Joan finally gave in to her unfulfilled desire as silently as possible. Her fantasies flipped between the memory of the servant wench with copious breasts who'd so nearly seduced her at the tavern in Frankia, and the thought of what Michael and Amadeus would be doing with one another right now if they could be together. Sometimes she imagined both things happening at once.

For a good while, this became her habit. She would lie quietly until Michael fell asleep and then relieve herself as subtly as she could. Then, one night, as she lay waiting silently in the dim light of their cell, Joan noticed that Michael's hand was moving under his blankets and realised he was fulfilling the same need. Tingling more than ever at the sight of the movement in the shadows, she waited breathlessly for him to climax and then sleep. When she finally touched herself, she was already saturated.

This continued nightly for a while and each time she witnessed his pleasuring, Joan became more aroused, sometimes barely able to wait for Michael to finish. She thought her friend was oblivious to her own actions until one night, assuming he had fallen asleep unspent, she started rubbing her phallus gently whilst massaging her centre with her fingers. As her rhythm grew, she became aware of a rustling noise. She stopped abruptly. Across the cell, she saw Michael staring at the mound she had created under her covers and giving himself pleasure. Realising he was caught, Michael halted too. Their eyes met in the moonlight. Joan, shocked but excited, nodded her assent and Michael's focus returned to where her hands were. Together they tentatively carried on until first he, then she, reached crescendo.

From then on, pleasuring themselves in tandem became their unspoken routine. Most nights she would wait for him to start and then join in hungrily and without shame. Joan did not desire Michael and felt certain he did not desire her either. However, watching him touch himself was doubly arousing and she assumed this was the same for him. It was exciting and gave them the freedom to touch themselves more vigorously. No longer did they have to be quiet or subtle, nor afraid of becoming breathless or whimpering from release…

CHAPTER 4

Over two years had passed since they had joined the Seminary Of St Joseph, and Joan, now nearly sixteen, could not remember ever feeling happier. She was so used to being treated as a boy and living in a male environment that the only time Joan remembered she was a woman was when she bled once a month. For even at night under the covers, she rubbed the phallus in her braies as though it were her own body part and it did not feel alien to her.

Joan was a natural scholar. The only academic subject she still struggled with at times was Mathematics. However, since rejoining Father Philon's group in recent weeks, even he treated her with greater respect because she was now more adept and had an excellent reputation as a student.

Generally, Joan was head and shoulders above the rest of the students in her class, even Benedict, her greatest competitor. Every day brought new joy and she loved everything about the vocation she pursued. She was certain, more than ever before, that becoming a scholarly priest was the only path for her.

Now, as members of the older class, some of their curriculum involved debating theological matters in the Great Hall with a public audience as well as the entire body of students and staff. Word had begun to spread of the didactic skill of 'Young John of Frankia' and over time the the public audience had grown from a handful of old men to an enthusiastic score of regulars who visited each Friday morning to hear 'John' speak.

"Do you believe there are different levels of sin or is all sin equally abhorrent in the eyes of the Lord?" asked one of the men at the end of her lecture on the purifying power of Christ's death.

"I believe our Lord examines the motivations of our hearts and judges accordingly. For example, if a poor man steals to feed his children, of course he has broken a sacred commandment, but is it not a greater sin for him to allow his family to starve? Therefore, in this case, surely our Heavenly Father would forgive such a transgression with little need for penance?"

"Do you believe it is sinful for women to participate in affairs of the Church?" asked a different man.

"It is our responsibility as men to treat women with respect and allow them to fulfil their potential whether intellectual, spiritual or domestic. For look at our Lord Jesus, did he not give Mary Magdalene a place at his side along with the disciples?"

"But," interjected Benedict, "did not St Paul forbid women to speak in church, but rather discuss spiritual matters with their husbands afterwards? Surely by allowing women to meddle with affairs of the Church, you break a clear rule from Scripture."

Joan took a deep breath and tried to remain calm. "We all know that Scripture can be used to justify or forbid almost anything. We would be fools to try to live by it word for word—it would only lead to conflicts and trouble. Is it not better to follow the *example* of

Jesus and try to love all beings unconditionally, enabling them to follow their talents as His own parable suggests? To see women as inferior would be to insult His blessed Mother Mary, after all."

At this, the crowd began clapping noisily and Benedict turned crimson with frustration at being silenced.

Later, when she left the lecture hall, he was waiting for her. "May God strike you down for your falsity! You do nothing but warp and twist His sacred word to bring yourself cheap fame and attention," he snarled menacingly.

"I love the Lord beyond all things and would sacrifice *anything* required of me to serve Him. He is my daily renewal and His word my inspiration. It is not my fault that He bestowed me with both wisdom and intellect and you with only the latter."

"I'm warning you, John," Benedict barked, pushing her violently against the wall. "I *know* you are not what you seem. One day I will find your secret and reveal it to all and then it will be *me* they listen to."

Joan was terrified, partly because of his physical strength and partly because Benedict sensed she had a secret that he might indeed uncover. To her relief, some of the other seminarians came around the corner and he released her immediately, pretending nothing had happened.

"The hatred in your heart makes your words ugly, Benedict," she whispered. "That is why people ignore you."

Joan strode away, head held high, trying to look as masculine as possible but inside she felt weak, girlish and vulnerable and had to work hard not to let welling tears fall. She looked around the grounds for Michael but he was nowhere to be seen. Then she remembered he'd said he would be dashing off straight after her lecture today to tend the goats. Two of the nannies were due to give birth any time now and he was anxious about leaving them even for his studies.

She went to the chapel, hoping to regain her equilibrium but when she entered, Joan saw it was being used for choir practice so instead she headed to the library. Whereas normally she could have lost herself in Scripture, now she was too restless to study. Benedict's words had gone straight through her, and she felt exposed. Joan worried that he might even be on the verge of working out her secret and this terrified her.

Unable to settle, Joan took a walk along the river and then deep into the woodland, exploring areas where she had never been before. As the woods thickened, the trees grew older and some trunks were wider than the torsos of twelve men. She felt safe amongst the trees and realised how rarely she embraced God's creation these days, always tending towards the library instead.

During Joan's two years at the seminary she had shied away from sports in the fields with the other boys, fearful of revealing herself by running like a girl or not being strong enough to keep up with them physically. In the heat of the summer, when the others had swum and played in the river, she had retreated to the chapel for prayer. But this feeling of sanctuary, here in the woods, was profound and would be something she'd reach for again.

Joan was by no means totally at peace as she walked back to the seminary but much of her fear had dissipated, and she felt ready to do whatever was necessary to protect herself from Benedict in the future. She was not expecting Michael to be back when she opened the door to their cell, but to her surprise, there he was standing completely naked. On seeing her, he grabbed his robe and immediately covered his private area. "Sorry, John. I had to wash. The goat-kids were just born, and I am filthy from kneeling in the dirt delivering them."

Joan was too distracted to think about goats. For having caught a glimpse of Michael's masculinity, she wanted to see more. "Michael, these past two years we have both been so careful not to show one another our bodies, in spite of what we share at night. But I realised today that I've learned how to be a boy, but not a man. I really need to see what it is that you have down there that I do not. I've only ever seen animals, my young brothers, and a brief glimpse of Amadeus when he was sick. I need to know now what people think I have in my braies—to believe I have it myself.

Michael hesitated for a moment and then placed his robes on the bed. Joan studied his body from head to foot. He was nineteen and a full-grown man now. The muscles in his arms, chest and legs were well defined and he looked strong and vital from all the physical activity on the farm. His flaccid phallus was only slightly smaller than the one she carried in her undergarments and Joan wondered what it would look like when aroused, for from what she understood, it would grow. Hanging below, were two large ballokes covered in thick dark hair, making the smooth leather mouldings at the base of her own phallus seem pitiful and unrealistic in comparison.

Her friend looked only slightly uncomfortable as she perused him with her eyes, and it wasn't until she stepped closer that he flinched and started to blush. Looking down she noticed that his phallus had begun moving upwards on its own. He moved to grab his robes again but she stopped his arm with her hand, "Michael, please. Let me see what it does. Can I touch it?"

Michael looked at her seriously. "John. It has been a long time since I thought of you as a girl. I am not in love with you, but if you touch me now I will become fully inflamed. Do you understand?"

Joan was dizzy with excitement and curiosity. "I want to see it. I want to feel it. I want to know how it works."

At that he grasped her hand roughly and placed it around his phallus, and began guiding it up and down. Within moments, it grew to over twice the size. Once a rhythm was established, he removed his hand from hers and she carried on. His phallus had become stiff and hot and throbbed with energy. Michael shut his eyes and started groaning as she continued to stimulate him. Joan felt herself ignite inside and a new need overtook her. To Michael's surprise, she spun him around pulling his buttocks into her body with one hand whilst continuing to pleasure him with the other. But now Joan was pretending it was not his phallus but her own.

As Michael's need became more urgent, Joan worked him furiously still imagining that she was doing it to herself and not to him. Their pace quickened to the point of frenzy, then suddenly Michael's entire body shuddered as he climaxed. She did not let go of him for a while, allowing him to lean into her until he got his breath back. Then she turned him around and held up her hand which was covered in his seed. "Thank you, that was incredible and amazing. But I still don't understand why being able to do *that* makes the difference between why someone is allowed or not allowed to read Scripture after the age of twelve..."

Michael looked at her for a moment, nonplussed, and then laughed. "Thank you, too. I don't understand either. But if you enjoyed it, we can do it again at night—if you wish?"

"Is it different when someone does it to *you* rather than using your own hand?"

"Yes. It is much more powerful."

"I'd like to do it again. But there are some more important things I need to start doing from now on, if I'm not to be found out."

"What?"

"I need to grow muscles like yours and start shaving."

"Very well," he replied. "We will begin tomorrow."

CHAPTER 5

Over the next two years, Joan worked diligently to turn herself from a boy into a man. Each day when lessons finished at three o'clock, she would join Michael at the farm for an hour to dig, chop or carry—whatever the heaviest work was that needed doing. In addition to this, she had collected a number of heavy stones which she practised lifting each morning before leaving her cell. At first, this exercise had been painful and tiresome, but over time, she had come to thirst it nearly as much as her academic work. She was proud of her muscles which had grown thick and powerful, adding to both her vitality and confidence. In this period, Joan had grown slightly taller as well and was now exactly the same height as Benedict who, although one of the shortest in her class, was by no means singled out as small.

In addition to her morning wash, each afternoon after working on the farm, Joan would scrub herself with the olive oil soap that Michael and Father Takis prepared in the medicine kitchen. She had noticed that her sweat smelled different from the other boys her age and feared that this might give her away. Only after this second wash, would she go to her beloved library and fulfil her duties there.

Shaving had been the most difficult task to master. She had no doubt that she wanted to live the rest of her life as a man; therefore, the idea of having a moustache did not bother her. It was the pain and effort it took to create one that caused the problem. Michael's shaving knife was brutally sharp. Trying to remove hair that was so light and downy it could barely be seen by the human eye, often left her bleeding. But as Amadeus Reichenbach had predicted, gradually over time, the hairs on her top lip and at the sides of her ears had become coarser, and where at first there had been only one hair sprouting; now there were two. By the end of her second year of shaving, Joan had a light but visible moustache and defined side burns, sufficient enough to delineate her as male. Michael, as suggested by Amadeus, remained clean-shaven so it looked like a Frankish custom not to have a beard. This ensured Joan did not stand out, because now they were getting older, many of the boys had chosen to let their facial hair grow.

She continued to pleasure Michael at night, always in the same fashion. She would stand behind him clutching him tightly to her, imagining his phallus was her own. They never kissed, and Joan assumed that whilst she touched him, it was Amadeus he thought of and not her. Joan was not in love with Michael but looked forward to this nightly union. She felt so close to him that it was sometimes as though they were part of the same soul. Oftentimes, she would climax along with him, even though she was not touching herself. When she didn't reach crescendo, Joan would wait for him to fall asleep and then continue on alone, needing very little more to be fulfilled.

They had remained together in the same classes, even though Michael was older because he'd had a more limited education before entering the seminary. Joan was glad to have him with her so much of the time. As well as being her best friend, he still acted as her shield. This meant that she could be friendly towards the other young men without becoming actual friends with them. Joan and Michael were a pair of Frankish boys who stuck together, pleasant to everyone, but not 'Greek' and 'different in their ways'.

Having lived and studied there for over four years, Joan was now more certain than ever that after her upcoming Ordination, she wanted to be a teacher at the seminary rather than take a parish. Michael also wished to continue on at the institution, working on the farm and in the kitchen, with Father Takis and teaching the new boys the way of the herbs.

Michael rarely talked about Amadeus now but Joan knew her friend still missed him in spite of so many years having passed. Sometimes Joan wondered where Amadeus was these days; whether he was still touring in his wagon and telling stories of the saints. Now when she thought about the entertainer's life from an adult perspective, it seemed so dreadfully isolated. *If he could do it all over again,* she pondered, *would he have made the same choice of running away with Wolfgang from their seminary? Were those two years of happiness together with Wolfgang really worth it, given the horror of how it ended and the subsequent years of loneliness?*

One thing was for certain. Joan knew that if *Michael* could rewrite history, he would have stayed with Amadeus despite the dangers of two men living together without women. Michael had found a modicum of peace working on the farm and learning the herbs but he was not truly happy in the way she was. The happiest and most fulfilled days of *his* life had been those few months spent in the arms of his true love, travelling from Austrasia to Venice. Nothing could ever match that perfection.

*

As she stood in the Great Hall, Joan was excited for the future. During today's public lecture, they were discussing what it meant to be a priest, and Joan was the last to have given a short talk. "So, it is with agapé, with this attitude of unconditional love, that priests should listen to others and refrain from judging their actions too harshly," she concluded, opening the floor for debate.

As always, Benedict was first to argue. "But surely it is the duty of priests to herd their flock down the narrow path and chastise them when they stray, so they will not do it again?"

"Yes, but even a sheep responds more willingly to a shepherd with a kindly voice than one who brandishes a stick," Joan replied, causing a murmur of agreement amongst the men who watched.

"It is fear of the stick that stops a beast from falling into the ravine. Without *fear*, at the first sight of something interesting, it would plunge into danger," Benedict quickly retorted.

"But surely, Scholar Benedict, the key is to make the environment of the flock so satisfying and secure that nothing would tempt them away from it? And only unconditional love can create that."

At this, the audience began clapping and once again, Benedict knew he was defeated and bowed his head to the floor. Father Nikolis smiled at the audience and began speaking, "Thank you, John. As always, you inspire us. And thanks to those of you who have visited us today to hear our bright young scholars speak. We hope that you will be present at their Ordinations next week. Let us now move to the chapel where we shall celebrate the Holy Feast."

It had been a long while since Benedict had last threatened her but today Joan was feeling so happy that she forgot to leave at Father Nikolis' or Michael's side and remained chatting to the visitors who wanted to ask more questions. She was last to exit the Great Hall and as she shut the giant oaken doors, Benedict stepped in front of her and pushed her violently as he had done two years previously. Now, however, Joan was physically strong enough to counteract his assault. Swiftly, she thrust him back against the doors, pinning him by his throat. Saying nothing, her unblinking eyes bored into him. Benedict tried to protest as he grappled against her powerful grip but she had trapped his windpipe, and he was struggling for air. Then, suddenly aware that she might kill him if she continued on, Joan dropped him and he collapsed in a heap on the floor. Horrified at herself and how close she'd come to committing the gravest sin of all, she dashed away, utterly distraught.

"I won't rest until I find your secret, John," Benedict rasped after her, still choking. "I still believe you are a fraud!"

Without looking back, tears now rolling down her cheeks, Joan raced through the seminary grounds towards the woods, passing the washing lines, laden with robes. She was nearly at the trees when a woman's voice distracted her. "Are you all right? You seem distressed."

Joan turned in the direction of the voice to see a striking, dark-haired woman not much older than herself looking at her concernedly.

"I'm fine, thank you...er...Miss. I was...just wrestling with a difficult theological point."

The young woman raised her eyebrows. "Ah, I see. What was it?" she inquired.

"What do you mean?" asked Joan, confused.

"The theological point?"

"What?"

"The theological point that has made you so upset?"

Joan felt flustered and did not know how to respond. "Oh...right...erm...You wouldn't understand."

"No? Why not?"

"Because you're a female," Joan blurted, not believing what had just come out of her own mouth.

The woman looked a little offended but then smiled politely. "Oh...I see...hmm...Females aren't capable of thought. I'd forgotten... But don't you think you have a duty to tell me—if it's really that serious?"

"What are you talking about?"

"The point! The one that's so grave that it has made you cry. I mean, even as a *female*, I think I ought to know—it might affect me!"

"What? Look. Who are you? I've never seen you before. What are you doing on seminary grounds?"

"I work here. I wash your clothes."

"But what's happened to old Mrs Andropolous? She's the washerwoman."

"She retired a month ago. I am her replacement," replied the young woman, matter-of-factly.

"Retired? But nobody told *me*!"

"Why would they? She was just a female servant. She had no value or significance."

"Of course she did!" cried Joan, indignantly. "Men and women are equal!"

"Oh, right. Yes—I forgot. You mentioned that earlier."

The woman was smirking now, and Joan felt totally beguiled by her. "Why are you doing this to me?"

"Doing what?"

"Making me chase my tail!"

"Oh, is that what I'm doing? Well, I'd best not distract you anymore then. You've got to get back to the point."

"What point?"

"The theological point that made you cry like a little girl when you thought no one else was out here!"

At this, the young woman picked up her empty washing basket and walked off in the direction of the cottage. Joan just stood, staring after her in shock, not knowing what had happened. Then just as the woman was about to leave from view, she turned and gave Joan a broad grin. Joan felt herself flush from head to foot, not understanding why. She raised her arm in a polite wave then darted into the trees where she steadied herself against a large trunk.

*

"Hello, Pickle," said Michael, as Joan entered their cell a few hours later. "What happened to you at Mass? Everyone was looking for you."

He rarely called her Pickle these days and her heart warmed at his affection.

"Oh...yes...sorry...it was Benedict...he caught me and it wasn't very pleasant. I needed air."

Over the last two years, she had told him of Benedict's unkind words towards her, but not about the violence, lest he intervene and make things worse.

"And did God's great creation help?"

"Well...yes...at least, I think so," she hesitated, remembering the somewhat disturbing encounter with the new laundry woman.

"Are you all right, John?"

"Benedict said that he would find out my secret. He's made me frightened. What if Benedict's words are really God's, warning me not to go through with the Ordination? Maybe God is trying to stop me."

Michael shook his head. "You're God's loyal servant, and one of the greatest theological minds in Athens. He would not have given you all this affirmation and success only to take it away just as you're about to offer Him the rest of your life."

"I know He let me get away with studying here, but that was just an education; becoming a real priest is something altogether different. What if He strikes me down for it?"

"He is *not* going to strike you down, John. Don't let Benedict's words become the words of God. You know in your heart they are not. Benedict is jealous of you and that's all there is to it. Anyway, why would God have bestowed you with so many other blessings if this were not His will? Your breasts have stayed tiny, your bleeding light and your profile strong. It *has* to be a sign."

"I suppose so. But..."

"No 'buts', Pickle. If God has anything to tell you, He will do it through a kindly face. Your devotion to Him is greater than all of the rest of ours put together and He knows it."

CHAPTER 6

During the next week, Joan spent much of her time lying prostrate before the chapel altar. As well as feeling immense guilt and horror at nearly choking Benedict to death, the rival seminarian's words had gone right through her. In spite of Michael's reassurances, she was still fearful that Benedict might be the mouthpiece of God, warning her not to sin further by continuing on with her guise and becoming ordained. She also started to question whether she was actually serving God or just her own intellectual needs. Would living as a theologian and scholar actually be what God wanted for her?

Yet each time she gave herself up to her Heavenly Father and asked for His will to be known, Joan felt so filled up with unconditional love that it was hard to think that He did anything other than approve of her intention to be ordained.

It was now the night before her Ordination and Joan had spent even longer in front of the cross than on the previous occasions. She rose from the altar to find Father Nikolis watching her from the front pew. The seminary head greeted her with a gentle smile. "I have noticed you in here even more than usual recently. Is something troubling you, young John?"

Joan looked into the kindly eyes that had given her so much encouragement over the past four years and decided to share some of her anxiety. "I am worried that I am not worthy enough to be ordained. I know I am clever and that people like to hear me speak, but that is not the same as being good and helping people. I want to be deserving of my appointment as a priest. I want God to be pleased with me!"

Father Nikolis gazed down at her for a moment then put his hand on her shoulder. "John…do you not know you are anointed? It is not because your mind is so sharp that people come to listen to you—it is because your words contain the power of truth and wisdom. When you speak, it is as though God speaks directly through you and men are moved by it."

Joan was flattered though still unconvinced. "But does that make me a good person? What do I do to really *help* others? When have I ever visited the sick or looked after someone in need?"

"Remember the words of Jesus in the Parable of the Talents: each of us has a different talent given to us by our Lord and it is a great sin to waste it. What makes you a good person is by fulfilling your God-given gift and doing so with great charity and compassion, which is the idea that St Paul reiterated in 1 Corinthians 13. When I watch you lecture, John, all I see is love—love of God, love of His word and love of the men to whom you speak. I whole-heartedly believe you are a good person who is following God's will."

"It is not enough, though. If I am to become a priest, I need to give people more than just intellectual insight. Will you show me how to help people receive the Holy Spirit? I do not mean the blessings we learn in our pastoral training, I mean bestowing the Holy Spirit on people so they experience being filled up by Him in the way I do during worship."

"Of course, I'd be delighted to," Father Nikolis smiled. "Now bow your head in prayer and ask God to forgive your sins."

Joan did as commanded and the priest pressed his hand to her head and started praying, asking for the Holy Spirit to fill 'John' up and heal 'his' agitated soul. Within seconds, she felt a wave of unconditional love rush through her and was totally at peace.

"To bestow the Holy Spirit on others, you go through almost the same process as you do for yourself. Simply ask for God's Spirit to flow through your head, down through arms and hands, and then into the recipient. In doing so, they will be filled up too—and sometimes even healed."

"Will I have the opportunity to help others like this after I become a priest?"

"Yes. After you are ordained, you will be expected to lead Mass once a week and people often stay behind to request extra blessings or healing."

Joan felt relief flood through her. Just as Michael had predicted, a kindly person had delivered her a sense of God's will. She would, as planned, take her vows the following day. However, from then on, as well as teach, she would try to live less selfishly. Joan decided to ask Michael if he would like to help too. Now that he was an expert in herbs; perhaps together they could travel around Athens, offering spiritual healing and medicine. In this way, she would do some genuine good.

That night as they sat in their cell, Joan broached another subject that she wanted to be clear about before becoming ordained. "Do you think that what we do at night would be a breach of the vow of celibacy we take tomorrow?" she asked Michael.

"It doesn't feel wrong," he replied. "I asked Father Takis a long time ago whether he thought it was a sin to give oneself pleasure. He said that from his point of view, it was only wrong if one's thoughts were sinful, such as violating a woman or committing adultery."

"I wish we'd discussed the matter in our Ethics class along with other sexual sins," stated Joan, frustrated. "I was always too nervous of asking. All I know is that St. Augustine thought that a man's seed is only meant to be released with the intention of procreation, so pleasuring oneself would be a sinful waste. Scripture says nothing, and every Pope seems to have remained silent on the subject. I am just not sure. Besides, in our case the issue is more complex—we don't just pleasure ourselves, do we? *I* pleasure *you…*"

"Yes, but it is just with your hand. It's not the same as me entering you as I would if we were married. My understanding is that to take a vow of celibacy is to refrain from being inside of someone and also to refrain from marrying and having offspring."

"Well, I certainly cannot marry. I would be found out!"

"And the person I wanted to marry is forbidden me because even though *I* do not think it is wrong to love him, the Church does…"

Joan felt saddened then. She had never been in love but it was not hard to see how powerful and enduring it really was. She took Michael's hand in hers.

"I love you, dear friend. What we do at night does not feel like a sin to me either, but I needed to check because if it were, and I took a vow of celibacy, then it would be a double sin to keep doing it, and I do not think I could stop myself now."

"I love you too, John, and what you do for me at night helps me manage both my body and my heart. I would be lonely without it."

She went across to his bed and put her arms around him, then kissed his cheek.

"Do you ever long for me to enter you?" he asked.

"No. I am perfectly content with what we do and will be for the rest of our days."

At this, Michael kissed her forehead and instinctively Joan pulled up his robes and moved behind him, taking his waiting phallus in her hand.

*

The next day Joan, Michael, Benedict and a handful of other young men from their class were ordained by the Bishop of Athens in the seminary chapel.

"Receive the power to offer sacrifice in the Church for the living and the dead, in the name of the Father, and of the Son, and the Holy Spirit," declared the Bishop, as he placed his hands on Joan's head to seal her Ordination. At his touch she felt the power of the Holy Spirit so strongly that she almost wept with joy, for God had clearly granted her heart's desire.

It was a beautiful ceremony. After the last of the seminarians was welcomed into the priesthood, more prayers were said and words of praise chanted to music by the choir. Then the Bishop spoke again, "Young men of God, it has been my privilege to ordain you into His priesthood today. May He bless your path in His service. Father Nikolis will now give you your Holy Orders."

Father Nikolis smiled lovingly at each of the young priests before addressing them. "Beautiful servants of God, as Head of this humble seminary, it has been my duty to help the Bishop discern our Lord's will for the next part of your journey."

The seminary head had already hinted that Joan would be made a lecturer, so she was not expecting any surprises.

"Father Michael," he began. "Because of your great compassion and understanding of medicine, it seems fit and necessary that you have a Church of your own where your pastoral gifts can be put to full use. There is a small community half a day north of Marathon in need of a new priest to serve both them and the leper colony above them in the mountains. I can think of no one better than you to take up that position."

Joan gasped in horror and quickly had to contain herself. She was truly shocked. Foolishly, she had assumed that because she would be staying at the seminary, Michael would be too. Everyone knew they were inseparable, and Michael was so busy with the farm that it seemed to her, and indeed to him, that he was indispensible. She looked across at her friend who appeared as dumbfounded as she was by the news. North of Marathon was nearly three days travel from there so they would barely see one another.

By the time she'd gathered herself together enough to concentrate on the rest of Father Nikolis' orders, he had already reached Benedict.

"Father Benedict. Your intellect, self-discipline and attention to detail are a fine example to any young seminarian. Therefore, I feel guided to keep you with us as a teacher, with a particular focus on Canon Law, where you have shown great flare."

From what she could see, Benedict was happy with this, but Joan was now doubly alarmed, as she'd hoped that it would have been Benedict that was sent away to run his own Church and not her beloved friend. Now she would be at the mercy of his goading and have no one by her side to give her relief and more worrisome, no one who knew who and what she really was. When Father Nikolis came to her, she was fighting back tears.

"Father John," Father Nikolis said, touching her shoulder with affection. "Your intellectual gifts astound us all, as does your wisdom, and it should be little surprise to you that we wish to keep you here amongst us as a teacher. You will be in charge of public lectures and have also been granted the esteemed privilege of a place on the Council of Athens so that your theological talents can be shared with those who foster the life of our great city."

The honour was more than Joan could possibly have imagined. It was a position that would normally have been given to someone several years her senior.

She looked at Michael totally overwhelmed, not knowing what to think or feel. Suddenly everything was going to change. Some of it would be wonderful but some of it painful beyond measure.

Joan then looked across at Benedict. For once he was not glaring at her. He was far too broken for that. Like her, he had an excellent mind and had worked tirelessly at his studies. If she had been given an equal position to him, he probably could have coped—indeed he would even have expected that to be the case. But Joan being given a place on the Council of Athens would wound him beyond comprehension, for it would likely take him a decade to reach a similar station. As she looked at him now for the first time with compassion, Joan said a mental prayer that Benedict too would find happiness one day.

*

"I can't believe this is happening. I can't even begin to imagine my life without you. You are the centre of my world," Joan cried, as they sat down on her bed three hours later.

Michael wrapped his arm around her shoulders. "And you mine, Pickle."

"Could you not talk to Father Nikolis and ask him to let you stay here or go to a church nearby? Surely he could arrange for you to be in one that is only a few hours away instead of days?"

"I'm sorry, Pickle, but I've already asked. Father Nikolis says I *must* go to Marathon. I have no choice. They need someone with knowledge of medicine. The old priest serving the leper colony passed away a few weeks ago and they haven't been able to find anyone qualified to serve in his place. God must have willed this for me, Pickle, or Father Nikolis would not have chosen me to go there."

Joan started crying then. She'd been fighting tears all afternoon. "But I won't cope. How will I keep up my disguise without you here to help show me what to do?"

"Of course, you'll cope," Michael said. "You've been getting away with it for over four years. You don't need me to help you anymore. You haven't asked me how to do anything for ages."

"But I'll miss you…"

"John, I love you. You are my family and I will miss you every hour of every day. But there is nothing I can do to change this. Just a few hours ago, I took a vow of obedience… I can hardly refuse to go, can I?"

There was no more she could say, so Joan just leant her head on his chest, defeated. Everything they had was shattered and her whole world turned upside down in the space of one afternoon. She was devastated.

CHAPTER 7

Within three days of their Ordination, Michael had gone. Their goodbye had been harrowing and unbearable. Joan thought back to when Michael had said goodbye to Amadeus four years earlier and now understood that she had not imagined even half of his pain at their parting.

For Michael, having to leave his best friend was a second great loss and so in many ways, he'd been in a worse condition than Joan. He'd also been beside himself with worry about going somewhere so far away from all that he had come to know at the Seminary Of St Joseph. And although he was now a man of medicine, the thought of working with lepers, having so little knowledge of the terrifying disease, had made things doubly frightening.

Joan's pain was exacerbated by the fact that she was now totally alone. There was no one with whom she could become close friends because such friendships were too great a risk, and no one with whom she could share her true self. Michael was the only person who knew her. He'd known the girl she had been and the man she had become and had believed in and supported the entire journey. Now she would be lucky if she saw him for a few days once a year. Joan was beyond consolation, even when at prayer.

Aching for solace, as she lay prostrate at the altar once again, Joan suddenly became aware of someone standing near her. She raised herself up to find that it was Benedict. She had managed to avoid being alone with him since their Ordination, but as she looked around, she realised it had gone dark and no one else was there.

"What's the matter?" he snarled. "Got no one to fornicate with now your friend has gone?"

Joan gulped and had to gather herself together. Benedict smirked, knowing he had hooked her.

"How dare you suggest such a thing!" she cried. "Michael and I are like brothers. We have known each other all our lives."

"Well, he didn't fight very hard to stay with you, did he? Maybe he's got a new boy to sodomise him in Marathon."

The look on his face was so smug that Joan had to work hard not to slap him. Instead, she went with a tone of righteous anger. "Father Benedict, this is the House of God. You should be ashamed of yourself!"

"Why? It is not me that indulges in perversion! God knows *I* am pure."

"As are Michael and I! You are just jealous because you have no friends and no power. You're pathetic!"

It was now Benedict who looked like he might be violent and Joan steeled herself in readiness for his assault. But as he raised his hand, he thought better of it. "I'll leave it for God to be the one who bestows wrath upon you, John. Believe you me, one day, He will!"

At this, he turned on his heel and marched out, leaving her exhausted with misery.

Her misery turned to horror when a few minutes later, she opened her cell door to see a stranger sitting on Michael's bed.

"Who on earth are you?" she asked angrily, of the short, young man with a long pointed beard.

"Oh, I'm sorry. Did they not tell you? I am Markos—your new cellmate."

"What? No, they did not! I apologise for my rudeness, but I was not expecting this."

"I arrived this afternoon from Thebes. Our seminary was burned down in a raid, and we were instructed to find hospitality elsewhere until it is rebuilt. Father Nikolis has taken in six of us."

Joan could not believe what was happening. She had been so upset about Michael leaving, that she had not even considered the possibility of a new arrival in her sleeping quarters. It sent her into a whirl of panic. *How will I maintain my secret, sharing a cell with someone whom I do not know? How will I get undressed? What will I do during my monthly bleed? This is going to be a nightmare!*

Joan had to work very hard to be polite to the young man still gazing up at her. "Very well. My name is Father John," she stated flatly.

"You do not need to introduce yourself to me. I've heard all about you. Whenever visitors from Athens came to our seminary in Thebes, your name was always on their lips. It is an honour to share your cell. I do hope I shall be worthy of it."

Joan smiled weakly at the compliment and then tried to work out how on earth she was going to get ready for bed without giving herself away. To her relief, Markos turned his back to her and started pulling up his robes, so she grabbed her sleeping shift from under the blankets and turned her back too. Swiftly she pulled off her new black priestly robe, but did not remove her camisia and braies in spite of the summer heat. Then she turned to the side just enough for the outline of her phallus to show through the shift. As expected, her new cellmate cast a furtive look in the direction of her manhood before pulling down his blankets and getting into bed. Joan sent a mental thank you to Amadeus Reichenbach—his wisdom about how to convince others she was male, continued to save her, even now...

*

The next morning Joan woke at dawn. It had been a restless night and she wanted to remove herself from Markos' presence at the first opportunity. She headed straight for the chapel, where she asked God to fill her with His Holy Spirit and show her the way through what now seemed like abject danger. *Please grant me wisdom and strength. I trust Thee, dear Lord, to protect me and help me find safety,* she prayed.

Joan remained in the chapel for over an hour and then decided to take a long walk in the woods before giving her first public lecture as an ordained priest. She had been so taken up with Michael's departure that she had not spent sufficient time preparing herself to talk in the Great Hall that morning to both students and guests. She hoped that the walk would clear her head.

It was still very early, as the days were long at this time of year and dawn had come well before six o'clock. She reached the far edge of the seminary grounds then walked deep into the woodland, deciding to explore a different route from her usual one. Joan was not afraid of getting lost, as although the wood was vast, it lay nestled between the River Eridanos and Mount Lycabettus so it would be easy to find her way home. As she walked, the trees gradually became interspersed with rocks and soon she was on all fours climbing upwards. It felt good to be using her body. She decided that because she probably wouldn't be working as much on the farm now Michael had left and that exercising in her cell was no longer a possibility with Markos there, she would walk and climb here every morning instead. As she got further up Mount Lycabettus and away from the tree line, she stopped and turned to take in the view. She could see the seminary again and beyond it the majestic Parthenon standing proudly on its own rocky outcrop. It was a breathtaking, panoramic vista and Joan could not believe that, in all this time, she had never explored this far up the mountainside. She had only ever followed the river's edge or gone into Athens itself.

In the opposite direction, away from the city, Joan saw that below her in the distance was a small mountain lake of turquoise water and she was immediately drawn to it. It did not take long to scramble down to the shore and once there, she was totally smitten by its beauty. The blue water glistened invitingly in the early morning sunlight and she longed to go in. Joan looked around carefully. There were no buildings or structures overlooking the small lake and she could see no one out walking on the mountainside. Finally, she overcame her fear at being spotted, removed her priestly vestments and dived in.

It had been over five years since she had last swum but Joan had not forgotten how. As she glided through the water, memories of hot summer afternoons in Austrasia flooded back. Michael, still just a boy himself, had taught her to swim when she was seven years of age, and she had loved it. As soon as the summer came each year, they would take every opportunity they could to go down to the river and have fun. Since becoming a boy, Joan had not dared swim in the River Eridanos with the other seminarians, even in her underwear as she did now, lest the outline of her breast-binding and the harness that held her phallus in place showed through the material. But here, where no human eye was witness, she felt both safe and free. She revelled in the glory of God's creation and found herself giggling and splashing like a child. Her only regret was that Michael was not there to enjoy it with her, for he would have loved it too.

After her swim, Joan found a large flat rock and stretched out in the warmth of the sun. Her lecture was not until ten o'clock so she estimated she had approximately an hour to dry off before returning through the woods. As she lay there meditating, she realised that God had answered her prayers from earlier that morning. Here she could exercise, here she could wash herself every day in private and when she bled each month, she could wash the cloths she used for that too. Here she could relax completely. Joan was overwhelmed with gratitude and totally at peace.

*

The Great Hall was much busier than expected and Joan had been nervous when she'd started to speak, especially as she was giving the last talk of the session and expectations were high. She'd decided to discuss the relationship of the philosophies of the great Greek thinkers to Christianity. Her argument was that embracing the views of Socrates and Plato ultimately led to Gnosticism—a doctrine similar to Christianity but claiming that Jesus' primary goal was to lead humans from ignorance to wisdom. Joan asserted that it was important for scholars to consider the claims of these two great men, but when trying to prove the existence of God to a heathen or discuss philosophy with the laity, it was better to fall back on Aristotle's views. "So perhaps by looking at Aristotle's work, we can show those who are sceptical about the existence of our Lord that his reality can be proven by logical means as well as through spiritual experience."

Within moments of Joan's conclusion, Benedict began to spar. "But Aristotle's God bears little resemblance to that of our Lord. We could end up encouraging paganism by employing such measures."

"I disagree. It is because Aristotle is so agnostic about the nature of God that he is safe for us to use. He concluded that an infinite regress of causes, changes and movements was impossible so there must be an Uncaused Cause, an Unchanged Changer and an Unmoved Mover who started off the universe. Aristotle provided no further embellishment. As Christians, once we have convinced our listeners of this philosophical truth, we can then tell them how this God has revealed His presence to us, first through His interaction with the prophets and then through the incarnation of Christ."

As always, the murmur of agreement in the crowd frustrated Benedict. "But philosophy does nothing but confuse a man, particularly a peasant man. It is better to tell him about his need for salvation than waste time on intellectual debates that he cannot grasp. A full description of the fires of Hell should suffice to bring any man to acknowledge God."

"To worship God because of fear of Hell is to worship a dictator. Where is God's love of humanity reflected in such an approach? If men can be helped to understand our Lord is real through intellectual means, then it can only be good news when they then find out that this God loves them and wants to give them a place in Heaven."

At this, there was clapping from the crowd and Benedict fell silent. Joan felt sorry for him. No matter how hard he tried, the audience always preferred what she had to say. He just could not win them over with his arguments. It was not so much that he was wrong in his views, but more that he was so rigid about the role of the Church and so negative in his assessment of human nature. Joan wished the audiences wouldn't be so expressive about their preference though. She liked that they listened to her and wanted to share in her wisdom, but it was so frequently at Benedict's expense. She also wished that he would simply avoid attending or go out during her slot at the Friday Lectures so that she would not have to witness this continuing ritual of public humiliation.

CHAPTER 8

It had been several days since Joan had discovered the sanctuary of the lake. She had since gone there every morning as planned to swim and then meditate whilst she dried off. The beauty of living in Athens was that the weather was extremely hot right through until October, so as it was still only May, there were many months yet before it would be too cold and dark for swimming.

After Michael left, Joan had still visited Father Takis and helped him a little on the farm but her heart was no longer in it; she was relieved when some of the refugees from Thebes had volunteered their assistance. So today, instead of going to the farm after lectures, Joan went straight to the library where she remained until Mass. Once the evening service was over, she stayed in the chapel to pray. She was not as distressed as she had been after Michael's initial departure, but her prayers had recently been focussed on staying safe in the new circumstances rather than being an active communion with the Deity. She wanted to be sure that she was sufficiently in union with God, as she would be leading her first Mass the following evening. To bless the bread and wine so it would become the flesh and blood of Christ Himself was the most sacred duty she would perform as a priest. She did not want to insult her beloved Lord by not being sufficiently humble and repentant at His feet whilst administering this Holy Sacrament.

The church was not empty today for there were others lying before the altar. Benedict was also present but rather than prostrate, he was sitting in a pew near the back. As she passed him on the way out, he stood up and whispered in her ear. "Anyone who spends as much time prostrating themselves as you, must have a guilty secret."

Joan was alarmed that he should say this as she left the church. She wondered, like so many times in the past when he had challenged her, whether his was really the voice of God, and that the feelings of love she experienced before the cross were some kind of demonic delusion that had ensnared her. She took a deep breath before retaliating in a low voice. "Perhaps if you spent more time worshipping the Lord instead of casting aspersions on me, He might actually help you get where you want to be, Benedict."

She walked out with her head held high, but she felt troubled and ached for Michael's soft words of reassurance. Although it was too late to go all the way to the lake, she did have time to follow the river into the trees and decided to calm herself with a brisk walk. The last thing Joan wanted was to return to her cell and make small talk with Markos. The only way she was going to survive the ordeal of sharing her quarters with someone who did not know her secret was to spend as little time there as possible.

But as Joan headed towards the trees, bathed in the incandescent light of the setting sun, the pain at Michael's absence only grew stronger. She remembered their first evening together at the Seminary Of St Joseph when they'd seen the resplendent view of Athens burnished in orange and red for the very first time. So often since then, they had walked to this spot and admired its breathtaking beauty. As she stopped and gazed back at it now, tears rolled down her cheeks.

"I can see you're grappling with theology again, Father John," came a woman's voice. Joan looked to her left to see the young washerwoman with whom she'd had the somewhat disturbing encounter just before Michael left.

"What do you...er...? Who told you I...?" she struggled. "How did you know I'd been ordained?" she finally asked, confusedly.

"Because I work and live here too. One tends to pick up on things like major Ordination ceremonies."

"Oh, right, I see, yes..." Joan replied, feeling her mind fogging up even further.

"You look terrible. When did you last eat?"

At this, Joan stepped back in surprise. She hadn't realised that she was ravenously hungry until the woman asked the question, but now felt like she might pass out if she did not consume something immediately.

"I...uh...this morning. I've been...er...busy."

"Let me get you some bread and cheese. Then you can tell me all about it."

"Tell you about what?"

"We're not really going to go through this every time I catch you out here in tears, are we?"

"I'm not in..." Joan gave up immediately, knowing full well that her face was still wet. "Some food would be nice, thank you."

The young woman moved to her cottage, which was not far from where Joan stood, staring after her and feeling totally befuddled. She could spar philosophy with boy or man of any age and stand lecturing three score of theologians, but the twice she had conversed with this young woman; she had been unable to construct a coherent sentence.

The woman returned a few minutes later with a basket of food and a small jug of mead. She indicated that they should sit by the riverbank and Joan followed obediently. Silently, she handed her a chunk of bread and Joan consumed it gratefully, not refusing when more bread, then cheese and then figs were passed in her direction. Finally, the woman poured them both a goblet of the mead, which they drank whilst watching the fiery red sun finally disappear below the horizon.

"I heard your friend left…" she said softly.

Joan almost jumped out of her skin but did not know whether it was from the breaking of the silence or the fact that the washerwoman knew why she had been crying. "Who told you that?" she snapped.

This time the woman was sharper in her retort. "I just said! I work here. Some people do deign to speak to me, you know."

Joan felt ashamed of her rudeness and turned to her, contrite. "Sorry, yes. You are right… I just didn't realise people were interested enough in my life to talk about it with a laywoman."

This time the woman smiled. "Not interested in the famous Father John? The greatest theological mind Athens has ever produced?"

Joan found herself blushing and lowered her eyes to the ground. "Well...I wouldn't say that...I just...have a lot of ideas."

"But you're feeling lonely now?"

"Lonely?" she asked agitatedly.

"Yes. Lonely now your friend has gone to Marathon."

"What makes you think that? I've lived here for years. I know everyone." The feelings of confusion were growing again and if the young woman had not been so kind to her, Joan would have risen immediately and gone straight to her cell.

"Yes, but no one knows you, except for him, or so they say..."

"What?" Joan cried, now feeling alarmed. "Look, who's 'they', anyway?"

"Good grief! It's no wonder no one knows you. I've never met anyone so difficult to have a conversation with. What do you do? Slice them up with theology then leave them in a pool of blood?"

Joan looked at the woman who was shaking her head in despair and surprisingly, she found herself amused by the analysis.

"I...I don't think I realised people thought me distant," she found herself confessing. "I've always had Michael—even before I came here. I've never really needed anyone else."

"Until now..."

"Well...yes...no...I mean...I'm sure God's work will keep me occupied...and Michael and I will write."

The woman nodded and smiled gently, and Joan could not help but feel kindly towards her.

"I wish I could do that," the woman stated solemnly.

"What?" asked Joan, becoming confused again.

"Write."

"Can't you do that already?"

"There are no places like this for girls, remember! And my parents weren't rich enough to have learned themselves, so there's no way they could have taught me to read and write, even if they'd wanted to."

"Oh, that's terrible!" said Joan, suddenly feeling a rush of gratitude towards her father. She sometimes forgot how lucky she was that he had taught her at all. Joan was a rarity. So many of the girls in her village had never learned. It was not deemed necessary so their parents hadn't let them, even though her father had offered to teach any child in his flock. She realised that if it hadn't been for him, everything that had happened since would have been impossible, as Michael could not have taken an illiterate boy with him to the seminary, even a clever one like her.

"Yes. It is...terrible," replied the woman.

"Do you wish you could learn?"

"Very much. I'd like to be able to actually *read* stories instead of just listening to them. But I doubt I will ever have the opportunity."

Joan felt an idea forming but didn't know whether to quash it or allow it to rise. She looked into the woman's eyes and saw how much she wanted to learn and again thought of how hideous her own life would have been if all that she had been subjected to had been women's work.

"I could teach you…" Joan found herself saying, even though she should have thought it through properly before making the offer.

"Really?"

"Yes."

"When?"

Joan hesitated for a moment as she tried to work out when on earth it might be possible. "Perhaps we could start tomorrow, after Evening Mass. Will you have finished work by then?"

"Yes. That sounds perfect. Where shall we meet?"

Joan paused again. She had to be careful. If a young priest who had taken a vow of celibacy were seen spending time with a woman, it would be cause for concern and possible scandal. But then it occurred to her where they could go. "I know exactly the place. Meet me on the path just inside the woods, and I will take you to the perfect spot. It will not be dark until around this time so we should be able to make a start."

The young woman looked excited and Joan felt an overwhelming urge to hug her, just as she would if she had pleased Michael. But instead, remembering she did not know her, Joan picked up the empty basket and jug and rose to her feet. The young woman, still smiling, took them from her. "Thank you so much. You don't know what this means to me!"

"I am more than happy to help. But please keep it to yourself, for as you probably know, people might think it unfitting for a young priest to teach a girl to read."

The woman nodded and once again expressed her thanks, then moved towards her little cottage.

"Wait! What's your name?" Joan called after her.

The washerwoman turned back and smiled so sweetly that Joan felt herself blush.

"My name is Thea, Father John."

Through the fog that had now eclipsed all reason, Joan bid the young woman goodnight, not understanding why her mental faculties were so befuddled.

CHAPTER 9

The next morning, before diving into the lake, Joan looked carefully around the shoreline for a good place to teach someone to read and write. Although she thought it highly unlikely that anyone would come there in the evening, for she had never seen anyone there in the earlier part of the day, Joan wanted to be careful. She finally selected a spot nestled between two large jagged rocks jutting out a few feet apart at the bottom of the mountain. Sheltered between the rocks was a raised flat slab of stone, more than wide enough to lay out parchment. It was ideal.

As she sat hidden from view between the rocks, Joan's attention turned to the needs of her body. Since her first visit to the lake, she had always swum in her undergarments and never taken them off, even to dry herself, just in case someone saw her from the mountainside. Going into the water naked would be far too risky, but she'd reasoned that no one from afar would spot the outline of her chest binding through her camisia or the harness through her braies and even if someone came closer, she would hear them in time to quickly don her robe.

Each day after her swim, she'd stretched out in the warmth of the early morning sun, longing to pleasure herself but knowing it was too exposed to indulge her needs. Equally there'd been no possibility of fulfilling herself in her cell because of now having to share it with Markos. Here between the rocks, Joan realised there was no way she could be spotted and her need welled up so strongly that she thought she might explode if she did not find release. She pulled off her robe and undid the drawstring of her braies, imagining herself standing behind Michael as she used to each night in their cell. It only took moments for her to climax and the relief was so great she knew that this would become part of her daily routine from then on.

When her skin hit the cool turquoise water, she felt doubly invigorated and worked her body even harder than normal before stretching out in her usual place to dry. This was a perfect sanctuary given to her by God, so that she could continue to serve Him. Joan raised her hands in praise and gratitude and instantly felt bestowed with love.

*

She was not lecturing today so passed her time fulfilling her duties in the library, which continued on in spite of her teaching position. Once finished there, Joan spent the afternoon illuminating a copy of the Gospel of St Luke which she had been working on for several weeks. After four years of hard practice, she'd finally reached the point where her work was deemed acceptable. "It will never be given as a gift to a Bishop," Father Amos had quipped. "But a humble monastery upon a hill might take it." This was high praise from the elderly priest and, although slightly insulting, in reality was the truth.

As she formed each letter, Joan thought carefully about how she was going to teach Thea to read. It had been so long since she had learned herself that she had to wrack her brain as to where to start, but by the end of her session she had decided on an approach that she hoped would work. She did not want to sin by stealing materials reserved for proper calligraphy, so Joan went to the table in the corner where scraps of linen and damaged parchments were kept. It was not uncommon for young seminarians to take these materials to their cell to practise on in their free time. She gathered a handful and folded them into a hessian sack along with an old over-used quill and a small pot of the lowest grade ink, secured with a cork.

Joan made sure she went to dinner that night. Her eating habits had become irregular since Michael had left because she did not like having to make small talk with the other men. She realised now that she couldn't keep on like that or by the end of the day she would have no energy to do what was required of her and she would become weak. Weakness was something she could not afford. She had to keep herself strong and muscular.

To her relief, Father Nikolis indicated that she should sit next to him to eat. "Well, Father John. How are you feeling about giving your first Mass this evening?"

"I have spent a lot of time in prayer this week and plan to go straight to the chapel once I've eaten, so I have time to commune with the Lord before the service begins. I hope that I have done enough to be sanctified."

The senior priest looked at her kindly. "John, you are Heaven blessed; you must never doubt it. We are honoured to have one such as you amongst us."

Joan felt more relieved than flattered by Father Nikolis' words. She'd missed Michael's constant reassurance and affirmation these past few weeks, especially when she was about to do something new. She hadn't fully realised until now that this was something he had done for her every single day.

To her great joy, by the time she had finished eating, Father Nikolis had instilled such confidence in her that she was ready to embrace this holiest of tasks without feeling inadequate.

The Mass went smoothly and as she consecrated the bread and wine for its transubstantiation, Joan felt the presence of Jesus more closely than at any other point. As she gave the Holy Supper to those present, she felt nothing but love for each of the men who participated. Father Nikolis beamed at her throughout the entire service, and it was a privilege to offer him the sacrament.

Much to her relief, Benedict did not attend the Mass so there was nothing to tarnish its perfection. Joan assumed that the rival priest could not bear to share in the sacrament if it was administered by her and had remained in the library instead. However, at the end of the service, she looked around carefully just in case he was lingering somewhere at the back, waiting to pounce, but he was nowhere to be seen.

As Father Nikolis had predicted, a few participants had remained behind to ask for her help.

Two of them were from the city and had regularly attended her public lectures; the other was a seminarian of about fourteen years of age. She tended the eldest of the men first. He said he did not know what was wrong but had been feeling fatigued and lethargic for several days and requested she pray for him. Nervously, Joan thought back to when Father Nikolis had laid hands on her, two weeks before. She placed her hand on the man's head and asked God to let His Spirit flow through her. In doing so, she felt a rush of tingling down her arm and then into her hand. "I bless you in the name of the Father, the Son and the Holy Spirit," she said aloud, letting her hand remain as the Spirit of God continued to flow.

A few minutes later, when the man finally looked up, he had tears in his eyes. "I have never known such grace. Thank you for bringing the Lord so close to me. I feel the strength of His healing," he said softly, in gratitude.

Joan smiled at him and nodded, knowing that none of it was her own doing and that she was just a conduit, a means by which God could reach His child.

She moved then to the other man who was not sick but wanted a blessing. He had experienced the deaths of several family members in recent months and felt himself distant from God. Joan repeated the ritual, again feeling the power of the Lord flow directly through her into the man who, like his friend, wept with gratitude at being bestowed with God's Spirit.

Finally, she moved to the boy who looked up at her innocently with hazel eyes the size of moons. "I just wanted to ask you something," he said shyly. Joan smiled at the two older men who indicated they were satisfied to leave them be. Once they had exited the chapel, she turned her full attention to the boy.

"Yes, young man. What can I do for you? I've seen you around, but I don't know your name."

"I am Andreas," replied the boy. "Could you show me how to receive the Holy Spirit, please? I asked Father Nikolis earlier and he told me that if I came to you tonight, you would help me."

Joan looked into the soft brown eyes of the young seminarian and nodded, remembering how anointed she'd felt when she had received the Spirit for the first time in the presence of her beloved father who had shown her how. It was a privilege to help the boy and witness him feel God's presence so viscerally.

She was so full of joy from taking the Mass and bestowing the Spirit of God on those in need, that Joan almost forgot her promise to meet the washerwoman for their first reading lesson. It wasn't until she exited the chapel into the warm spring evening that she remembered. She rushed to her cell which, thankfully, was empty; pulled off her white robe, used only for administering sacraments, and changed back into her black one. Then Joan grabbed the hessian bag full of writing materials and darted out towards the woods. She was already late, and it would not be fair on the young woman to make her think she was not coming. She desperately hoped Thea would still be there.

As she entered the woods, Joan soon saw Thea waiting for her just inside as arranged. The woman did not look cross in spite of her tardiness and greeted her with a broad smile, which instantly made Joan feel fuzzy in the head. She just did not understand why this female rendered her incapable of focussing and was annoyed by it happening yet again.

"Thank you so much for coming, Father John. I was worried you might change your mind..."

"Not at all. Do you still want a lesson?"

"Of course! I can't wait. Where are we going to have it?"

"At one the most beautiful secrets of God's creation," Joan declared, regaining her mental faculties.

As they moved in the direction of the mountain slope, Joan asked Thea to tell her about how she had ended up working at the seminary.

"My great aunty is old Mrs. Andropolous," she replied. "She was washerwoman here for nearly forty years but simply could not manage anymore. So my mother agreed to let her move into our family home if she could organise for me to take her place here in exchange. There have been members of my family working for the seminary since it was built two hundred years ago. Mr. Andropolous, my great uncle, died a few years back. He used to do all the maintenance and helped out on the farm. But their only two children, both boys, did not want to work here and joined the army instead. There were no daughters to assist my aunty with her duties as she got older, so my sisters and I helped out from time to time."

"Do you have many brothers and sisters?"

"Two older sisters and five younger brothers. What about you?"

Joan had to pause. She rarely thought about her old life in Austrasia, except for her father and their times together in the library at Fulda. And because she had never felt very close to her siblings, she had not even wondered what they would look like now, let alone what they would be doing with their lives. "When I left at the age of thirteen and a half, I had four younger brothers and one younger sister, but there may well be more by now. I lost touch with my family a long time ago."

Thea stopped and put her hand on Joan's arm. "Oh, you poor thing. It's no wonder you are so lonely."

Joan stared down at Thea's hand. It felt like it was burning through her robes and it threw her even more off kilter. She stood there dumbstruck. After a moment Thea must have realised she'd made Joan uncomfortable and she removed her hand, her cheeks reddening slightly.

"What does your father do?" Joan asked, starting to walk again, still flustered.

"He is a blacksmith. What about yours?" the young woman replied politely.

"I don't want to talk about my family any more," Joan replied curtly, forging ahead.

The atmosphere was now awkward but to Joan's relief, the terrain became more challenging and she had the perfect excuse to concentrate on their ascent, rather than answering difficult questions.

However, she was regretting the decision to teach this young woman. Amadeus Reichenbach stood correct yet again. As soon as she offered the hand of friendship to anyone, they would begin asking about things she did not wish to discuss—questions that would make her feel vulnerable and ill at ease.

When they finally reached the lake, the mood changed again, for Thea was full of delight. "It's beautiful! I had no idea it was here!"

"I don't think many people do. I only discovered it myself recently, and I haven't seen anyone else around. I guess this side of the mountain is too steep and barren to graze sheep, and it's so far from the edge of the city that no one has any reason to come here."

It was still very warm and the light good enough for a short first lesson. Joan took Thea immediately to the spot she had chosen earlier that day and unpacked the writing equipment.

"Thank you so much for doing this," Thea said again.

"I am glad to. It's not fair that women don't get to learn like men."

"I thought you didn't think we had brains," Thea laughed.

Joan looked at her seriously. "Believe me when I tell you, there are some women who are even cleverer than men. Do not ever doubt that I know that."

Thea smiled again and Joan found herself mesmerised by the woman's deep brown eyes. Then a feeling once familiar to her rose up inside and she realised what was happening. It was the same feeling of want she'd had for the serving wench all those years ago when they were travelling across Frankia. *Oh, Heavens!* she said to herself. *That is why I haven't been able to concentrate when she speaks...*

It was then that it occurred to Joan that she had not actually spent any significant time in the presence of women since leaving the convent of The Sisters Of The Virgin Mother at the top of the mountain in Bavaria, four years previously. The only woman at the seminary had been Thea's aunty and she was old and kept herself to herself. Priests who taught there were celibate, and women were not allowed to attend the Public Lecture or to worship in the seminary chapel. Occasionally, when she had been into Athens, she'd seen younger women but had never conversed with them.

Until now, Joan had simply believed that God willed it that she would not fall in love with a man because He wanted her to serve Him. Her intimacy with Michael was as close to a sexual relationship as she thought she'd ever want. Now Joan realised it was more complicated than that. Suddenly her body was awash with desire, and it was clearly because Thea was a woman and a very beautiful one at that. *I wonder why she hasn't been married off by now...* Joan found herself thinking.

They sat side by side and Joan spread out a tattered piece of parchment on the flat rock, securing the curling edges with small stones. Then she drew an 'Alpha'.

"This letter is called 'Alpha'. It is said 'AY' like apron and 'AH' like apple."

Thea studied the letter for a moment and then repeated nervously, "'AY' for apron and 'AH' for apple... so 'AY' for apricot and 'AH' for abacus?"

Joan was pleased that Thea had instantly made this connection and smiled delightedly. "Yes, Thea. That's good. Would you like to try to form it yourself?" she asked, holding out the quill.

Thea took the writing implement but as she moved her hand towards the parchment, it began to tremble and instinctively Joan reached out and steadied it. The contact made them both jolt and look startled at one another. Joan felt herself turning pink. Thea had also blushed and quickly averted her eyes. But the letter had still not been formed, so in spite of the tingling sensation travelling up her arm to her thumping chest, Joan kept her hand on Thea's and helped her write the 'A'. On its successful completion, Thea was so happy that she seemed to forget her nervousness and, instead, threw her arms around Joan saying, "Thank you!"

Joan was so overwhelmed with desire that she pushed the woman away roughly. "Thea! It is not fitting for a woman to hug a priest, and you know it!"

Thea looked shocked and immediately stood up and started moving away. "I'm sorry, Father John," she said, as she walked. "This was obviously a bad idea."

Alarmed, Joan sprang to her feet and dashed after her. "No. It's me who should be sorry. Forgive me. I was rude. It's just that I am not used to sharing such affections. Please come back and let me continue with the lesson."

Thea looked unsure, but Joan continued to press until finally she agreed that they go back and carry on with the lesson. This time, they sat further apart and Joan was careful not to touch the woman or make too much eye contact. But when Thea bent over to practise writing, whilst saying aloud a plethora of words beginning with the letter 'Alpha', Joan found her eyes wandering first to the arc of the woman's neck, then to her collar bone and then to her cleavage, the flesh of which peaked out enticingly over her dress. Joan's insides began to melt and she longed to reach out and run the back of her hand across the woman's cheek. *I am in such trouble...*

For the next half an hour, until the light became too poor to carry on, Thea practised the letter 'Alpha' so she could write it perfectly. Joan continued to struggle with burning need and thought seriously about finding an excuse to make this their one and only lesson. But because her student was so excited and so very eager to learn more, Joan knew that it would be wrong to stop teaching her just because she was tempted by carnal desire. *I shall swim twice as hard in the morning! Maybe that will get it out of my system...*

"Am I doing well?" asked the woman, tentatively.

Joan, realising that she must have been grimacing, forced a smile. "Yes. You are doing brilliantly. You are a fast learner, so tomorrow we will study the letter 'Beta'."

Thea smiled shyly and Joan felt a rush of pride for them both. The young woman was obviously bright, and she was doing a good job of teaching her. Unable to hold eye-contact without exacerbating her lust, Joan reached over to the parchments, placing them back in the hessian bag and securing it with a heavy stone. "I think it will be safe to leave these here. They're sheltered from any breeze," she stated confidently.

Thea nodded in agreement and rose to her feet. For a moment they stood opposite one another, and the young woman's cheeks reddened again.

Does she desire me too? Or does she know what's going on in my mind and body and is blushing from embarrassment? Joan asked herself.

Both options were too alarming to countenance; so quickly, Joan turned and began walking back towards the trees.

"Tell me why you left Frankia," Thea requested, catching up with her.

Joan found herself startled again by the intrusion. "I told you already! I really do not wish to discuss my family history. It would be better if you stuck to other subjects," she snapped.

Thea looked offended. "Well what *would* you like to talk about, Father John?"

Joan thought for a moment. She did not want any more discussions about the personal but it would be strange just to walk in silence. "Well, perhaps I could tell you about the saints. Would you like to hear all about the female ones?"

Thea beamed at her. "Yes. The only women I ever hear about at Church are Mary Mother of God and Mary Magdalene! Please tell me about these other women. I want to know!"

Joan grinned, trying to fight back the urge to push the young woman up against a tree and tear off all her clothes. "Great. Let's start with St. Hilda who was baptised by St. Paulinus. She was in charge of both women and men in the days before the Church changed its mind about women's leadership. She was a Benedictine Abbess and became the head of a double monastery in England where she trained five Bishops!" Joan began.

"How did you find out about this St. Hilda, if the Church doesn't want us to know that women used to be in charge as well?"

Joan took a deep breath. It was actually impossible to have this conversation without talking a little about her past. "My father was originally from England and was aware of a time when women were priests there, before everything changed. And an old friend from Frankia possessed countless stories of the saints, both male and female."

"How incredible!" Thea stated, in wonderment.

"Yes, 'incredible'!" Joan laughed.

Joan continued telling Thea about the marvels of St. Hilda until they reached the edge of the woodland and had to part. They decided that Thea should leave first so they would not be seen together. The young woman looked at her again with gratitude. "Thank you so much, Father John. You have no idea what this means to me."

Believe you me, I do, thought Joan, as she said her goodbyes.

After Thea left, Joan remained in the woods and found herself a giant tree to lean against. Being together with this woman had been both wonderful and terrifying and her whole body raced with energy. It took Joan several minutes to calm her breathing, and still her heart beat furiously in her chest. *Oh, Heavens! This must have been how Michael felt around Amadeus. I had no idea...*

CHAPTER 10

Joan could not sleep. She'd returned to her cell long after dark to avoid having to talk much to Markos and he, as hoped, was already in bed when she'd arrived. He'd said a sleepy goodnight to her as she'd pulled back her covers and within moments he was snoring gently once again.

Now all she could think of as she lay in her bed was Thea. It was as if something had possessed her. She could not stop imagining kissing the woman, and she was throbbing with need. But Joan dared not touch herself in the presence of someone she did not know or trust. If Markos needed to self-pleasure like she and Michael did, he had plenty of opportunity when she wasn't there. Whether he did so or not she had no idea, but for all she knew he might think it a sin.

Joan struggled to gain control of her thoughts and say her final prayers as she normally would, but she just could not concentrate on the Lord and as a result felt guilty. She then tried contemplating a paradox of Zeno: *Why is it that logic shows that Achilles cannot ever pass the tortoise, yet in reality he does?* she asked herself, before the memory of Thea's neckline returned to the forefront of her mind. *Aargh! This is totally useless...*

She continued to toss and turn until the crack of dawn, at which point she got up, dressed quietly and went running to the lake. Breathless, Joan arrived at the spot between the rocks, pulled down her braies immediately and pressed her fingers into her saturated need. It frightened her how powerful her lust had suddenly become. Thinking of Thea seemed to quadruple the strength of her climax and whereas once was normally enough, now she pleasured herself over and over, her fantasies becoming increasingly graphic.

By the time she was finally sated, her thighs and the stone she was sitting on were dripping. But even more surprisingly, rather than now forgetting about the woman and getting on with the rest of her day, all Joan wanted to do was see her, hold her and talk with her. She may have released the needs of her body but her heart and her mind simply would not let go.

She jumped into the cold blue water and swam faster than ever before. Yet no matter how vigorous her stroke, still Joan yearned to see Thea's face. It felt like she would fall apart if she had to wait a moment longer to witness the beautiful woman's smile. *What on earth is happening to me? How can I have become so obsessed so quickly? Have I been possessed by some kind of demonic force? I don't understand why one moment I felt just a dart of lust, and now I can do nothing but think of her...*

However, Joan was determined to quash her emotions. She swam and swam and swam. It wasn't until she was so exhausted that she was struggling to stay afloat that she finally got out and laid on her favourite rock to dry. Yet even then, meditation proved impossible. Finally, she took her robe and pretended it was Thea tucked into her side, and as she gave in to the comfort of fantasy, Joan fell into a deep sleep.

When she awoke, she was disorientated and it took several moments to work out where she was and what had happened. She did not know the exact time of day but the sun was high in the sky so it must have been approaching noon. "Damn!" she said aloud. For the first time in all the years she had been living at the seminary, Joan had missed a class and more embarrassingly, a class she was supposed to be teaching. It would be deeply shameful. *What have you done to me, woman?* she thought crossly, realising it was because Thea had disrupted her equilibrium that this situation had arisen. The only consolation was that the lesson was for the younger students rather than the public but even so, she felt dreadful.

As she ran through the woods, Joan tried to think up a suitable excuse. *Could I say that I went for a walk and got lost? No, that wouldn't work. It's easy to find a way back—mountain on the left, river on the right—it's impossible to get lost. Could I say I wasn't feeling well? No because then I would have been in my cell, and someone was bound to have been there to check on me. What am I going to do?*

The answer came by accident, or at least she hoped so and that she had not somehow willed it. Sprinting fast and preoccupied with worry, suddenly Joan found herself tumbling over a stone and landing on her left arm with a sharp crack. When she hauled herself up to sitting, she could barely move the arm and had to breathe deeply to stop herself from screaming. Joan sat there for several minutes feeling wretched and helpless, trying to work out what to do next until finally she saw someone moving through the trees. To her relief, it was Thea.

"Are you all right?" the young woman asked concernedly, as she hurried up to Joan.

"I had an accident," she groaned, trying to get up.

"Here, let me help you," Thea offered, going over and steadying Joan as she rose from the ground. "They've sent people looking for you along the river path, but I thought I might find you here. They don't know I'm looking too, but I'm sure they won't mind if I help you."

When she was finally standing, Thea took a look at her arm but as soon as the woman tried to move it, Joan yelped with pain.

"It's definitely broken," Thea stated solemnly. "Let me make it easier for you to bear whilst we get you back."

Thea removed the light scarf she was wearing around her hair and deftly turned it into a sling. Joan's pain eased a little, but tears were still streaming down her cheeks. She was grateful that it was this woman who had found her and not one of the men, lest her reaction arouse suspicion. They walked slowly towards the main path, stopping regularly to allow her to breathe. As they neared the river path, they soon spotted the search party led by Father Nikolis.

"Father John, what on earth happened to you?" he asked, in an anxious tone.

"I went for a walk on the mountainside, and I fell. I'm so sorry I missed my class."

"Oh, my poor boy. Let's get you to Father Takis immediately. He will give you something for the pain."

Father Nikolis looked at Thea who was still supporting Joan's arm. "Thank you, young lady. It was kind of you to help us find him. You can run along back to your washing now. We will look after him from here."

Thea looked at Joan worriedly. Joan knew the look she gave in return revealed just how much she wanted the woman to stay but neither of them had any choice, other than to part. The last thing they needed was for the Head of Seminary to become aware that they had started spending time together. So Joan allowed Father Nikolis to take Thea's place in supporting her and within moments Thea, who had no excuse for walking at such a slow pace, had disappeared down the path.

When they emerged from the trees several minutes later, the young woman was nowhere to be seen and Joan felt nothing but sorrow. All she wanted now was to lie in bed while Thea stroked her head as though she were a child. *I can't believe I have become so pathetic,* she thought through the agonizing pain, as she moved in the direction of Father Takis' kitchen, still assisted by the Father Nikolis.

On seeing her condition, the first thing Father Takis did was prepare a large tankard of poppy and valerian tea. Within a few moments of the first gulp, Joan felt her head turning giddy and the pain began to dissipate. Though disorientated, she smiled at Father Takis gratefully.

"Will he be all right now?" Father Nikolis asked, still concerned.

"He will need to drink this tea several times a day for the next fortnight, so he will be too drowsy to teach. In a while, when this medicine has fully taken effect, I will reset the bone, cover his arm with ointment, and bandage it with linen. That should further ease the pain and take away the swelling."

The seminary head looked relieved but shook his head as he spoke. "Oh, Father John! What are we going to do without you for two weeks? You will be sorely missed!"

Joan was too woozy to answer properly but tried to nod her head and smile.

Once assured his protégé was going to be all right, Father Nikolis left. As a result of the poppy and valerian tea, the pain had turned to a dull ache, and Father Takis indicated Joan lie down on one of the treatment beds at the far end of the room. She'd become extremely drowsy but even through the medicinal fog, Joan was still concerned about revealing her arm. Thankfully, as she had been doing so much swimming recently, her muscles were strong and well developed. She hoped that this would be enough not to arouse suspicion.

Before he reset the bone, Father Takis made Joan take another swig of tea and then instructed her to bite down on a roll of cloth. He was swift in his execution of the procedure but it was still excruciating.

Even muffled by the wad of material, her howl of pain echoed around the kitchen. Afterwards, when the tankard met her lips again, Joan gulped down the liquid desperately and was resistant to giving it back when Father Takis indicated she'd had enough.

The old priest let Joan rest for a few minutes whilst he went over to the large wooden table to mix a treatment for her arm. As he worked, Father Takis started listing the ingredients of the unguent, which included bishopwort, wormwood, helenium and hollowleek, but Joan found it difficult to concentrate on the plethora of herbs and her mind fogged over once again. As he pulled up her sleeve and began pasting her skin with the ointment, Father Takis still gave no indication of seeing anything out of the ordinary. Joan trusted him completely, but as he continued applying the herbs she found herself crying, wishing it was Michael who was healing her and not him.

"Don't worry, Father John. The tea can make you weepy along with the pain," said the old man, noticing her distress. "Here, you need to drink more now before I start binding it."

Joan swigged back the remains of the tea and found her head becoming fuzzy to the point where she could barely focus at all. Father Takis applied the bandage, but this time before she could react to the searing pain, everything went black.

When she awoke it was almost dark, and Father Takis was working at his long wooden table by candlelight, pounding herbs with a giant pestle and mortar.

"Aargh!" she cried, as she tried to sit up.

"Don't move, Father John. Let me come to you."

The old priest brought over a fresh tankard of tea and Joan supped at it gratefully.

"You will need to sleep in here tonight, and then tomorrow we will move you to the private cell next door so I can keep an eye on you."

Even in her disorientated state, Joan knew that this could only be a good thing. The thought of sharing a cell with Markos if she had to rest in bed for two weeks was horrendous. At least on her own, she could tend to herself without witnesses.

Then she became sad again, realising that she would not get to see Thea. Joan thought about how keen the young woman was to learn how to read and write and how disappointed she would be not to have their next lesson. Joan also remembered how wonderful it had been to see Thea come to her as she'd sat helpless in the woods—how glad she'd felt at the sight of the woman's beautiful face and how comforted by the look of compassion in her eyes. *You are in love...*came a voice from within. *I know I am...*another voice replied.

CHAPTER 11

By the third day of lying in her cell, Joan was starting to feel restless in spite of the drowsing effect of the poppy and valerian tea. She wasn't used to being incapacitated for she'd been lucky enough not to succumb to serious illness since living at the seminary. She'd had a light fever once that had been treated expertly by Michael and, of course, the odd headache, cold and stomach upset here and there, but nothing that had kept her from her duties and studies. It was hard not being active and not having enough mental capacity to even read the most basic of texts. What's more, although she was sleeping a lot, her dreams were vivid and bizarre and she had woken more than once in a start, not knowing where she was.

In addition to this, she missed Thea terribly. All Joan wanted to do was see the woman, but she was effectively imprisoned until the pain had lessened enough for her to stop drinking the tea. In the hours that passed, Thea consumed her thoughts and Joan found herself giving in to more and more elaborate fantasies of what she wanted to do with the woman. For the first time in ages, she found herself really wishing that the phallus in her braies was real. If she were a man, she would simply relinquish her vow of celibacy and seduce Thea without question. But how ever much she ached for it, there was no way that her desire for this woman could ever be fulfilled. The minute Thea found out she was female, it would all be over and she, John, would be exposed as Joan. She might even be killed for it.

Joan pleasured herself as best she could with her right hand, trying to reduce her pent up longings. But even when doing it gently, the climax was so powerful that it sent agonizing streaks of pain through her broken left arm.

Prayer had been intermittent because her thoughts both tea-blurred and Thea-obsessed, kept drifting away from God and into the arms of human love. Joan tried her hardest to keep connected to the Deity in spite of this constant distraction and begged forgiveness for having become so divided in her devotion. As she lay there struggling to concentrate yet again, there was a gentle knock on the door and Father Takis entered with a fresh bowl of ointment and bandages.

"Do you have enough tea to cope with this or shall I make you some more?" he asked.

Joan picked up the tankard and saw she had about half left from earlier. She drank it down quickly whilst Father Takis prepared the bandages at the small table by the side of her bed. After a short while, Joan felt the rush of giddiness the tea always brought run through her body and indicated that she was ready for the priest to begin.

The pain had lessened in comparison to when she'd first broken it, but still she winced as Father Takis covered the broken limb with the herbal paste. When he'd finally finished binding it, he looked at her softly.

"We've known each other a long time now, haven't we, Father John?"

"Yes," she replied foggily.

"So you know that you can trust me to help you?"

Even through the haze, alarm bells rang in her head and she felt herself tensing up. He saw her reaction and put a gentle hand on her right shoulder. "It's all right, John. You're perfectly safe. But I can make it even safer for you, if you wish."

"What do you mean?" she asked, still not wanting to believe that the old man had found out her secret.

"I mean that I can provide you with things to make this journey smoother for you. Such as a rosemary-based oil to stimulate the growth of your moustache..."

Joan gasped with horror. For he really did know the truth, and it terrified her how easily she had been found out. In spite of the medicine, she now felt wide awake. "How long have you known?" she asked anxiously.

Father Takis smiled kindly, patting her shoulder again in reassurance. "I always knew there was something—that you had some kind of secret—but I would never have guessed it was this until I treated your broken arm. You have done so very well to maintain your guise, and I'm not sure anyone other than a man of medicine would even have been able to tell from your limbs. But I assume my dear boy Michael always knew?"

"Yes. He helped make it happen."

"Then, if nothing else, I owe it to *him* to help you carry on. For a start, if you agree to assist me with the herbs every day, I could persuade Father Nikolis to give you this single cell permanently so that I can call on you in an emergency."

Joan was astounded by his kindness, but still shocked at just how easily she had been found out. She felt hugely vulnerable. "Thank you so much, Father Takis," she whispered. "It is very generous of you to help. But you won't tell Father Stefanos, will you?"

"No, John. Of course not."

"I do love God, Father..."

"That, my son, is something none of us can dispute. I do not believe that God would have protected you from discovery for so long had He not wanted you to be here, which is the other reason why I shall ensure that your secret remains safe."

Still smiling down at her, he rose from the bed. Joan looked at him gratefully, thanking him once again. Then just before he exited, he turned and spoke. "Oh. I meant to tell you yesterday. The young washerwoman came by to ask if you were all right. It was she that found you after your fall, was it not?"

Joan felt a wave of nausea overcome her. *Did Takis know about Thea too?* She gathered the last of her wits and nodded. "Oh, yes it was... that's very kind of her to ask about my well being."

Father Takis gave her a long look, and she tried to appear as innocent as possible but had no idea whether he could tell that she was in love with the girl or not. After he finally exited, she sat in opened mouthed shock. *I am so exposed without Michael...*

*

By the end of two weeks, Joan had reduced her intake of the poppy and valerian tea. However, she found it difficult to give it up altogether, not only because of the lingering pain (for she could manage that more easily now) but also because drinking the tea calmed her nerves. Since Father Takis had revealed he knew her secret, Joan had been on edge. Taking sips of the tea was the only thing that could steady her, as prayer did not seem to be working. She knew that her dependence on the concoction could not go on indefinitely because she would never be able to study with such a foggy mind, but the sensation of the drink when it hit was like being wrapped in a warm lamb's fleece and held in gentle arms. It was difficult to relinquish so deep and soothing a comfort.

Father Takis had not mentioned her secret again and still referred to her as 'son' or 'my boy' or 'John'. The old priest had already kept to his promise— he had brought rosemary oil to her cell the following day and also made her meals that were extra heavy in meat, saying they would help her get stronger. But even though Father Takis was doing all he could to assist her, Joan felt more vulnerable than at any point since she had been living as a male.

She took a small swig of tea to steady her resolve and then opened the door to her cell. She had not been outside since the accident as she was too woozy to cope with interacting with others. Even though her mind was fuzzy, she had enough sense of self-preservation to know it would not be wise to mix with people when her wits weren't fully about her. Now she was drinking less tea, she decided to go for a walk.

Joan tried to deny to herself that she would be turning right and walking straight to where Thea hung out the washing. She could not bear to admit that the pull of her love was already as powerful as the moth's to a lighted candle. And in spite of the abject danger, there was no resistance in her body when she headed straight towards the woman's domain.

It was not long before Thea came into view. She was down at the riverside, scrubbing her way through a pile of light-brown robes. The woman did not see Joan arrive and jumped when she said, "Hello."

"Father John!" she said, quickly rising to her feet and brushing down her clothes with her hands. "It's so good to see you up and about. How is your arm?"

"Much healed," Joan smiled, trying not to gaze at the woman's bosom.

"Are you still in pain?" Thea asked concernedly.

"Only a little now. Father Takis knew exactly what to do to fix it quickly."

"Oh, I am pleased. I was worried about you."

The woman blushed, averting her eyes to the direction of the washing. "I wanted to thank you again for helping me that day. It may have been hours before they came in that direction, and I would have been in terrible agony by the time they found me."

"I was just glad I knew where you'd be. But it was awful to see you in such pain. Will you get the full use of the limb back?"

"Yes. It will take a while but Father Takis says it was a clean break so there should be no problem in making a full recovery."

"Ah, good," replied the young woman, smiling shyly.

Joan could feel the tension rising between them and was sure that Thea, too, was experiencing its potency. They both stood there awkwardly not knowing what to say until finally Joan broke the impasse. "Do you still want to learn how to read and write?"

"Oh, yes. I thought you might change your mind because of what happened."

The girl looked so delighted that Joan had to resist from sweeping her up for a hug. "Of course not. I made you a promise and I intend to keep it. Another week and I will be ready to take a walk to our 'classroom'!"

"Thank you so much, Father John. You'll never know just what this means to me. I only wish there was something I could do for you in return."

Joan felt herself blushing at the thought of exactly what it was that she wanted from Thea, and this time it was she who averted her eyes. "I look at it as my duty as a priest to help all those in need, whatever that need may be. So you owe me nothing."

They continued to smile at one another but something in Joan tensed and from the corner of her eye, she became aware that someone was watching them in the near distance so turned in that direction. It was no surprise to see that it was Benedict. It was something malignant in the air that had made her feel so wary. She acknowledged his presence with a polite nod and then turned back to Thea speaking softly. "We must not be seen together in public again. It will cause suspicion. I will meet you a week from today, after evening Mass at the place where you found me when I fell and we can walk the rest of the way to the lake together. If anything changes, I will find a way to let you know. I'm going to walk away now."

"Yes," Thea whispered, with a blank expression.

At that, they turned in opposite directions, Thea, back to her work and Joan towards the herb kitchen.

CHAPTER 12

The next day, Joan decided to go to the chapel for Morning Mass, with a view to staying on to meditate after the service. She still felt dislocated from God. Over two weeks without participating in the sacrament and failure to concentrate on prayer had made her feel weakened in her connection to her beloved Heavenly Father and His Son, Jesus Christ.

She took a gulp of the tea to ensure she could manage the pain for the duration of her outing, and then hauled herself up from the bed. When she reached the chapel, she was greeted with an array of smiles and warm welcomes from the boys and men assembled for worship. She had done well over the years to keep the 'friendly-distance' that Amadeus had recommended and had made no known enemies except for Benedict, for even Father Philon treated her with respect these days.

Father Nikolis was taking the service and he looked more than pleased to see her. They sang in worship, two passages from scripture were read; then the Holy Eucharist was served. Joan had felt like she was floating for most of the ceremony and when she drank from the golden chalice, the wine hit her with a power previously unbeknownst to her. It was as if a golden fire had raced through her body and set light to everything around her. Everyone present was laced in a dazzling hue and then suddenly the cross became so ablaze with white light that Joan could barely behold it. She looked up at Father Nikolis who was smiling, and she saw the Holy Spirit, like a dove, enveloping his shoulders with Its wings. Father Nikolis turned to her and looked deeply into her eyes and then rested his hand on her head. "The Lord bless you and keep you. The Lord make His face to shine upon you and be gracious unto you. The Lord lift up His countenance upon you and give you peace." In receiving this blessing, Joan, drenched in the Spirit, sank to her knees in gratitude, silently weeping with joy.

When she finally looked up, her surroundings had returned to normal and the only person remaining was Father Nikolis. "Welcome home, Father John. We missed you," he said softly.

"I thought I…" but no more words would come.

Father Nikolis nodded his understanding. "I felt it too."

"Did anyone else?"

"I'm not sure but the atmosphere was so anointed, that you were not the only one who fell to their knees. Our Lord was happy to see you, I think."

Joan felt humbled that the seminary head would think it was her return that had brought forth God's presence so palpably. But it also made her concerned. If he knew her secret—that she was not actually a man—would he instead think that they had just been visited by the devil, disguising himself as the righteous? When he exited a few moments later, Joan remained in the chapel, now wanting to be reassured about the veracity of her experience as well as simply meditating as previously planned.

Whereas before the service Joan had struggled to connect with the Lord, now the moment she lifted her arms into the air she was drowned in His presence, just as she had been a few minutes earlier. And in her blissful union with God, her concerns over Father Nikolis' hypothetical perceptions of her, should he discover the truth, were instantly washed away. She simply worshipped. She found herself singing in the language of tongues described in the Letters of St. Paul, and her voice resounded from the stonework so deep and rich that no one hearing her could doubt that she was anything other than a man.

Then, once she had sung until no more words of either Spirit or man were forthcoming, she simply bowed her head in thanks. *I love Thee, Oh Lord. How great is Thy mercy. How beautiful Thy grace. Please grant me wisdom and strength to follow Thy law. I am sorry for my many sins. Please forgive these transgressions and let me find the courage to forgive all those who trespass against me. Amen.*

*

She was so strengthened from her reunification with the Lord that Joan soon found herself participating again in seminary life. She would not be teaching for a while but she attended those lectures of others that interested her and went to every Mass.

It would be another two days before her lesson with Thea, and she was already tingling with excitement about seeing the woman again. Her desire continued on in spite of her reconciliation with the Heavens.

As Joan walked along the riverbank, secretly hoping that she might run into Thea, she thought about what it would be like to genuinely be a young male priest, who had fallen in love. There was a divide within the church as to whether a man could truly love and serve God and be in love with and married to a woman at the same time. Some felt that the power of one love would sustain the other, whereas others argued that women were a distraction, and devotion to God must involve the necessary sacrifice of pleasures of the flesh. At the moment priests who chose to marry stood little chance of rising to the higher echelons of the church and had to content themselves with running small parishes as her own father had. Even at the seminary, to stay on as a teacher, a priest had to have taken a vow of celibacy as well.

When Joan had taken her own vow of celibacy a few short weeks ago, she had not fully realised what the argument was about. In spite of having witnessed Michael and Amadeus falling in love, until this point, she had not known what it actually *felt* like and how very powerful it was. But now she was falling in love with Thea. Her relationship with God had already come under threat because of it, and she finally understood the complexity of the issue. For being in love was almost totally consuming, and it was hard to keep God in first place.

On the other hand, this state of being in love also felt so euphoric and unalloyed in its joy that it was hard to see how God would have created creatures to feel it so powerfully as a positive urge, if they were then supposed to deny themselves it in order to follow Him. So it was by no means obvious which side of the celibacy debate was correct. All Joan knew today was that, in spite of her revitalised relationship with The Deity, the new and ardent feelings she had for Thea had not diminished. However, she was determined to double her efforts to keep in union with the Lord, so that He did not feel her devotion had lessened.

I wish I could lie with her though... came a voice from within, immediately distracting her from all thoughts of determination. This was the hardest issue. She was fairly certain that Thea was attracted to her, and if she were a real man, she would risk going in for a kiss, but there was no way she could let herself. *Perhaps this is my test...perhaps God is trying to ensure that my will to follow Him at all costs is still truly rigid.*

As she continued to walk, Joan reached the place by the river where Thea scrubbed the washing with bars of olive soap, but the woman was nowhere to be seen. Rows of brown, black and white vestments swayed softly in the gentle breeze but there was no young woman obscured amongst them. Joan could not help but be disappointed. Just a glimpse of her new love would have been enough to set her heart alight. She lingered for a short while in case Thea returned, but not wanting to rouse curiosity from even a casual observer, she soon went on her way.

When Joan returned to the kitchen, Father Takis and Father Stefanos were deeply involved in creating a fresh batch of medicine. There had been an outbreak of sickness amongst some of the young men who had eaten food cooked at the market, so they were chopping up ginger, peppermint and chamomile ready to brew in the giant cauldron on the fire. Joan chatted with them briefly before returning to her cell. Father Takis did most of the talking whilst Father Stefanos, reserved as always, nodded and smiled where appropriate.

Once sitting on her bed, Joan picked up the Gospel of Saint John and closed her eyes, letting her finger point randomly to a passage of the text. When she opened them, it had landed on chapter eight, verse twelve. 'Then spake Jesus again unto them, saying, I am the light of the world: he that followeth me shall not walk in darkness, but shall have the light of life.' She meditated on the verse for a few minutes, but found herself restless with thoughts of Thea. No matter how much she tried to concentrate, she could not focus. Exasperated, Joan put the scripture to one side and took a swig of poppy and valerian tea from the large tankard by her bed, hoping it would steady her enough to forge ahead with her contemplation. Feeling its soothing effects immediately, she gulped down the rest. But this time, rather than being soothed, instead she experienced an upward rush so powerful that it felt like she was pushed outside of her own body by its force. She tried to get a grip of herself but no matter how hard she fought to come back to earth, there was no return. It was as though she were being scooped up into the heavens by a giant hand.

Suddenly everything was brilliant white and a dazzling figure stood before her. As she gazed at its ethereal brilliance, Joan felt nothing but overflowing love. She found herself drawn towards it by a force she had no control over until the Being became her and she became the Being, entwined with one another in rapture. So powerful was their union, that Joan's senses as she knew them disappeared and all she felt was absolute 'oneness' with Love. There was no differentiation between herself and this Being; yet conversely, she knew Its magnitude and distinction from her more forcefully than ever. Suddenly, nothing on earth was important. All that mattered was this Heavenly union of unconditional love that felt as though it might last a whole eternity.

As Joan soared in blissful unification, somewhere in amongst it, words began to form again, and she found herself asking, "Do I sin by being a man?"

"No," came the reply. "Thou art my devoted child and I love thee."

Then, in an instant, Joan felt herself land with a thud on her bed, and she was back in her cell. She looked around her, totally disorientated wondering what had happened. Then her mind began to race. *What was that? Did I just unite with God in a spiritual dance? Was it real or was it some kind of delusion?* Joan looked across at the empty tankard and grimaced. *Or was it the amount of poppy and valerian tea I gulped down?*

She could not bear the thought that such unadulterated ecstasy had really been an herb-fuelled illusion, so Joan staggered to the library to consult the texts of the Mystics. There, she hoped to find confirmation that her exultation had indeed been real. On arrival, she went straight to the far right corner where texts referred to as 'Mystikos' were kept. Joan perused the many shelves. In addition to the account of St. Paul meeting Jesus on the Road to Damascus, and the many startling encounters with God described by the prophets, Joan also knew of a mystical interpretation of the Song of Solomon, which she had not yet fully studied. So this was the first text she pulled from the shelves. Penned when Christianity was still in its infancy, Father Origen's exegesis of Song of Solomon reflected that rather than being about man and woman, this piece of Holy Scripture really referred to the union of God with man. On encountering God so overflowing is the love, man feels like a bride meeting her bridegroom in the bedchamber. Once she had completed reading Origen's analysis, Joan turned to the writings of Father Macarius of Egypt. In his 'Homily', Father Macarius wrote of his own encounter with God, saying, "The face of the soul is unveiled, and it gazes upon the heavenly Bridegroom face to face in spiritual light that cannot be described."

The power and intimacy described in both of these accounts was reassuring for Joan. During her experience just a few short minutes ago, Joan had felt like she was madly in love with God and He was madly in love with her. Its potency had been astounding and she understood why these writers had evoked such bridal language, as nothing else in human experience was remotely akin to it.

Whilst reading these texts, Joan found herself side-tracked musing on another fascinating aspect of these men's understanding of their experience. Neither of these male priests had thought it shameful to refer to the man as 'the bride'. This assertion of a male being able to become a female in a holy context made Joan question whether the concept of human beings having fixed 'maleness' and 'femaleness' was a creation of human society, rather than the reality which was far more flexible. This covert assertion that there was fluidity when it came to one's sex certainly made more sense of her own position.

Once she had finished contemplating the works of Origen and Macarius, Joan then searched for a text she had once read by St. Augustine. She remembered Augustine describing a specific experience he'd had which was similar to hers. The sainted scholar wrote of how he had perceived God through his 'Soul's eye' as a brilliant light far greater than any light perceived on earth. He also described being transported into the heavens.

There are times when the soul is raptured into things seen that are similar to bodies, but are beheld in the spirit in such a way that the soul is totally removed from the bodily senses, more than in sleep but less than in death.

This account by St. Augustine of leaving behind the physical body and joining with God in a spiritual body was uncanny in its similarity to what had just happened to her. Joan was glad that she was aware that such texts existed so she at least had a frame of reference for her own experience; it meant that it was not so frightening. But nonetheless one question still lingered in her mind: *Did any of the mystics drink poppy and valerian tea first?*

When Joan returned to the herb kitchen over two hours later, Father Takis was working alone, so she broached the subject with him. After explaining what had happened to her, she asked him what his thoughts were. The elderly priest raised an eyebrow and then smirked a little. "Hmm...well...who knows how the Lord might choose to communicate with His children, but the last time I drank poppy and valerian tea, I imagined that the little white cat that Michael was so fond of had sprouted wings and was flying in circles around the rafters."

Joan looked at him seriously to check he wasn't joking and then deflated, she stated, "Best not drink anymore then..."

CHAPTER 13

Coming off the poppy and valerian tea was easier said than done. Father Takis had warned her she might be a little nauseous, but Joan was not really prepared for how hideous it would actually feel. She felt very low, like she had experienced a great sorrow and had been physically sick on several occasions. It was hard not to walk back into the kitchen and start brewing up the concoction again.

By the time she was heading through the woods for her planned meeting with Thea, Joan felt truly dreadful and was tempted to turn back and hide in bed. With only the ointment, bandages and sling to soften the pain, her arm ached terribly, particularly now she was walking rather than resting. However, on reaching their rendezvous point she was glad that she had not gone back for Thea greeted her with a smile so broad that Joan's heart thumped eagerly in her chest. The woman was wearing a dark red linen dress, with a pattern of butterflies stitched in gold thread. The garment was simple but elegant and made her look more appealing than ever.

They walked amicably towards the lake, and Thea asked about Joan's arm and how she had been coping during her recovery. Joan wanted so much to discuss with Thea the two such profound experiences she'd had with the Lord. She yearned to know Thea's thoughts on whether or not they were genuine, but she found herself holding back. For Joan to talk too much about her inner thoughts would take their relationship a step closer. It did not matter how much her heart desired that, her mind told her to resist. At the end of the day she could not have what she wanted with this woman, even if she relinquished her vow of celibacy. She had to prevent herself from making it more intense than it already was, how ever hard that might be.

As the terrain became more difficult, Thea instinctively grabbed Joan's good arm and steadied her across the rocks. This time Joan did not shrink from her touch for she needed the woman's help. Normally Joan would scramble up quickly, but now it was much more of an ordeal and by the time they'd reached the top, she was panting with exhaustion.

"Here," Thea indicated, "sit on that flat rock for a moment and get your breath back. We have plenty of time before we lose the light."

Joan sat down gratefully holding her damaged arm close to her chest whilst trying not to wince. But Thea sensed her distress anyway. "Did you forget to drink your painkilling tea?" she asked sympathetically.

"I...er...I was worried I was getting addicted to it so I stopped taking it yesterday."

The woman nodded her understanding then paused for thought before speaking. "Hmm, I think I know something that will help you. Wait a minute, and I'll see if I can find some nearby."

Thea disappeared back down into the trees and was soon out of sight altogether, so Joan allowed herself to whimper a little from the agony. After a short while, the young woman reappeared with a handful of greenery. "They're willow leaves. They're awfully bitter but they should ease the pain."

Joan smiled gratefully and started stuffing leaves in her mouth. They did indeed taste horrible, but she was so in need of relief that she continued chewing. The painkilling effects were not as immediate as with the poppy and valerian tea, but while they walked slowly down to the lakeside, Joan found her arm easing enough to concentrate again.

When they reached their outdoor classroom, Joan was pleased to discover that the teaching materials had remained secure in the bag under the stone and, apart from being a little dusty, were unharmed during her absence. Joan pulled out the battered old quill, a scrap of parchment and the ink, then found a comfortable position in which to sit. It was a relief that it was her left arm she had broken and not her right for she could draw the letter as required. "This is 'Beta'," she explained. "We use it for 'Bee', 'Butter', and 'Birds'."

Thea studied the letter and then used some examples of her own. "Beta for 'Bugs', 'Bath' and 'Bed'!"

The beautiful woman smiled so enthusiastically that Joan forgot the lingering pain in her arm and instead tried to fend off the swirl of flapping butterflies that seemed to have jumped from Thea's dress and into her stomach.

As in their first lesson, Thea was quick to master the art of drawing the letter and after a few attempts could write it without hesitation. Joan was confident that if they met most evenings, within no time at all the woman would be forming words. She liked it that the object of her desire was intelligent. It excited her, and she could not help but imagine them together tucked up in bed reading scrolls by candlelight and discussing their theological implications.

"Would you like to hear another story about a female saint?" Joan asked, once their lesson was done and they moved slowly back towards the woods.

"Yes," replied Thea smiling. "But first, I want to tell you about the woman who once ruled these lands from her seat in Constantinople. Did you know about her?"

Joan raised her eyebrows in surprise. "No. No one has ever mentioned that to me. When was it?"

"About thirty years ago, I think."

"What! Really? That recent and nobody told me?"

Thea laughed for a moment. "If a woman rises to power, once she is gone, men will do all they can to pretend it never happened. Of course, no one will have told you about it. The only way you would have known her name was if she had done something so terrible that she was used as an example of the moral badness of women. You men are all the same. You don't want to believe a woman is capable of leadership."

Joan looked at her guiltily. Thea was more correct than she realised. For Joan had become so used to thinking like a man that she no longer sought out stories of women who had been sainted or held power, in order to affirm her own choices. She simply lived as a man and conversed as one, barely giving women a second thought. It wasn't until she had started telling Thea about the female saints at the end of their previous lesson that she had even thought about them for a long time. She had simply gotten used to the fact that the only examples ever given of holy human beings were male ones; the only thinkers' works that were discussed were those of men; and that the Scriptures were all written by men as well.

"I expect you are right," she said apologetically. "But please tell me about this female ruler. I'd like to hear her story."

"Well, she is known as 'Irene of Athens' because she originated from here even though she ended up ruling from Constantinople. Sometimes she referred to herself as 'empress' and sometimes as 'emperor' like a man."

Joan was immediately excited about this revelation and desperately wanted to know the whole story. "Tell me everything you know about who she was and how she got to rule like a man, I'm intrigued!'

Thea smiled at her, obviously pleased that Joan's interest had been piqued. "Her husband, Emperor Leo IV, ruled for a short while but died when their eldest son, called 'Constantine' like many before him, was nine years old. After Leo's death, instead of conceding the throne to Leo's half brother, Nikephoros, Irene took the throne for herself and became Empress with young Constantine as Regent. Whilst she ruled, she fended off several attempts to dethrone her and caused great controversy by condoning the use of icons in worship. In fact, the very reason why your seminary chapel is still full of icons is because *she* had her way against those who believed they should be abolished."

"Good grief! I can't believe I didn't know all this. I'm ashamed. Especially given how important those icons are to my own worship. We have debated both sides of the argument concerning icons but her name has never been mentioned!"

"See, what did I tell you? Men don't want to tell her story in spite of the good things she did for them."

"How long did she rule for in total?"

"About five years. She managed to defend her lands against attacks from the Franks and the Arabs, who thought she was a weak target being a woman. But in the end, it was her own son who challenged her authority and the loyalties of the people became divided."

"Who won?"

"She did, at least in the first instance. She got wind of a plot to kill her and had Constantine arrested. However Irene was no saint and instead of just imprisoning him, she had his eyes gouged out to stop him from ever trying again. Unfortunately, though, instead of just blinding him, he died from his wounds, which was not what she had intended. Shortly after this incident, because the 'Regent' was now dead, the Patrician governors across the empire conspired against her and exiled her to the Island of Lesbos, giving Nikephoros the throne."

"And how did you know all this?"

"Because, I listen to the stories told me by my parents, grandparents, aunties and uncles. Just because I can't read or write doesn't mean I'm an ignoramus!" snapped Thea.

"Sorry, I didn't mean to imply that you were! I just don't know how knowledge is dispersed in a non-academic environment—especially to women..."

"A woman has to glean all the information she can from wherever she can if she is to keep her own power and not be sucked into a life she does not want."

"Is that why you aren't married?" Joan found herself asking, unable to control her curiosity. The woman was at least twenty and Joan had often wondered over the last few weeks why there was no contender for her affections.

"I don't want to talk about my past any more than you do yours!" Thea snapped, quickening her pace so she was ahead.

"I'm sorry. It was rude of me to ask. Please forgive me," Joan cried after her.

Thea continued at a pace that was hard for Joan to keep up with, given the lack of balance from only having the use of one arm.

"Thea, please!" she pleaded, when the woman still did not reply.

Thea turned around and looked at her crossly. "I know you are a priest and unused to dealing with the female of the species, but you must understand that there are some questions that should never be asked."

"Yes. You are right, and I really do apologise. I should not have raised it."

The young woman nodded her acceptance, then turned back facing the path. But this time she walked slowly enough for Joan to keep up. Once they reached the rocks, Thea's mood was calmer and she held out her hand to steady Joan where their descent became difficult. Each time their palms met, Joan felt pins and needles dart up her arm and travel down through her body. By the time they finally landed on the ground, Joan was so overwhelmed by the tingling effect that she could not let go of the woman's hand. Instead, she stared deep into Thea's dark brown eyes— transfixed by them. Thea returned the ardent gaze, and Joan knew that all she needed to do was bend to meet her lips and they would end up making love amongst the trees. It was only because she suddenly remembered that she was a woman not a man and realised how little it would take for Thea to discover the truth, that she pulled her hand away and walked on.

The rest of their walk was silent. Joan knew that Thea, like her, was fighting back feelings and was probably hurt by the fact that 'John' had not kissed her. For no matter how much she offended the woman by her ignorance and assumptions, when they were in harmony the energy between them was terrifying in its power.

On reaching their parting place they both stood awkwardly, neither wanting to leave but neither being able to say what was in their hearts.

"Would you like another lesson tomorrow?" Joan finally asked.

"Yes, please," Thea replied, smiling nervously.

"Good. Meet me in the same place," said Joan, walking off towards the seminary without looking back.

CHAPTER 14

Joan barely slept that night. Between trying to resist brewing up poppy and valerian tea, and working out how she could possibly teach Thea again without jumping on top of her, it was impossible. She felt truly dreadful. Eventually, she went into the kitchen and made herself a strong tankard of chamomile, sipping at it gratefully as it took the edge off her nerves.

She wished she could go swimming in the lake to get the pent up energy out of her system, but even if she got in and tried floating on her back just kicking her legs, it could be perilous given how very deep the water was. And besides, she would never make it up those rocks without Thea's assistance.

On returning to her cell she pleasured herself for the seventh time that night, yet still it was not enough. All she wanted was to be inside Thea, on top of her and underneath her. Only that would sate her need. It would be easier if the woman did not want it too, but even though Joan had never been in a love relationship before, it was obvious that Thea was feeling the same desire as her. *Oh Lord. Please help me. How can I go on like this? I have barely known her a month yet I feel like I cannot breathe without her. Please show me the way. I am not strong enough to fight this alone, and I fear so much the consequences if I fall.*

After her prayer, Joan finished the chamomile tea and then sat cross-legged on her bed. With her hands on her knees, palms facing upwards, she stared at the flickering flame of the candle on her bedside table. Remembering how it got her through the peril of the mountain ridge whilst trying to save the life of Amadeus Reichenbach all those years ago, Joan instinctively started repeating the first three lines of Psalm 23 over and over again.

> *The Lord is my shepherd; I shall*
> *not want*
> *He maketh me lie down in green*
> *pastures*
> *He leadeth me beside the still*
> *waters*
> *He restoreth my soul*
> *He leadeth me in paths of*
> *righteousness for His name's sake*

After chanting this quietly for several minutes, Joan felt herself enveloped with peace and her mind became light and feathery. Then suddenly she found herself travelling up through the crown of her head and floating above herself in the room. She looked down at her body sitting cross-legged on the bed and from the vantage point of the ceiling, saw that a silver thread attached her to it. Instinctively knowing that so long as the thread joined her to her physical body she would not die, Joan allowed herself to travel to her heart's desire. Within a heartbeat, she was inside Thea's cottage hovering above the woman as she lay in bed. As she gazed down at the sleeping woman, Joan felt her soul oozing with love, and she allowed herself to travel downwards to merge with Thea's soul, which lay just above her body. The instant their souls connected, Thea sat bolt upright, eyes wide open and shouted "John!" out loud. Joan was immediately flung back up to the rafters. She stared down from on high at the woman she loved; overwhelmed by the power of how it had felt for them to be joined for just that single moment.

"I love you," whispered Thea into the darkness.

With a violent jolt, Joan suddenly returned to her physical body, still cross-legged on her bed, in her cell. "I love you too, Thea," she whispered, before trying to work out what on earth had just occurred.

Joan reached for the tankard to check that it was indeed chamomile tea she had drunk and that she had not made poppy and valerian tea accidentally on purpose. A sip confirmed it was definitely chamomile. She sat there puzzled, wondering what on earth was going on. She had never heard of anyone hallucinating due to chamomile tea, and what she had just experienced felt so very real that it was hard to see how it could have been just a fantasy. It felt like she had seen Thea with her own eyes and she was still ablaze from the ecstatic joy of just one moment of their souls colliding. *But then again, maybe it was just a fabulous and wonderful dream*, she thought. *I've had so very many weird and fantastical dreams since I've broken my arm...*

Joan went over the experience again in her mind. She had been meditating deeply and then suddenly found herself out of her body. She had then seen that she was now a spirit body joined by a silver thread to her physical element. When she'd had the powerful experience of being at one with the Lord just a few days earlier, she had no memory of seeing a thread, but she'd had the same sense of leaving a living body behind and experiencing existence as a spirit body. The main difference seemed to be that in the first experience she'd felt as if the hand of God had scooped her soul up, whereas in the second she'd exited her body of her own volition. Both experiences felt totally real; they did not have the fading edges that a vivid dream might. They were perfectly clear, and one felt no less valid than the other. The one with the Lord was more satisfying and blissful than anything she'd conceived possible. But the one with Thea, albeit only lasting for a short moment, produced a different kind of fulfilment and completion. She did not know if she would ever be privileged enough to experience either again, but she knew that she would like to. One thing was for certain—she would be spending much more time at the 'Mystikos' section in the library.

The only scriptural reference she could think of that spoke of a silver thread was in Ecclesiastes near the end where the reader is urged to remember God 'before the silver cord be severed'. When they had studied this passage in Biblical Exegesis classes the interpretation offered was that it referred to the spinal cord. No one had suggested it was a cord or thread that tied the spirit to the body. Now she wondered whether this was what it really meant.

Joan's thoughts then turned to Thea. If what she'd just experienced was real and not an hallucination or dream, three amazing things were true. Firstly, Thea had fallen in love with her too; it wasn't just an attraction, they were 'in love'. Secondly, she had visited her love in a way that no else could witness, which meant that if she could learn how to travel like this again, she could go to Thea at night and no one would ever know. Thirdly, Thea had called her 'John' which meant that her spirit did not give away her sex which, in turn, meant that either spirits are not defined by masculinity or femininity and are without a 'sex'; or she was a male spirit somehow trapped in a female body, which was why God had let her live as a man. Either of the two possibilities would make perfect sense, and she had no preference for her own self either way. However, in terms of the bigger picture, she hoped that the first scenario was the real truth, as this meant that 'men' and 'women' were equal and had the same type of soul in the sight of God. This would make separation of their roles and the subsequent permissions as to what they were or were not allowed to do, human constructions not Heavenly ones. From God's perspective the difference in bodies was simply for the purpose of procreation and nothing else. This would indeed illucidate Saint Paul's words in Galatians 3:28, "There is neither Jew nor Greek, there is neither slave nor free, there is no male and female, for you are all one in Christ Jesus."

In addition to these insights, Joan now finally understood what 'two souls being joined before the eyes of God' actually meant with regards to the sacrament of marriage. Her soul had literally melded with Thea's, and she wanted nothing more than for them to meld again with God's blessing—that God would indeed bind them together like that permanently so that no one could put them asunder.

Her next questions were: Had God shown her a way for her to have such a union that didn't involve her being 'found out' in physical reality but could satisfy her emotionally? Or was she in fact now permanently deranged due to the overconsumption of poppy and valerian tea?

*

Later that day after Mass, Joan saw Benedict lingering in the chapel. She had successfully avoided him for several weeks, and it was disappointing that he should choose tonight of all nights to loiter, given how much she wanted to ensure her relationship with God was intact. Joan needed the steadfastness brought by participating in the sacrament now more than ever before, as she still worried that she was being deluded in some way either by malevolent design or mental incapacity. She wanted the reassurance that she was righteous and sanctified before her Lord.

To her surprise, Benedict did not approach her as she remained quietly seated in the first pew on the right. Rather, he took the other pew on the left and simply sat there. Joan tried to concentrate on prayer but just Benedict's presence distracted her so instead, she imagined God sending her a giant angel to stand over her and protect her with its wings. Whether or not there was really an angel received on request she could not see, but as she sat there imagining the large white feathers blocking Benedict's energies from her own, Joan felt stronger and more at peace in his company than she had in a long time. Then, after several more minutes of her holding this visualisation, Benedict stood up and marched out without coming near her. *Thank you, God. Thank you, angel,* she said silently.

Once Benedict had left, Joan's meditation became easier, and it did not take long for her to feel awash with God's unconditional love. Half an hour later when she met Thea in the woods, she felt calm and confident. After exchanging the usual pleasantries, they gazed upon each other longer than ever before. Thea looked at her searchingly but did not speak, and Joan remained silent also. This made Joan wonder whether she had indeed visited Thea in the night and whether the woman had somehow sensed it.

Once their gaze finally broke, they walked in amicable silence for a while before halting simultaneously at the sudden appearance of a pair of young roe deer just ahead of them. The two creatures were chasing one another in and out of the trees, lost in their own world of fun and frolic, unaware of their audience. Every so often they would stop together and nuzzle one another lovingly before one of them darted off and the chase recommenced. Joan realised that at some point during their silent watching she must have grabbed hold of Thea's arm with excitement. As the woman turned to her, beaming with joy from watching the beautiful animals at play, Joan felt a rush of love run through her so intense that her centre literally ached with passion. Quickly, she turned her attention back to the deer and breathed deeply in through her nose and out through her mouth trying to regain her composure.

Eventually the creatures disappeared from view, and Joan indicated they should make their way to the lake. Thea steadied her as she climbed up the rocks, but thankfully the ascent was easier today as Father Takis had given her tincture of willow bark in a corked glass bottle so she could take a few drops as and when required. Joan felt the loss acutely when Thea let go of her arm as they reached the natural path that led gently down to the lake. It felt so good to be touching—and she craved it—in spite of what danger it might lead to.

Her pupil had been so quick to learn during the first two sessions that Joan decided to teach two letters that evening to see if she could cope. Thea mastered 'Gamma' and 'Delta' without problem and was excited that the pace of her learning had increased. "Maybe we can try three next time?" she asked excitedly.

"Yes, but you need to practice at home too if we're going to pick up speed. Why don't we take back some of the scraps so you can work on them in your cottage?"

"I have some fabric dye I could use as ink, but do you think you could get me another quill?"

Joan thought for a moment. "That should be all right, but you will have to wait until tomorrow night for that as I don't want to be seen with you in the day if we can help it."

Thea paused before speaking. "Yes...all right...but I can't meet with you tomorrow or Sunday. We have special family time at weekends. On Saturday, the wider family gather together and we sing and tell stories; and on the Sabbath, we take Mass twice at the church at the bottom of the hill and then eat a frugal meal together at home."

Joan could not help but feel disappointed. She had simply assumed that they would spend every single evening together because she was free herself then. She had been arrogant to think that Thea would not have any other life or interests outside of her.

"Very well," she smiled politely. "I will find a quill for you ready for Monday evening."

They got up from the stone writing table and stood together for a while taking in their surroundings. Joan gazed at the aquamarine bliss of the lake. It was a very warm evening, and she would have liked nothing more than to dive in naked with her loved one and swim around with her, entwining in the water like the river otters used to back in Austrasia where she'd lived as a child. *This is going to be nothing but agony every single time...*

"So," Thea stated, breaking Joan's reverie and turning towards home. "Whilst we walk back may I hear another story of a female saint?"

"That would be my pleasure!"

By the time they reached their parting point, Joan had in fact told Thea two stories of strong women in the history of the church. St. Adele who founded her own abbey in Trier—without the permission of men—and was known as a great leader, both powerful and compassionate; and then St. Eustadiola who did a similar thing in Bourges, using her money as a widow to build her own convent and run it single-handedly.

"If I'd been a boy, I would have begged to join the seminary. I've always thought my brothers foolish to want to follow my father as a blacksmith. Not a single one so far has shown any interest in the priesthood. I would have loved to be a priest like you—studying and thinking all day."

Joan tried not to give away her euphoria at hearing her love say those words. "Why didn't you become a nun?" she asked instead.

Thea's face dropped and she turned away, speaking with clipped tones and not making eye contact. "I'd best be on my way now. It's getting dark, and I don't want to keep you. It's my turn to go first."

Without looking back, Thea sped off down the path and left Joan wondering what on earth had changed the woman's mood. As she walked back, she felt deflated. It had been a beautiful evening, but something had gone wrong and she did not know what it was. *Why would Thea be offended with my asking why she didn't become a nun? I don't understand...*

*

Later that night, when Joan returned to her cell, she did not want to sleep. She couldn't believe that she wouldn't see Thea until Monday, and they hadn't even left one another in a positive manner. She thought again about why she might have offended the woman by asking her about not choosing to be a nun. *Perhaps her family would not let her...or perhaps she was refused because she was not seen as pious enough...*

Whatever it was, Joan just wanted to make things right with the woman. She hated the thought of Thea in that cottage, alone and upset. She just wished she could go to her and wrap her arms around her, telling her how much she already cared.

This image of being with Thea was strong and it made Joan restless, until finally she realised that there might actually be a way to make it a reality. She went to the kitchen, brewed chamomile tea as she had done the night before, then returned to her cell and sat cross-legged on her bed, staring at the candle flame. This time she did not repeat a Bible verse but instead whispered Thea's name time and again whilst visualising her spirit coming out through the top of her head and travelling to the woman's cottage. But nothing happened. It did not matter how determined she was, she remained there trapped in her body. In the end she was so frustrated that she got under the covers and pressed the fingers of her right hand deep into her need. Although it still hurt to move her left arm, she nonetheless gripped the phallus tightly, imagining plunging it into Thea with all of her passion.

It was just before her moment of climax that it happened. Suddenly she found herself hovering above Thea's body only to find that Thea was doing exactly the same as she, rubbing the very centre of her most private area and moaning. As their souls touched, the woman juddered and started moaning the words, "John! John! Oh, John!" Then in a violent crescendo which made her torso rise from the bed she cried out, "John, please..." before landing back with a crash.

Joan's soul did not leave the woman but instead basked blissfully in her essence. Thea brought her pillow to her chest, kissing it and rolling around the bed with it before pleasuring herself again. This time the woman put the fingers of her left hand inside herself whilst the fingers of her right hand massaged the small mound that nestled between folds of skin. When Thea had climaxed for this second time, she no longer moved about but instead just held the pillow tightly. "I want you with me, John," she whispered.

Joan's soul, filled to the brim with love, remained immersed and entwined in Thea's soul until the woman finally drifted into sleep. Then she followed the silver cord back to her cell.

When she jolted back into her body, she suddenly found herself crying. Partly because she had experienced such joy and partly because she knew that if her body had been in the room along with her spirit then she would have reached absolute perfection.

CHAPTER 15

"And what makes you think that you know anything of how we should manage law and order in the city?" the grey-bearded man asked gruffly.

Joan was surprised by the tone of the man whom she had not met until this morning. She was sitting at the Council of Athens for the first time and had just suggested that they should stop stoning people to death for stealing. It seemed inexplicably unchristian and harsh to her that such punishments still existed, so she decided to press her point.

"Was it not Christ himself who said 'Let he who is without sin cast the first stone?'"

"Look, son. We're not at the Seminary Of St. Joseph now. This is the big wide world where real people live," retorted the grey-bearded man.

There was a murmur of agreement amongst the older men, and Joan now knew that she was totally out of her depth. He was right. She had not lived in the 'real world' as he put it, since she was a child. And that was a very different world from Athens. What made her more uncomfortable, though, was his total lack of respect. She simply was not used to it. Apart from Benedict, and perhaps Father Amos and Father Philon who were more cynical about such matters, everyone at the seminary believed her to be anointed by God's spirit and wise beyond her years, so treated her with the appropriate deference. Now suddenly, in this environment she was being treated like a mere boy and one perhaps more naïve than a normal boy her age precisely because of the life she led at that religious institution.

She looked around at the wall of men. They were sat in the resplendent narthex of what used to be called 'The Parthenon', where the ancient peoples of this land had once worshipped the goddess Athena. It was now one of the most important centres of Christian worship in Greece. In the main church, separated by a wall from where they were currently sat, the original statue of Athena had been replaced with a giant effigy of Mary, Mother Of God, and the whole complex had been renamed the 'Church of The Virgin Mary of Athens'.

Out of the fifty men present, elected from esteemed occupations and stations across the city, she was by far the youngest, and now she realised that she was also perceived as the most inferior. It was an honour to have been given a place, which Father Nikolis must have organised with the Bishop, but in reality she had no status amongst them yet.

She sat quiet for the rest of the session, just listening to the men and how they conversed. As well as the Bishop of Athens who had ordained her, there were several priests there, all of whom were much older than herself. The rest of those present, although Christian in name, were clearly men of the world who had little respect for the traditions and guardianship of the Mother Church in the way they believed the city should be run. They were more aggressive than 'men of God' and some even sat in a manner that suggested they were ready to take on anyone who challenged them, with their fists as readily as their minds. Some of them wore armour, others robes of office, be it law or politics. The strongest amongst them sat upright with legs apart, and more than one had arranged his posture to flaunt the size of his masculinity.

As she sat there, arm in a sling and one of the shortest and weakest-looking in the room, she knew that whatever else happened, she needed to get to know this world and fit amongst its occupants as easily as she did those of the seminary, if she wished to continue successfully passing as a man as she left behind her teenage years. Learning masculinity from churchmen was not enough, she realised, to pass in the wider world too.

Her exercise routine had almost been destroyed since breaking her arm, and walking would not be enough to maintain the level of muscle she needed. She would have to start lifting heavy stones again. Even though the left arm would be out of action for a good deal longer, there was nothing to stop her exercising the right, and she would also devise some work for her legs too. Then, when she was back to full movement, she would swim harder and longer in the mornings and, equally, start doing heavy work again on the farm. If she wanted to have time to keep teaching Thea too, she would simply have to give up her work illuminating texts.

The next stage of development would be to find out more about Athens. Although she knew the main areas, she really did not know much about the city or the lives of people within it. The grey-bearded man was right. She was sheltered away from 'ordinary life'. And if she were indeed going to win the respect of these men of stature and repute, she would have to be seen amongst them more and know about the lives of the common folk they were there to serve. She would talk with Father Nikolis about it when she returned. There had to be something she could do to get to know the city, its people, and its politics more than she did currently. One thing was for sure. She did not want to feel as humiliated and infantile as she had in this meeting today.

When she returned to her cell later that day, she practiced sitting like the army generals. Upright, shoulders back, head held high and fearless. It made her feel strong and virile, and within moments of taking on the posture she was on fire for Thea. Instinctively she put her hand to her phallus but instead of rubbing it, she tightened the harness so that it stood out from her body. *I want a bigger one...* she thought as she looked down.

*

As they greeted one another, Thea gazed at her with large brown eyes more intense than ever before. This time Joan was even more convinced that the woman was acknowledging their spiritual meeting in the night. She realised though that it would be a subject they would never speak of out loud. Neither of them would want to seem mad or deluded to the other and, of course, to talk of it would also mean having to discuss what was actually going on between them—that they were falling in love and wanted to be together.

However, now that she was more certain that her experience of them merging in the spiritual world was not just an hallucination, she did not know how she was going to make it through another lesson without touching the woman. Thea wanted her as much as she wanted Thea. And even though it had satisfied her to experience this truth in a different dimension, in *this* dimension Joan's cunte, heart and the area just above her naval now physically hurt with longing. It was a pain of absolute desire that could only be fully sated by their bodily union, and such union could not happen under any circumstances. *Aargh!* she howled in her mind.

To distract herself from being consumed by need as they walked through the woods, Joan asked Thea to describe her weekend. It was a good strategy, for Joan was genuinely curious about the lives of the woman's family. She needed this insight into how people who were not of the church actually lived. Thea described her relatives and their activities; the stories they told, the songs they sang, and the arguments between the boys and young men who tried to outdo one another in tests of stamina and strength. One of their favourite stories, according to Thea, was of how the Athenians had outwitted the arrogant and facetious Trojans by fooling them with the gift of a giant wooden horse with soldiers hiding inside. Although the tale was ancient and some disputed whether it really happened, Thea said that amongst the common folk of the city it was always used as an example of the natural supremacy and wit of the Greeks.

On reaching the rocks, Joan refused to take Thea's help, even though she needed it. For she remembered the men at the Council of Athens earlier that day and how strong and powerful looking most of them were. Joan now wanted to have that presence herself and one way to gain it would be to learn to override pain. She scrambled up the rough and rocky incline using her free hand and the strength of her legs in new ways to create balance. When she finally reached the top she was proud of herself, and although she had sacrificed touching the woman she wanted most ardently, it was worth it for the feeling of achievement. And besides, it was probably better to diminish any more touch between them, given that it only made things worse.

Thea excelled again in her lesson, learning the letters 'epsilon', 'zeta' and 'eta' with ease. Joan was deeply proud of her pupil and was further delighted by Thea's expression of achievement. The woman's smile was so broad that Joan felt she might be totally absorbed by it. Seeing desire rising in Thea's face made her gravitate forward, and Joan was only a moment from kissing her before she pulled herself back and jumped to her feet instead.

As she looked back at Thea, she saw the woman trying to hide her disappointment, and Joan felt sorry to the core. Thea was in love with her and all she wanted was the man she loved to kiss her. Thea also knew that Joan wanted her too. The only thing between them in the woman's eyes would be Joan's vow of celibacy. Little did she know that in reality that was the least of Joan's reasons for pulling away.

Determined to regain her equilibrium, Joan marched ahead. Her arm ached as she walked at a pace up hill but at the same time the rest of her body thanked her for the exercise. She had missed working her legs like this and could not wait to push herself even further. When she reached the incline where she would descend, she looked back to see that Thea was far behind her, but knowing it would take her an eon to climb down unaided she did not wait and pressed ahead. Finding the necessary balance to get down safely was her greatest challenge yet, but by focusing her concentration she eventually reached the ground without injury.

It was not long before Thea joined her but instead of returning Joan's smile, she looked upset and walked on ahead. Joan felt guilty then. She had sped away without talking to her, and the woman was hurting inside because of it. She'd been unfair.

She caught up with Thea, matching her pace. "Would you like another story of a female saint?" she asked gently.

"No thank you," Thea replied, looking ahead.

"Well, perhaps you'd like this, instead?" Joan pulled the spare quill and a bundle of linen scraps from her robe pocket and handed them to her. Thea, although clearly still cross, could not help but be grateful to her. "Thank you. I shall practice all evening and a little tomorrow morning as well."

"Good, because we're doing three more letters next time."

After that, their silence was more companionable but the unsated passion between them was still palpable. Joan found it nothing short of agonizing.

"I'll go first tonight," she said firmly. "See you here tomorrow evening." She then walked away fast and determinedly, without looking back, knowing that if she turned for just one glimpse they would end up running into one another's arms.

When she returned to her cell, the first thing she did was work her fingers vigourously against the small mound that had been throbbing with lust all evening. She would not be able to concentrate on anything else until she found relief. Then, once she had taken away the worst of the ache, she went about arranging her small cell for exercise. She lay on the floor with a large stone between her lower legs and tried to pull up her body from the ground without using her arms. After that she took a smaller stone and started exercising the right arm as she used to when she shared her cell with Michael. Finally, she lay down again and began lifting her heavy wooden bed with the power of her legs.

Her broken arm was in agony by the time she had finished, and she had to fight the temptation not to boil up poppy and valerian tea to soothe the pain. Instead, she consumed twice as much of the willow bark medicine as recommended by Father Takis and brewed herself a large tankard's worth of chamomile tea.

Before drinking the tea, however, she took a long swig of the bitter tincture of tribulus herb that Father Takis had made especially for her. He had never prescribed tribulus before but understood it would help her increase muscle and feel more male. Normally, it was given to men of war who wanted to be stronger in battle, and because this was a holy institution, he had not deemed it necessary to grow the plant. But a few days previously the elderly priest had bought a large clump from the market, potted some up and prepared the remainder for her to start taking straight away.

After drinking the tribulus, Joan then rubbed rosemary oil into her light moustache and massaged even more into her chin, hoping to stimulate growth there as well. Then she pulled off her robes and sat upright in bed drinking her chamomile tea.

The exercise had helped calm much of her pent up desires but her mind was still churning. Up until meeting Thea, she had only wanted to know what it *felt like* to be a man so she could continue to 'pass' enough to keep studying theology. Growing facial hair and gaining muscle had been a necessary part of continuing on with her guise. The prize of first being a seminarian and then becoming a priest had been worth sacrificing her feminine appearance for. But now feeling like a man and looking like a man was not enough. She found herself deeply wanting to actually *be* a man, because if she were, she could have Thea— and she wanted Thea more than anything else in the world.

As things stood, there was no way that this was possible and nor could it happen if she became a woman again. For not only would she have to give up being a priest and everything she had worked so hard for, it was a man that Thea had fallen in love with not a woman. Thea would probably be horrified by and abhor the idea of sexual intimacy with a woman. And besides, she had never heard of two women living together like a man and wife. Joan suspected that society would react to it with the same violence as it did towards two men. They would be in as much danger as Amadeus and his lover Wolfgang had been.

The only reference to women being with one another she'd ever seen in the Bible was in Romans 1:26 where it listed it amongst an array of sins that St. Paul had described taking place in another city, 'For this cause God gave them up unto vile affections: for even their women did change the natural use into that which is against nature.' In her studies, this passage had never been discussed, but it was clear to Joan that if same sex union was banned for men it was also banned for women.

However, for her to become a full man, which she would happily do if it meant she could be with Thea, would also be impossible. For all his help with outward appearances, Joan knew it was beyond even the powers of Father Takis to help her grow a real phallus. Instead, from now on, she would be stuck floating somewhere between male and female, and be unable to fulfil herself as either for the rest of her life. Joan thought back to Amadeus Reichenbach's words the night she'd asked him for help disguising herself as a boy, 'Child, you know not what you sacrifice,' he had said. Now, nearly five years later, she finally understood what he meant…

She longed for Michael then. Things had been so much simpler when it was he and she together, fulfilling one another's basic needs. Even though she was so in love with Thea and her heart soared at the thought of her, part of her wished she had never met the woman. Then she would not have known what it was to be in love and have one's body taken over by such an all-consuming passion. She would have remained satisfied as she was.

Joan and Michael had written to one another twice each since he'd left for Marathon but their letters had been very limited in content. They'd agreed that there must be nothing in writing that would give away her secret, talk of his need for men or mention the intimacy they'd shared in their cell. They'd kept to the basic facts such as Joan having broken her arm and Michael having visited the lepers for the first time and how frightening that was. Joan had not written anything about Thea, nor her experience of being swept up by God, nor feeling like she could travel out of her body. In fact, she might as well have been writing to a stranger, for there was nothing of her real self shared and vice versa. She just hoped that she would get to see her best friend soon. Michael had been gone only two months, yet it felt like she'd been through two years worth of experiences since his departure.

Thoughts of Thea drifted through her mind. She wondered whether her soul would go to her tonight, or whether like Saturday and Sunday nights, she would try again and fail. Joan was not yet sure what the key ingredients were to guarantee that her soul would leave her physical body and travel, but things with Thea had been so upsetting tonight, she longed to visit her. She yearned to wrap her soul around Thea's in comfort. So when she finished sipping the chamomile tea, Joan lay back on the sheets, repeating Thea's name over and over, and imagining the woman lying in bed. But to Joan's disappointment her spirit remained where it was.

CHAPTER 16

The next day, Joan taught her first lesson since breaking her arm. It was to the older students, and they discussed the role of confession and penance in the church.

Just like the issue of the role of women in leadership, the issue of penance had been viewed differently by the two wings of the Church, which had been fairly isolated from one another for centuries. In the traditions of Rome and Greece, unless the individual *wanted* to confess to sin publically and be given penance to do by the community as a means of supporting themselves in their faith, small sins were confessed directly to God. This personal penance was a matter of asking for forgiveness and doing prostrations in front of the altar. Only serious sins such as murder and adultery were confessed officially—and that was to the Bishop, whose job was to determine what course of action was necessary for the individual to be reconciled with God and be able to participate once again in Holy Communion. But in the Celtic lands a different practice had emerged where each individual was to confess *all* of their sins, both large and small, to a priest or monk and was then given a tariff according to the nature of the sin itself—such as several days of fasting for the sin of greed. Only then, when they had completed their tariff, were they forgiven.

Whereas on the role of women, Joan wholeheartedly believed that the Celtic church was right; with regards to this issue she agreed with Rome. Confession to another individual for every single little sin to ensure being on right terms with God seemed unnecessary. After all, Jesus had died in order for people to be forgiven of their sins. So if someone was genuinely sorry for a small sin, such as a moment of jealousy, it seemed perfectly reasonable for them to say sorry to the Deity directly and perhaps spend more time at the altar without needing the intervention of another person to make things right.

Her students had mixed views on the matter. Some of them liked the idea of tariff-based confession, as they felt that it would make a person more mindful of their actions if they had to speak of their wrongdoings aloud and be told what the price of such sin was. Other students preferred the Roman position that only really serious transgressions required confession and penance.

Joan was relieved that the Celtic practice of confessing all had not been taken on board in Greece. She had survived living in the seminary as a young man because her absolute privacy had always been respected. If she'd had to tell someone every time she'd committed a tiny sin, that person she confessed to would have started to get to know her, which was dangerous.

She was glad Benedict was not present in her lesson. He was teaching his own class that afternoon. Now they were both ordained and teaching, the only time they found themselves in the classroom together was during the public lectures on Fridays. Joan saw him at mealtimes, in the library and in the chapel, but generally they had spent years keeping as far away from one another as possible except, of course, when he chose to goad her. Joan did not have to think long to know which position Benedict would prefer on the issue of penance. The more control the priest had the better in his eyes. She was sure he would take great pleasure out of making people pay tariff for even the smallest of their failures.

It was great to be teaching again and have enough clarity of mind to really think deeply about theological complexities and discuss them so thoroughly. She had missed this mental stimulation. By the time she finished her lesson, she was feeling deeply invigorated. However, as she exited her classroom, an unfortunate incident occurred. Three of the youngest students came running up to her excitedly, each with a massive grin. They were particularly vocal about how much they had missed her whilst she'd been away, and one boy called Iaret literally shouted at the top of his voice, "We missed you, Father John. You're the best teacher in seminary!" just as Benedict came out into the corridor.

"I wish we could be taught by you *all* the time," chimed in his friend.

Knowing that the boys had just been taught by Benedict, did not make the situation any easier, and Joan could see that he had to steel himself against the insult it caused. The humiliated priest turned away and marched off, and the young seminarians did not even know what they had done.

After this incident, Joan went back to the kitchen to work with Father Takis. She actually found herbs very interesting. She had never really had the time or inclination to learn them before, as she had been too absorbed in theology. So long as Michael knew how to treat her if she was sick, then her knowing them for herself did not seem necessary. Now, as she started learning them from Father Takis, she thought back to Sister Hildegund, the striking woman who had saved Amadeus Reichenbach's life back in Frankia. Joan remembered how impressed she had been by the woman's skill and knowledge, and how she'd loved watching the nun work. But, nonetheless, Joan had still rejected choosing convent life for herself because there was no room for real academic learning.

Now she had achieved what she'd set out to do—to study and become a scholarly priest—there seemed more space for her to expand her knowledge. Self-interest was, of course, a highly motivating factor. Michael was no longer here to look after her if she became ill, and Father Takis was a very old man and would not be around forever. She needed to ensure she knew how to maintain her own health without dependency on anyone else. After all, as Father Takis said, she could fool anyone but a man of medicine.

Before they started the lesson, there was something Joan wanted to discuss. "Back in Frankia, some of the monks who helped people in our village talked of 'balancing the humours', but I have never heard you, Father Stefanos or Michael mention this."

Father Takis frowned. "Urgh. I don't like that practice. When I first came here as a young man, the old priest who taught me believed in the humours and did things like put goat's dung on open wounds. Even though most of the so called 'balancing cures' clearly did not work, he insisted that they were the correct practice."

"So, how did you learn to do things differently?" she asked, curiously.

"When my first teacher died, not long after my training began, the new priest who took over was more in favour of the 'Doctrine of Signatures' which asserts that God has provided a specific herb for every illness. The closer the herb is in shape and texture to the part of the body that is afflicted, the more likely it is to heal it. God has left us direct information in His creation of how to cure our ills."

Joan smiled at this idea. It did indeed sound plausible. She liked the idea that God left clear signs of how to treat each sickness; it made perfect sense. "Would you show me an example, please, Father?" she requested, wanting to learn more.

Father Takis went out through the kitchen door, indicating for her to follow. He then pointed to a plant with slightly spotted looking pink flowers. "This is 'lungwort'," he stated. "Notice the shape is similar to that of the human lungs. The spots symbolise the diseases that afflict them."

Joan carefully examined the flowers and soon saw the resemblance. "So, would this be used to treat people with breathing problems?"

The elderly priest smiled. "Yes, precisely. It's very straightforward, isn't it? The world may have been besieged by Lucifer, but God has given us signs of his goodness and love everywhere we go!"

Joan nodded in agreement. This approach seemed much more in keeping with common sense than pasting wounds with stinking faeces or other practices she'd seen as a child, like applying leeches to suck out blood. If God loved his creation, it would make sense for Him to bestow them with obvious ways to heal themselves when in need.

"So will it be the 'Doctrine Of Signatures' you'll be teaching me?"

"Yes, along with a great number of other herbal recipes. It is important not to be too rigid about any one practice or theory. There are many, many treatments for the myriad sicknesses humans can succumb to. Over the years, I have read countless books and conversed with many different men and even some women." He looked at her then with a wry smile which, although making her nervous, she returned. "The most important thing," he continued, "is to always try the treatment that has worked for most people first and then, if that is not successful, try other methods."

They returned to the kitchen to start her first official lesson, which focussed on cures for headaches. Father Takis first showed Joan how to create oil from lavender to rub on the forehead and then tea from the feverfew plant. As she already knew, both willow leaves and willow bark could also be used for pain relief, and sometimes Father Takis prescribed those if the headache was bad. Then, even stronger again, was poppy and valerian tea, but Father Takis preferred not to use that unless the person was literally crying in agony.

Just the thought of poppy and valerian tea made Joan twitchy. She missed that heady rush and warmth rippling through her body. She wondered whether, if she drank some now, it might dull her need for Thea, which today seemed more ardent than ever. However, in reality, she dared not take any at all, as she knew it would make her both too hazy to teach and too altered in her mind to make safe communication with others.

Joan took a sip of the feverfew tea to test it. Like most herbal medicines it tasted foul, and she would not be in any rush to try it again. Father Takis said that she was better off sticking to the willow bark tincture for the pain in her arm anyway, as feverfew really only worked for headaches.

Once she had finished her lesson in the kitchen, Joan went to the chapel. It was quiet in there, and she took time to really meditate on the statue at the altar of Christ crucified. 'Justification by grace through faith'—God loved humans so much that He sent His only Son and sacrificed Him so that those who believed could be clean in His eyes and enter the Kingdom of Heaven—Christ having been punished on their behalf. A high price for the Heavenly Father to pay for reunion with His own creation. It was such a powerful message: that all could be saved who genuinely believed, so long as they repented of their sins. Joan thought again about the lesson she'd taught on the concept of confession and penance. Now, as she contemplated the figure of the suffering Christ, she felt repentant for even the smallest of her sins. *Dear Lord, I am sorry for all my trespasses known and unknown. Please forgive my inadequacies and my lack of devotion to Thee. If I sin by loving Thea, please make me stop. Please help me know Thy will, and then give me the strength to follow it.*

She was still unable to prostrate because of her broken arm but she knelt in prayer for over an hour, repenting and asking for absolution. When she was done, she felt close enough to the Lord to ask Him to send his Spirit, and she lifted up her right arm and allowed the flow to come. It was so powerful that she fell back on the ground and tears of joy streamed down her cheeks. She did not have to travel out of her body to feel the depth of God's love for her, as He could just as easily meet her within.

Because she was feeling so uplifted and consumed with thoughts of God as she left the chapel, she did not see Benedict coming towards her from the left. In fact her first knowledge of his presence came with a sharp pain. The rival priest had grabbed hold of her broken left arm at the wrist and was twisting it behind her back. The pain was so intense, that Joan howled in agony and instinctively punched him in the face with her right fist to make him stop.

Suddenly he was down on the ground, yelping in pain. Even covered in blood, it was clear to see his nose was broken and Joan, now consumed with regret, reached out to help lift him back up.

But as soon as she touched him, Benedict beat her away. "Get off me, evil creature! Spawn of Satan! Devil in disguise! You twist the minds of the young and the weak with your poison! You are doomed to Hell!" he yelled, ferociously.

Joan did not respond as yet more violent curses spewed from his mouth. Instead, she ran to her cell as fast as her legs could carry her, terrified by both his words and her own actions.

When she reached the kitchen, Father Takis was nowhere to be found and nor was Father Stefanos. Her arm was in excruciating pain from Benedict's vicious assault and there was only one thing she knew of that could take it away. She grabbed a jar of poppy seeds and big lump of valerian root and began boiling them. Whilst she waited, she swigged on willow bark tincture and even drank the bitter feverfew tea left in the pan from earlier. Then, she gulped back copious amounts of mead—anything to relieve both the agony and the misery.

Once satisfied the boiling brew was strong enough, Joan filled a tankard three quarters of the way up and added a quarter of cold water so she could drink it straight away, then downed it all in one go. After this, she swigged back another tankard of mead to wash away the foul taste.

The rush the concoction gave her was far greater than anything she'd experienced before and her pain disappeared completely. Joan now had an overwhelming urge to run to her special lake, where she would pound through the water to vanquish Benedict's denouncements of her. Excitedly, she headed from the kitchen towards the woods, getting faster and faster as the prospect of the aquamarine paradise drew nearer.

On reaching the washing lines, laden with dripping robes, Thea stepped out in front of her, causing Joan to stop abruptly and nearly fall over herself.

"Father John. What are you doing?" asked the woman, concernedly. "You look totally deranged!"

Joan tried to concentrate on Thea's her face, but it kept coming in and out of focus. "I'm going for a swim," she stated, trying not to sway. "Do you want to come?"

"What are you talking about? You can't possibly swim with that arm. You'll drown yourself!"

"No I won't. God will protect me. He loves me, and I'm His special servant."

"John. Have you been drinking?"

"How dare you think I'm drunk!" Joan shouted, making Thea look around anxiously.

"John! Listen to me. You're not right," she spoke firmly. "I need to take you to Father Takis."

"No!" Joan shouted. "Come with me to the lake."

Suddenly, Joan found herself grabbing Thea by the arm and dragging her towards the trees. The woman looked alarmed, but followed without resistance until they were deep inside the woods. Then she stopped dead, and Joan, who still had her by the arm, was jolted to a standstill.

"Right. We're out of sight and out of earshot. Talk to me, John. What have you taken and why?"

Overcome with a rush of emotion, Joan started crying as she spoke, "Benedict twisted my arm on purpose. It hurt so much I drank poppy and valerian tea."

"And what else?"

Through the blur Joan explained what she had consumed and Thea's expression increased in worry. The woman moved herself so she could keep Joan in full eye contact, and she placed her hand on Joan's right arm. "All right, Father John. I understand what's happened. But I think you've had a little too much of everything you took, and you need looking after properly. Will you *please* let me take you back to Father Takis so he can help you?"

"No!" shouted Joan, more ferociously than before. She started swaying again and had to fight to regain her balance.

Thea, still looking anxious, put her hand on Joan's arm to steady her. "Then we must get you to the lake so you can drink water."

Joan looked deeply into Thea's eyes and a familiar ache rose up through her body. All she wanted to do was make love to her there and then. "I love you," she heard herself say, before leaning forward and taking the woman by the mouth.

The feel of Thea's lips under her own was astonishing, and Thea kissed her back passionately for a few moments before suddenly pushing her off and staring at her open-mouthed. Alarm resounded right through Joan's body and the world began to spin, then suddenly she was floating in a sea of white clouds.

When she finally awoke from countless time immersed in heavenly bliss, it was almost dark and Joan discovered she was lying with her head resting in Thea's lap and the woman gently stroking her hair. Panic overtook her instantly, and she tried to sit upright, looking around frantically, worried they might be being watched. Thea steadied her, comforting her with soothing words, "It's all right, Father John. No one is here. You passed out; that's all. Do you remember what happened?"

Joan stared at Thea for a moment, trying to work out why she was in the woman's arms. Then she remembered Benedict's assault and her bloody retaliation as well as her frenzied attempts to dull both the physical and mental trauma.

"I'm sorry," she whispered, recalling how she had dragged the woman into the trees. Their eyes met and then she remembered the kiss. Everything started to blur again as her anxiety returned tenfold. But Thea shook her gently and she came round enough to refocus. "It's all right, John. You did not offend me."

At this, Joan saw love oozing from Thea's eyes and instead of resisting when Thea moved forward, she allowed the woman to take her lips once more. The beauty of the woman's mouth moving against her own was beyond measure as was the relief from finally giving into love. All she wanted now was to continue on like this deep into the night.

Thea did not seem anxious to touch her phallus and so as not to lead them in that direction, Joan limited her embrace to running her hands up and down the woman's back. It did not matter that she could not enter her lover like a man, because just the kissing gave Joan fulfilment that she could not have believed existed. It was not until Thea touched Joan's tongue with her own that Joan suddenly pulled back, for it caused such a violent explosion deep within that she became soaking wet. She was embarrassed and did not know where to look.

Gently, Thea took Joan's chin in her hand. "Are you all right?" she asked softly.

"Yes..." Joan replied, reddening further. "...It's just...that I've never kissed anyone before..."

Thea smiled shyly, before reaching up and running her finger across the feathery moustache which Joan had worked so diligently to grow. "You are the sweetest man, I have ever met, Father John," she stated.

"I love you," Joan found herself saying for the second time that day.

"I love you too," replied the woman, before pressing her lips against Joan's once again.

Thea moaned softly as Joan caressed her back and shoulders whilst they kissed. Joan felt her spirit melding with Thea's like it had on the nights when she'd travelled by silver thread to the woman's bedroom. But this time, she knew for certain it was real, and its power was ten times multiplied. *You are my completion*...she thought as they entwined even deeper.

They remained like that until late into the night. Joan was still barely strong enough to stand up again without going dizzy, but she had no choice but to head back. Neither of them wanted to leave, but they had both been absent for several hours and that absence, particularly of 'Father John', would be noticed. Thea steadied her as they walked to the edge of the trees; then as they neared their exit point, she moved Joan behind a large oak and held her arms firmly as she spoke. "When you return home, you need to drink lots of water and go to bed otherwise you will feel truly dreadful. Meet me in our usual place tomorrow evening, and we can work out what to do next..."

Joan nodded and bent forward for one last kiss before staggering back to the kitchen alone. When she stumbled through the door, Father Takis met her with a worried look. "Are you all right, young man? I was starting to worry where you'd got to." he asked softly.

"My arm was hurting so I took some strong tea. It was a mistake to have so much I think."

The old priest nodded gently. "You will have ups and downs with your arm over the next few weeks but eventually the pain will disappear altogether and you will be as you were before. But next time you are in distress, you must find me. A mistake like that could kill you. These medicines are strong and need to be administered properly, and you don't know what you are doing yet. Now here, take this chamomile and get some rest," he said, pouring her a tankard from a pot he was brewing on the stove.

Remembering Benedict's bloody nose, which she was still convinced she had broken, Joan looked across to the far end of the large kitchen. To her relief, the rival priest was not lying on one of the beds. If he had come for help, he had already been treated and gone back to his cell long ago. He could not have told Father Takis or anyone else that she'd hit him or she would know about it by now.

When she reached her cell Joan sipped at the tea. She found it difficult to think clearly, for between her earlier 'medicinal concoction' and the memory of what it was like to finally come together with Thea, no rational processes were available to her. Finally, she gave up and lay her head against the pillow and let herself bask in the memory of her love until she drifted off to sleep.

CHAPTER 17

When she awoke the next morning, Joan was hit by a swirl of panic. For she remembered the events of the previous evening and realised she had made herself hugely vulnerable. Not only had she almost poisoned herself to death with medicine and mead, but also she had ended up in a passionate embrace with Thea.

She was in so much danger now. *How on earth could I have let myself become so exposed? I am such a fool! An idiot! A half-wit!* she cursed to herself. In the state she'd been in, Thea could easily have undressed her and discovered her secret, and she would have been defenceless to do anything about it. *What am I going to do?* she asked herself.

Joan was at a total loss. The memory of the fulfilment and passion was powerful and she wanted nothing more than to run straight back into the woman's arms, but that would not be possible. Thea had not expected anything of her last night, probably because she was intoxicated by herbs and mead. But if they were to come together again, it would not be long before the woman would want more, and even if Thea were chaste and wanted to maintain her virginity, she would soon have an expectation of marriage. Yet, if Joan put a stop to it, she knew that she would also have to put a stop to Thea's lessons too, for there was no way they would be able to carry on now that such love and ardour had been so honestly declared. It would be just too hard.

What's more, she knew she would really wound the woman if she ended it now. Thea was in love with her, and they had come together. Thea had looked after her and protected her when she was in danger and then given herself over to her in their embrace. How could she possibly hurt her like that?

The situation was impossible. She had no idea what to do. She knelt at the side of her bed and prayed hard and long for wisdom, but still the dilemma remained. There was only one person who would know how to resolve this kind of a fix and that was Amadeus Reichenbach, but Joan did not even know where he was, or whether he was still alive.

*I wish Michael were here...*she found herself saying, not for the first time that morning. It was then that it came to her. She rushed into the kitchen and found a bag, then grabbed her spare robe, underwear, the willow bark tincture, the tribulus and the rosemary oil, and stuffed them inside it. She then headed straight to Father Nikolis' cell.

It was a barefaced lie that she told Father Nikolis and one Joan knew she would have to repent of at the first opportunity. She said to the seminary head that she'd had a word from the Lord that Michael needed help with treating the lepers for there had been a sudden increase in numbers and he could not cope. She insisted that God had urged her go to Michael's aid until the colony was back under control.

"And in what form did this word come?" Father Nikolis asked with one eyebrow raised.

"Two days ago I had a dream about Jesus healing the sick, then yesterday morning Michael's letter came saying they had been inundated with more lepers, and then last night when I was reading the Gospel of Saint Matthew, the verse 'Heal the sick, cleanse the lepers, raise the dead, cast out devils: freely ye have received, freely give;' jumped out at me."

Father Nikolis looked at Joan sternly. "I really could do with you back in the classroom, Father John. Your absence has been felt very deeply whilst you have been recovering—not only by your students but also by those of us who have taken over your lessons. But, if, as you illustrate, this feels so strongly to be God's will, then I shall permit it."

Dying of shame inside, Joan nodded at him.

"Then go in peace and with my blessing," he relented.

He indicated she kneel and placed his hand on her head. "Heavenly Father, I beseech Thee to protect Thy devoted servant, Father John, as he follows Thy will to heal the lepers. Please keep him safe and steadfast on his mission and may he return unharmed. Amen."

Father Nikolis then took her to his office and gave her enough money for transport and food for a month, in case it was difficult for Michael to support her.

Within an hour, Joan was being taken by horse and cart out of the city and deep into the countryside. The guilt was overpowering, but it was all she could think of to do. She prayed God would forgive her for lying about His intervention and promised Him that she would indeed help Michael with the lepers. At least that part was true. There had been a sudden increase in numbers, and Michael had felt overwhelmed by the task of settling them in. She would make it her duty to do double the work expected of a genuine helper and hope that this, along with prostrations and fasting, would suitably atone for her sin.

The other guilt would be less easy to assuage. She was leaving Athens without word to Thea. The woman would expect her at seven o'clock in their usual spot in the woods, and Joan would not arrive, nor the next night nor the one after that. First, Thea would be alarmed there was something wrong, and then she would devastated when she realised the priest she loved had deserted her from shame of breaking his vow.

However, Joan could see no other course of action that would lead to anything other than disaster and misery. At least this way she would be able to talk things over with her friend, who, if nothing else, was in a position to listen and give an honest opinion. Joan was excited then, in spite of the guilt. She had not thought she would see Michael for another few months, but now she was on her way to him. He was her best friend, her confidante and her only true family. She had missed him so deeply it gladdened her heart to think that within three days she would be greeting him at his new home.

*

When Joan walked into the Michael's church just outside Marathon, he was trimming a candle at the altar. On hearing someone enter, he looked up and greeted her with surprise. "Pickle! What are you doing here?"

"Father Nikolis let me come," she said running into his arms for a hug.

Afterwards, Michael looked at her seriously and held her by both hands. "Pickle, what is wrong? I thought from your letters that you were managing…"

"I was…until yesterday…"

Her friend looked at her expectantly, but Joan struggled to begin.

"Tell me, John," he said gently, pulling her into him for another hug.

"Michael, I am in trouble, and I have even fallen into sin…"

"Sin? Why? What have you done?"

"Promise you won't judge me too harshly. I just couldn't help myself in the end."

"You know I'd never turn my back on you. No matter what you have done. You're my oldest and greatest friend. Whatever it is, you can tell me."

"I…I…I have kissed a woman. I have defiled myself and put myself in great danger."

Michael looked worried for a moment but then broke into a smile. "I didn't realise you knew any girls. Who is she?"

"She works at the seminary. She does our washing and cleaning."

"Oh, yes, I remember her. She came just before I left. She's pretty. Very, very pretty.

"Why are you smiling? Aren't you shocked? Aren't you worried that I'm going to be found out?"

"Of course I am, but from what you've said, you had a quick kiss with the washerwoman and now you think you're going to either get found out or burn for eternity in the flames of hell."

"But don't you see? I want to break my vow of celibacy, and I want to be with her even though she is a woman."

"Why would *I*, of all people, be shocked at that?"

"Because we are priests now. It is a sin to break our vows, and it is a sin to lie with someone of the same sex. It is stated in Leviticus and repeated by St. Paul."

"Look, I appreciate the vow of celibacy aspect, but you know that I do not think it is wrong for two people of the same sex to lie with one another. You knew full well that Amadeus and I had a proper relationship, and I have never thought that was a sin. I can understand why some might argue that God would not want us to commune without love as the motive. However, I cannot believe that our Lord would be so cruel as to make us love and then tell us it is evil."

"Yes. I think I've always believed that too about you and Amadeus. I just...never expected to find myself in the same position... Beside, that's not the biggest part of the problem, is it?"

"Then what is?"

"I am in love with her and she is in love with me. Yet, I don't even have the choice of relinquishing my vow of celibacy and...I...want to be inside of her like a proper man... "

At this Michael finally understood, and he drew her even closer to him.

"Oh, Pickle. I am so sorry. I never considered this would happen to you. I always assumed that if you fell in love it would be with a man and that you'd simply discard the disguise."

"I'm going to break her heart and mine..."

"Tell me all about it from the beginning."

CHAPTER 18

The parish of the Church of Saint Lazarus was scattered across a sweeping valley half a day's cart ride from Marathon. Above it, further into the hills, lay the leper colony. According to Michael, the people of this parish were friendlier than those of Athens, and he had been accepted as much as one could expect to be, replacing an old priest who had served the community for decades. Nevertheless, Michael had been feeling lonely since his arrival and was as relieved to see Joan, as she was him.

Joan missed Thea dreadfully, but to be with Michael again was like finding water after drought. She felt safe and protected, and could truly be herself. The two months that had passed without him had left such a huge void in her life, but now the gaping hole was filled with kind words, laughter and understanding.

After she'd arrived yesterday, they'd chatted extensively and although no solutions had been found to her dilemma, she'd felt much calmer and started having faith that she would eventually work out what to do.

Once Michael had said Evening Mass, they'd retired to his quarters and lay on his bed together holding one another tightly. Then later, once they'd told one another everything about their separate existences down to the very last detail, she had pleasured him as she used to in their cell. Joan had found great comfort in the familiarity, but for the first time too, she'd felt a twinge of jealousy—for if she had this appendage herself she would be able to be with the woman she loved. Yet, in spite of this moment of envy, she'd been grateful for the contact and afterwards, not wanting to separate, she'd fallen asleep in his arms.

The next morning, as they readied themselves for the day, Michael told Joan how much he had missed her and how difficult he was finding it to live without human touch. "I was not born to be alone and celibate..." he sighed.

Part of Joan felt guilty then, remembering that she was responsible for severing his connection to the one person who could have given him true happiness. She wished there was a way she could remain with him and serve the community there, even if it did mean less access to scholarly activity. She was certain she could obtain anything that interested her from the library at Marathon or one of the nearby monastic collections. But it would be impossible for her to stay. The community was too small to be served by two priests; besides, it would have to be sanctioned by Father Nikolis, and they both knew he would never allow it.

Of course, the other reason why it was so appealing for Joan to stay there was that she would not have to deal with the reality of her relationship with Thea. If she simply never went back, she could blot out the feelings and the complications that their love brought. She could devote herself to prayer and service, and hope that eventually the passion, which consumed her entirety, would diminish to a distant memory.

After Michael took Morning Mass, they set out together for the leper colony in the hills. Joan had never mixed with lepers before. Leprosy was a disease that brought fear to the hearts of men and women alike, and Joan was not without trepidation when she entered their designated living area. In spite of Michael's assurances that a healthy, well-nourished young person like her would be unlikely to succumb to it, she was still terrified.

The Church's position on the status of lepers always seemed to be a contradiction to Joan. On the one hand, it was referred to as a 'curse from God' and then on the other hand, it was only priests, monks and nuns who seemed to do anything to aid those affected.

The actual cause of the disease was still a mystery. And even though it had been around for thousands of years, still no one knew how to cure it. Michael explained that using hellebore to attack the disease had shown some minor results. In the pagan past, apparently bathing in the blood of virgins had been prescribed to men of wealth who could afford it. Michael had also heard of using snake venom and bee stings to try to cure the disease as well. But her friend was cynical about the efficacy of any of the 'cures' including the hellebore and, instead, had reconciled himself to helping the community as much as possible by providing medicines that simply relieved the symptoms. Today they were carrying baskets containing several large pots of ointment made of fox's clote, radish, garlic and yarrow root that would soothe swellings and ulcerations.

The lepers in this colony lived far enough away from the unafflicted parishioners not to cause them too much distress, but they were required to wear robes died bright yellow and bells around their ankles so that unaffected folk would know if they were in the vicinity and could avoid them. As Joan and Michael walked deep into the mountains, she soon started to notice yellow figures moving around in the distance.

The first group they approached were seven adults, sitting together outside a wooden structure that Joan assumed was their home. They looked so miserable and afflicted that she could not help thinking that a diet of poppy and valerian tea would do wonders for their troubled existence. Internally Joan chastised herself for such an idea. She and Michael had chatted a lot last night about her relationship with that tea and she had promised him she would not touch it again unless it was specifically prescribed for her by Father Takis. But just the thought of it made her twitch from craving.

The lepers were deeply courteous and rose to their feet and bowed as Michael and Joan reached them. Michael had instructed her not to touch them, and the lepers themselves were also careful not to make physical contact. Ointments and food were taken from the baskets and laid out in front of them on the ground and then the baskets taken away from the area where they were assembled. Gradually other lepers appeared from different wooden houses scattered across the hillside; men, women and even some children gathered ready for a blessing.

By the time Michael was about to say Mass, over fifty individuals of all ages had arrived. Michael gave a short speech and Joan read from Matthew

Chapter 1, "And there came a leper to him, beseeching him, and kneeling down to him, and saying unto him, 'If thou wilt, thou canst make me clean.' And Jesus, moved with compassion, put forth *his* hand, and touched him, and saith unto him, 'I will; be thou clean.' And as soon as he had spoken, immediately the leprosy departed from him, and he was cleansed." Joan felt tears of pity welling up and hoped with all her heart that these poor creatures would also be relieved of their burden through their faith in Jesus Christ, for it was truly terrible.

The bread was broken and the wine shared amongst the afflicted congregation, but neither Joan nor Michael participated. The wooden cup used for the wine was left amongst them and not returned to the basket, and having passed the blessed bread to one of the older men, it was he who handed it around to each of the participants whilst the two of them stood back. Once they had finished, prayers were said and Joan and Michael left.

Joan still felt sorry to the core, as they walked slowly down the steep rocky mountainside. She said a silent prayer to her Lord, thanking Him that she had not been subjected to such a hideous disease and asking Him for further protection. Some suffering seemed incomprehensible to her, in spite of her faith in a greater plan, for it was hard to see how such an affliction as leprosy could aid in spiritual growth. Nonetheless, she hoped with all her heart that these poor souls would eventually find absolute peace in paradise.

On reaching the church complex, they went into the herb kitchen where Michael prepared an ointment to help Joan's arm. Gently, he massaged in the fragrant mixture before applying fresh bandages and returning the limb to its sling. Although Benedict had hurt her with his attack, the break had already healed enough not to have gone out of alignment. However, it did hurt more than before her rival's assault and not being able to drink poppy and valerian tea made the pain harder to bear.

"I'd hoped he'd leave you alone once he started teaching and no longer had to spar with you in class every day," Michael stated solemnly.

"So did I. But he just can't stand the fact that I have more status than he does. Nor can he cope with me being treated with more reverence than he is. He bubbles over with rage every time I am acknowledged publically. My very existence wounds him beyond measure..."

*

Over the next few weeks, Joan worked tirelessly beside Michael, creating medicines for the lepers and those with ailments in the wider community. Although it was a small parish, it was still a lot of work for one man to prepare all the necessary treatments as well as tend the flock for spiritual matters. There used to be a convent further again into the mountains whose mission was to serve the lepers, but it was now almost derelict. Many years before, several of the nuns had become infected by the disease and eventually, the healthy ones had abandoned the institution believing it had become cursed by the devil. Since then, it had fallen to the priest alone to look after the community. Joan was glad she was there to help her friend build up stocks of medicine so that his burden would be easier when she left.

No matter how much she occupied herself making medicines and enjoying Michael's company, Joan's need for Thea had not diminished during their separation. Sometimes she would be in the middle of a conversation or complex task when she would almost collapse from the intensity of her feelings. The pain in her sexual area would ignite to unbearable proportions, along with an intolerable ache above her belly button and in her heart. Then, when she lay at night in Michael's bed, and tended herself after he had fallen asleep, it felt as though Thea was present in the room.

Joan wondered whether Thea's soul had somehow started travelling to her, just as she herself had done on those two occasions back at the seminary. It was as though they were now connected to one another by an invisible thread, with the same pull as the thread that attached spirit to body.

Eventually, Joan talked about her experiences with Michael. He had never experienced such spiritual travelling himself, but said that for years after their separation he'd felt as though Amadeus was with him each night and sometimes during the day. From Joan's description of how she believed she'd travelled to Thea's cottage, Michael thought it quite possible that Amadeus had travelled to him too. The man had been such a phenomenon in his own right; it would be of no surprise to either of them if he were capable of such a feat.

It was a concept that frequently occupied their conversation because if it were true, then this possibility of the soul being able to travel opened up boundless questions. Could anyone do it? Do you have to be in love to do it? Can you go anywhere you want to or just where you are most drawn to emotionally? Can you simply explore? Can you travel to different lands, even across the sea? Is it a God-given gift or something dangerous and demonic? Is it related to how Jesus was able to walk through walls and other miraculous events surrounding his post-resurrection existence?

The possibilities were endless, and Joan was glad to be able to discuss the issue with someone who was open to it being real. However, she purposely decided not to try to travel back to Thea whilst away from her, even though her soul ached for it. For between them, after hours of conversation, she and Michael had concluded that she had to put a complete stop to the relationship. It was her only option if she were to safely maintain her guise as man. Although it would be heartbreaking and seem cruel, in the long term, Thea would be better off because inevitably that heartbreak would come anyway when there was no marriage proposal.

One of the hardest consequences would be letting the woman down with the reading and writing. Thea had been so enthusiastic and had learned so quickly, that it felt mean to be cutting off her lessons before she had reaped the fruits of her labour. But, it was the only way. The only place she could teach Thea was at the lake and the temptation would be too great. Even if Joan managed to be disciplined for a few lessons, it would not be long before their passion would overflow again and she would be back in danger of discovery. Thea would not be permitted to learn to read and write within the seminary, and there was no one else who could take over as her teacher for that very reason. She was a woman and past the age of twelve. It broke Joan's heart almost as much to deprive her of this learning as it did to deprive her of a relationship, but she had no choice.

CHAPTER 19

Leaving Michael after a month of reunion was actually harder than when he'd gone in the first place, for they both now knew the depth of misery caused by their separation. Joan had pleasured him every night and felt at peace sleeping in his arms. Although it was not a union of passion, like between her and Thea or him and Amadeus, it was the only touch that either of them had and, in its own way, had sustained them both for several years. It would be many, many months before they would see one another again and knowing that their letters had to be sparse in detail, they left one another devastated by the magnitude of their severance.

They waved until they were no longer able to see one another, and then Joan slumped down in the back of the cart in which she travelled. It would be an uncomfortable journey lasting three days and two nights, stopping at small monasteries along the way.

When Joan reached the first monastery that night, she was tempted to ask if she could join them. For if she lived this close to Michael, then perhaps she would have the chance of seeing him more often. She would also not have to face dealing with Thea. But although the monks were educated, it was not a scholarly order. Their ascetic living conditions along with the paucity of any real privacy would be extremely difficult to bear—harder even than at the monastery she had stayed in with Michael and Amadeus in the foothills of the Bavarian Alps. In addition, if she lived as a monk, she would be living a life of total submission—far more so than as a priest. She would struggle with the lack of control over her own choices and would continually feel threatened at being put in some circumstance where her secret might be discovered. She would also find it hard to live without status, particularly given the level of standing she now had at the seminary back in Athens. So when dawn rose the next morning, Joan climbed back into the cart and continued with her journey back to the Seminary Of St. Joseph.

On returning home, the first person she visited was Father Nikolis. He was so thrilled to see her that he rose from behind his desk and embraced her. "Father John. You have been sorely missed. Do tell me of your travels and the progress of Father Michael."

Joan recounted the conditions of the parish and Michael's care of the lepers and the many medicines she'd helped her friend prepare for the months ahead. She also explained how seeing more of the real world had helped her understanding of the human condition and requested that she start visiting the sick and needy of Athens as part of her service. Father Nikolis, not wanting a 'man' of her scholarly talents to be wasted on medicine, was not keen on this idea. But when Joan explained how out of touch she'd felt when she'd attended the Council of Athens those few weeks previously, Father Nikolis finally agreed that she did need to know more about the city and its inhabitants if she were going to have the respect of the men with whom she served.

The next person Joan saw was Father Takis. He too, was thrilled to have her home and even more excited to hear about Michael. He missed his protégé, and Joan was glad to spend several hours telling him about Michael's work with the lepers and how all the lessons in herbs had given Michael the knowledge and understanding he needed to really help those miserable souls living isolated in the mountains.

By the time they had finished talking it was dark, and Joan had still not seen Thea. It was too late now, so she decided to wait until tomorrow after lessons.

She rose early the next morning and walked to the lake. It was not safe to swim yet, but her arm was healed enough now for her to clamber up the mountainside unassisted. On finally seeing the beautiful water, Joan felt overcome with sadness from remembering how much Thea loved it up there too. She walked over to their outdoor classroom and found the hessian bag still secure in its place, and pulled out the ink and quill, then the parchments. Studying them made her recall the expression of achievement on Thea's face when she had successfully drawn the letter 'Alpha' for the first time. Joan's heart was so full of sorrow that she let out a howl, then threw herself down on their 'writing table' and wept.

"So you're back then?" came a woman's voice.

Joan jumped, startled to find Thea standing over her with her hands on her hips. She did not look happy.

"Thea, I…"

"How could you do that to me?" cried the woman angrily. "I waited and waited and you did not come. I was worried sick and had no way of knowing if you were alive or dead. It wasn't until I risked my livelihood and went to see Father Takis to ask if you were all right that I even knew you'd gone away. He could have easily reported me and had me removed from my position."

Joan looked at the woman's distress and her guilt tripled. She rose to her feet and faced her. "Thea, I'm truly sorry. But you must know that what happened between us before I left was wrong. I went away to try to sort out my mind."

"You went away for a whole month without even telling me you were going. You know that I love you and you treated me with such disregard—right after we shared our love so tenderly. How could you?"

"Thea…I was alarmed. I cannot be with you the way we both might desire…you must know that."

"Why not?"

"It would not be right…"

"What wouldn't be right about it?"

"I took an extra vow of celibacy the day I became a priest."

"But other priests marry. Surely you could change your vows…"

"Yes, but I wouldn't be able to stay here. If I did that, I would end up having to take a normal parish elsewhere and everything I've worked so hard to accomplish would be gone."

"And I'm not worth it?"

Joan looked at her, flabbergasted. She had not expected to get into an argument like this, and her heart ached from the knowledge that if she were a man that she would, without question, give up the seminary and take her own church so she could marry the woman. She was lying, and the lie she was telling was so insensitive and hurtful that it was twice as wrong as telling the truth.

"Of course you would be worth it...Thea, I can't explain...you have no idea how difficult this is for me..."

"John. I know it's hard but you're not the only one suffering here. I have been in agony since you left. All I can think of is that union we shared in the woods and all the precious moments leading up to it. I know that you love me and what's more that you need me too. I feel it all the time."

At that point, Joan found herself wanting to cry again and sat down on the edge of their stone writing table with her head in her hands so Thea would not see the tears that were already breaking through. Then suddenly her head was being pulled up and Thea was taking her lips with her own. Joan was too weak to fight it, especially given that she wanted it more than anything else in the world and it felt so very right.

"I love you, John," Thea whispered when she finally broke away.

"I...I love you too, but we must not do this...I cannot marry you...and I don't want to make you with child..."

Kneeling before her, Thea looked at her for a moment with an expression Joan could not understand. Then the woman gently caressed her moustache as she had the last time Joan saw her, after she'd collapsed from drinking too much poppy and valerian tea, along with feverfew and mead. "I've been thinking about that whilst you've been gone..." Thea said tentatively. "I was wondering whether perhaps you could love me in a way that is different to what people normally expect... If you do not sow your seed, then perhaps you are not really breaking your vow..."

Joan looked at her shocked. "Thea! I cannot believe you even know about such things! Where did you learn about that?"

"John! I am a woman. I have a mother, sisters, cousins. Do you think I grew up in silence? Of course I know how a child comes into this world and how our bodies work!"

Thea was cross and Joan now felt totally bewildered. She had been so determined to end it once and for all, and yet here she was being offered a solution to how they could be together without her being found out. She looked into the woman's eyes, which although frustrated, still oozed with love. "I cannot let you touch me, Thea..."

"I know," Thea smiled gently, "but we can still have love."

Thea took Joan's hand and as she placed it on her breast, saying, "You need this, John. Probably even more than I do. Let me show you..."

Joan did not require Thea's assistance to know what to do to express her deep desire—for her fantasies had explored this moment a thousand times before. On contact with the woman's breast, she was like a hungry wolf taking full possession of her catch. Joan kissed Thea passionately and the woman moaned underneath her touch, which explored ample bosom before moving greedily to equally full buttocks. In the privacy of the rocks, she had no qualms about unlacing the woman's dress and pulling it down along with her underwear. Thea was truly beautiful. She had the body of a woman who was strong and ate well but not excessively. Her breasts were large and round, the planes of her stomach were sweeping and curvaceous.

Joan continued kissing Thea fervently as she explored every inch of the woman's body with her hands. When she took Thea's nipple between her fingers, the woman shuddered and gasped, and Joan was not surprised as she started swaying beneath her embrace. Joan moved them further back onto the flat stone and brought the naked woman deep into her lap, holding her safely with her right arm whilst her left hand travelled from her welcoming breasts down to her most private area. After teasing her several times, Joan could see that Thea was aching to be fulfilled so she plunged her fingers inside the woman's saturated flesh. Within moments, Thea's cunte opened up deep within and she began pressing harder and harder against Joan's thrust. And as Thea moaned from her touch, Joan felt like she was playing an exquisite musical instrument that sang out nothing but heavenly tunes. She basked in the delight of what it meant to give her true love such unadulterated pleasure. The woman's need became more fervent, and Joan matched her quickening pace with her fingers, which glided through Thea's velveteen wetness as though especially created for the task. Then suddenly, Thea's body shook violently underneath her and she let out a scream of pleasure so loud that it echoed across the rocks causing Joan look around to see if they had been spotted.

Thankfully, their isolation and the time of day meant they were not in danger, and she found herself smiling with such unabated joy that she believed God Himself must have engineered the moment. Thea moved up into her arms and kissed her again.

"I love you, Thea," Joan whispered.

Thea looked at her and started crying, and Joan became alarmed. "What's wrong? I didn't hurt you, did I?"

The woman shook her head. "No. It's just that I never thought this moment would come. I thought I'd lost you, John. You broke my heart."

At this point, Thea wept so hard that Joan could do nothing but rock her in her arms until she was finished.

"Promise you won't run away from me again!" Thea pleaded.

"I promise."

Joan kissed her again then, and the woman's lips were soft and tender underneath her. She knew that if Thea's body worked anything like her own that she would need more intimacy now. Joan's left arm was already aching from activity, as it was the first time she had used it so vigorously since the break. But she wanted nothing more than to keep pleasuring this woman whom she loved so utterly and completely. So gently, Joan moved Thea across so her back was leaning into her chest. Then, she placed her tired left arm across the woman's stomach to steady herself, whilst exploring her breasts with her right hand. They swayed lovingly together as the early morning sunlight bathed them in its glorious rays and gradually Joan's hand moved from Thea's breasts across her belly and down to the triangle of black curls between her legs. This time she did not go deep inside of her lover but instead found the small mound nestled between the folds of skin not far from the surface. As soon as Joan touched the mound, Thea juddered. Remembering how she had gained such pleasure from doing this to herself all these years, Joan smiled at the thought of what she would now make happen for her love. Slowly she massaged the nub between her finger and thumb until a natural movement built up and Thea's urgency became apparent. Then Joan moved her left hand to Thea's breast and pressed her face into her long dark hair. She caressed the silken nub rhythmically with her finger and in each moment their pace quickened. Thea groaned, sighed, and wailed with delight as her pleasure increased under Joan's touch. As she moved against her, the top of the Thea's buttocks pressed against Joan's phallus, hidden under robes and braies. Joan was happy that the woman would feel the hardness of it and think this was caused by their union. Although, she knew that if she were a real man, she would be twice as hard and large again. As the friction continued, Joan felt her own pleasure rising as the sculpted leather rubbed against her centre in unison with her fingers upon Thea. When finally Thea reached her crescendo, Joan exploded at the same time, and it was as though they were soaring through the sky. Then, as they came back down to earth, Joan swept Thea around, looking deep into her dark brown eyes and said, "I love you more than anything in the whole world. I will never leave you again."

CHAPTER 20

Joan and Thea remained in one another's arms, kissing and declaring their love, until the sun was so high that it was obvious they needed to return to the seminary. They arranged to meet again that evening in their usual place in the woods and walk to the lake for their lesson and, of course, to make love again.

Once they were away from their private sanctuary they were careful not to hold hands except for when helping one another down the rocks, just in case they were seen by someone taking a morning stroll. They chatted harmoniously, and all Joan's cares and worries dissipated. God had found her a way to be with the woman she loved, and the woman she loved was happy with it. Thea had agreed not to touch her but at the same time had responded to her need when it arose in a way that satisfied them both. She did not know why this was enough for Thea, when most women wanted a husband and children, but perhaps she was wrong in that assumption. Perhaps there were far more women like herself who could not settle for that life and Thea, in her own way, was one of them.

Their conversation was lighthearted as they walked. Every now and then, Joan would look around to make sure no one was watching so she could steal a kiss on her lover's cheek. Thea was truly radiant and almost skipped her way through the trees. When they reached their usual parting place, again they checked they were unobserved but this time, Joan kissed her passionately on the mouth. Afterwards, Thea stroked Joan's sandy hair and looked into her eyes. "You are the most beautiful man I have ever met, Father John."

"And you are the most beautiful woman," Joan replied.

At that, Thea kissed her on the nose and giggled, before turning on her heel and leaving.

As she watched the woman walk away through the trees, Joan's heart somersaulted in her chest. Then, just as she was about to lose sight of her altogether, Thea turned around and smiled at her once more. Joan felt her insides melt, and she was compelled to kneel down on the ground and thank God for letting this happen.

Then, still in a state of absolute gratitude, she went to the chapel where she lay prostrate before the altar in absolute supplication. For God was truly good to have given her this gift. He had found her a way out of the torment and had protected Thea from heartbreak too.

After giving thanks for her own situation, she prayed for the happiness of Michael all alone at the Church of St. Lazarus, asking that he too might find a companion who could help him through the dark, lonely nights.

Finally getting up, Joan saw Benedict sitting at the back of the chapel looking miserable as always. His nose was no longer bruised from where she'd punched it a month ago, but it was clearly a different shape. Joan still had no idea what he had told people concerning its breakage, but he had not implicated her for she would surely have known about it by now. She felt a small surge of guilt then, but soon remembered what he had done to her arm, and that her punch had been a reaction not an intention. As she moved towards the back of the church, he glared at her fiercely but, in spite of their previous altercation, even his presence could not perturb her today. She was far too elated from her union of love. Instead, she greeted him with a large smile and said, "Morning, Benedict!" before exiting without giving him a further glance.

Joan's lesson that morning was excellent. She taught better than at any point before, and she enjoyed getting the young seminarians to think about the nature of God. They were discussing whether God was inside or outside of time. It was one of the harder philosophical debates because each view had consequences that affected the Christian position on other issues.

If God was timeless—if He literally invented time and existed outside of time, which He created, then it followed that He could see both the beginning of time and the end of time, along with every event in between, simultaneously. This made God hugely powerful and knowledgeable, but such omnipotence and omniscience left questions about exactly how much free will humans actually had. Did we really freely choose to do anything in our lives, including follow Jesus Christ Himself or was it actually all predestined because God created the beginning, the middle, and the end before we experience them for ourselves?

The Christianity of Rome and The Celtic Church that had gained dominance over all other forms during the last eight centuries, had always maintained that we did have free will. Indeed, the salvation of human beings depended on them exercising that free will by making an active choice to accept and follow Jesus as their personal Saviour. But at the same time, this dominant form of Christianity wanted to hold that God, being timeless, knew absolutely everything in advance, and therefore taking this stance created a giant paradox.

Alternatively, there were some theologians who posited the idea that God was 'eternal' rather than 'timeless' and exists 'within time' like human beings. This would solve the problem of whether we have free will because God would not know the future other than His own intentions. An eternal God, inside of time and subject to time, would have a high chance of predicting the future based on His vast knowledge of the here and now, but He would not know it for certain. However, many Christians felt that not having total omniscience regarding the future meant that God was not big enough or powerful enough. The dominant form of Christianity had also traditionally believed that God had created absolutely *everything,* including time itself. If time was already there, then this was a contradiction, not to mention a reduction in His omnipotence.

It was a philosophical problem that was not easy to solve, and Joan had vacillated on her own position over the years. In general, theologians seemed to prefer believing God was timeless because it made

Him seem more powerful, in spite of the seemingly insolvable paradox this created.

In Greece this view was also preferred as it distinguished 'true Christianity' from 'Gnostic Christianity' that built its ideas around those of the philosopher Plato. Plato had believed that although there was a God or 'Demiurge', this being did not create time or matter but, instead, shaped pre-existent matter into the world we know and tried to imbue it with a reflection of 'The Forms', which he believed were the only timeless entities that existed. These timeless 'Forms' were qualities such as 'perfect justice', 'perfect love', 'perfect honour' and 'perfect beauty'. The Demiurge could only really create an imperfect world of 'shadows' from them—for how could that which is material and subject to the corruption of time truly reflect the timeless perfection of such entities?

Gnostic Christianity, so influenced by Plato's concepts, had long been seen as dangerous and heretical by the version of Christianity endorsed by the powerful Roman Empire. Following Plato's assertion that the goal of human beings is to attain 'higher knowledge', Gnostic theologians had argued that Christ's purpose was to liberate humans from ignorance. In giving us higher knowledge, Christ's teachings allowed humans to become free of the shackles of the material world and all of its illusions.

Roman Christianity held that the Gnostic view was dangerous and misleading. Jesus had come to save people from *sin,* and this was what human beings needed to know above all else if they wanted to be given their place in Heaven. So in spite of the paradox of believing in a timeless God and having free will, Christian theology had favoured it so that their God was seen as the one true God: omniscient, omnipotent and omnipresent; creator of all things including time.

Joan's students loved the way she taught the lesson because she did not impose a 'right' or 'wrong' view upon them but, instead, allowed them to argue fiercely with one another. Joan knew that by facilitating debate in this way, they would remain fired up for the subject and in the long run it would help them be more tolerant of a range of views and not get bogged down in dogma and rigidity of thinking.

After her lesson was finished, Joan went to the kitchen and helped Father Takis with the herbs. She then went outside and tended the animals. Joan liked that she had chosen this new aspect of her life so she could have her own cell. The farm work would keep her body strong and her hands rough and masculine in appearance. The herbs would keep her in optimum health and, of course, both things would make her feel closer to Michael. As if sensing her thoughts, the little white cat that Michael adored came up and rubbed itself against her leg, purring, and Joan sent thoughts of love in her friend's direction.

Later, as she went about her duties in the library, Joan found it hard not to make a huge noise. More than once the desire to sing welled up within her and she had to stop herself at the last minute. She could barely eat for excitement at dinnertime and fidgeted through Mass in spite of her absolute gratitude and piety that morning. Too many hours had passed since she had last seen her love and all she wanted now was to go to her.

When Joan finally met Thea in the woods an hour later, she ran into her arms and they kissed furiously before heading to the lake. On reaching their open-air classroom, the last thing Joan wanted to do was teach Thea the alphabet and, instead, started undressing her immediately. Then, as the woman stood naked before her for the second time that day, Joan gulped at how beautiful she was. Thea's skin was the light olive of the people indigenous to these lands, so much warmer and welcoming than her own marble complexion. Her nipples were a deep rich red like wild raspberries ripened and ready for eating, and as that thought crossed her mind, Joan found herself moving towards the woman and hungrily taking a breast to her lips. Gasping from the contact, Thea brought her hands to Joan's back and shoulders. Joan continued to explore the hardening nipple with her tongue, whilst clutching Thea's ample buttocks with her fingers. She moved her mouth from breast to breast causing her lover to sigh and moan underneath her lips. Thea's skin tasted exquisite, and now Joan wanted to kiss every part of it and savour the woman's piquancy.

Joan moved her tongue up to Thea's collarbone and then to her neck, enjoying feeling her lover sway from the sensation. Gradually her lips moved back downwards to the woman's breasts and then across her stomach. The aroma from the nest of curls between

Thea's legs was intoxicating, and as Joan pressed her mouth against them, Thea started trembling all over.

"I don't think I can stand up if you keep kissing me there," she gasped.

Joan rose to her feet and met Thea's eyes. "Then would you like to lie down, my love?" she asked softly.

Thea nodded and sat down on the flat rock that had once been merely a writing table. But as Joan gestured for her to lie back, she became shy and embarrassed. "Are you sure you want to know me in this way?" she asked anxiously.

"Every part of me knows that to kiss you there will be the most joyous experience of my life. But if you think it isn't fitting then I'll understand..."

Thea kissed her before answering. "I never knew such intimacy existed, yet I long for it now more than anything I've ever wanted before. But, please, John, if it is in any way unpleasant you must stop. I shall not be offended."

Joan could not understand why Thea might think that the enticing scent would give her anything other than absolute felicity. She kissed her again, this time more fervently, before travelling down her body once more with her tongue. When she reached the area of her desire Joan moved to the end of the rock and stared up at Thea who was still looking at her nervously.

"I love you, Thea. Do not be afraid," she said softly. Then she parted the woman's legs and knelt into her.

The moment her tongue made contact with Thea's centre, Joan felt a wave of pins and needles surge through her own body, and she was as soaked through as the woman under her mouth. Thea tasted like ambrosia to the gods, and Joan imagined that she may have died and reached a truly Greek Heaven. She drank greedily from her lover's flesh and Thea, shuddering with delight, overflowed with nectar. Thea's climax was deep and primal and as it came to an end, she clutched hold of Joan's hair and screamed. Joan was about to travel up Thea's body to kiss her on the mouth when she sensed that the woman already needed her again.

This time, Joan pulled Thea's legs even further apart and as well as caressing her with her tongue, she plunged two fingers deep inside of her. This combination of being both inside and out was so potent that it made Thea shriek from ecstasy which resounded like music all around them. Joan had to fight not to lose concentration from an overwhelming need to smile. She felt like a magician witnessing the secrets of Alchemy unfold before him. When Thea finally reached her crescendo, so much silken liquid spurted from her centre that it coated Joan's chin and hand. Joan was intoxicated from giving such joy and having such power, and she knew now that never a day would pass without her wanting to do this to her lover again.

When she took Thea in her arms a few moments later, the woman was still shuddering.

"What have you done to me?" Thea asked, staring up at Joan in shock.

Suddenly Joan was alarmed. "I'm so sorry. I thought you were enjoying it."

"It's just that..." Thea's words fell away and she simply stared at Joan unable to carry on.

"Thea, I love you. I am truly sorry. Have I hurt you?" Joan said, panicking that she had somehow caused damage.

"No...Don't be sorry...It was the most incredible experience I've had in my life...I just...I just didn't know my body could do that."

Joan was filled with relief. She looked into the soft brown pools of Thea's eyes and saw herself reflected there, smiling. Their souls were truly joined now, just as they would have been if they had been married in a church. They did not need a ceremony or a priest to call them 'man and wife'. For God had sewn their spirits together for all eternity irrespective of what the Church's view on such matters was.

As if reading her thoughts, Thea stated solemnly, "I do not need to marry you to know that I am your wife."

"Nor I to know that I am your husband," Joan whispered, before claiming Thea's lips with her own.

CHAPTER 21

The next morning, not long after dawn had broken, Joan and Thea met up again as planned. This would be their routine now. They'd decided on it whilst walking back the night before. They would meet at the beginning of the day and the end of the day whenever they possibly could, and have absolutely no contact with one another in between. That way, no one would ever see them together or have the slightest inkling of their union. They had found a spot deeper into the woods as a meeting point and Joan decided that she would vary her route to the edge of the trees as best she could, in order to avoid curiosity or detection from anyone at the seminary who might notice if they saw her walk in that direction at the same times each day.

Their arrangement suited Joan perfectly. It meant she would experience emotional and sexual bliss twice a day in a place where she could give herself to her love undetected. Then she could devote the rest of her day to scholarly and spiritual matters.

Like yesterday, as soon as they reached their private sanctuary, she tore off Thea's clothes. She had always been diligent in whatever task she'd pursued, always striving to excel, and giving this woman pleasure would be no different. She intended to learn every possible way in which she could make the Thea happy so that the absence of a phallus inside her would not even be an issue. From what she had discovered last night, a phallus really wasn't required to make a woman reach the heights of ecstasy, and Joan wondered whether she had discovered some special secret known only to a few pioneers in this area. Most men, she imagined, would simply enter a woman until they were satisfied themselves and not even consider whether all of *her* needs had been met. In fact, Joan now felt she might actually be at an advantage—for Thea would never discover she was born a woman and, at the same time, would be given so much unadulterated pleasure that she would think she had met the most amazing man ever to walk through the world.

At the lake, Joan took Thea by the mouth, pulling her close to her body. Thea rubbed her body gently against the hardness under Joan's robes but like before did not attempt to touch it with her hand. As their need became more urgent Joan lifted Thea up and Thea wrapped her legs tightly around Joan's waist. The pressure against her and its rhythm became frenetic and although her weaker arm had to work hard as the pace and movement became even faster, Joan's own pleasure was so great that she overrode the pain in favour of much greater joy. Thea squeezed hard with her thighs and allowed Joan to set the pace but Joan could see that she was experiencing the same delectation as herself. As their climax came nearer, they stared deep into each other's eyes, then on reaching their peak, both threw back their heads simultaneously, groaning with delight. Thea became limp in Joan's arms but made no attempt to let go. "I love you so much, John. I hope you take enough satisfaction from our love. I want so much to make you feel as special as you do me."

"You have given me more than I could possibly have hoped for, my love, and we have only just begun," she replied.

Joan knelt down with the woman's legs and arms still around her body until they were level with the flat rock and then she gently moved them back until she was on top of her. She prized Thea's right leg from around her waist and plunged two fingers deep inside of her wetness, still pressing the weight of her body down upon her. As Joan thrust into her saturated need, Thea cried out, "John! Oh, John!" over and over again. And when she reached her crescendo, Thea exploded all over Joan's hand and juddered for several minutes in its wake.

Later, after she was certain the woman had climaxed enough times, Joan sat behind Thea and pulled her back into her chest. Joan's breasts were so tightly bound and so very small anyway, it did not feel like a risk to let this happen. She rocked Thea gently and the woman smiled up at her adoringly.

"I don't understand why someone as beautiful, intelligent and lovely as you was not married years ago," Joan stated.

Suddenly Thea became stiff and began to extract herself from Joan's arms, gathering her clothing. "I told you before. You should not be asking questions like that."

Joan jumped to her feet immediately, grabbing the woman's arm. "I'm sorry, Thea. It just slipped out. But anyway, things are different now. Don't you know you can tell me anything? I love you with my whole being."

Thea looked at her sternly. "You might not love me like that if you know why I'm not married."

Joan stared at her concernedly. She could not think of a single thing that Thea could have done that would make her love her any less in that either moment or at any time in the future. "I love you unconditionally, Thea. You must know that. Please don't walk away from me. I want us to be without secrets from one another."

At this, Thea turned around looking fierce and speaking harshly. "Do you, now, Father John?"

John felt panic rising up in her chest and everything started to blur from worry that Thea might know she had a secret. She sat back down on the rock to regain her equilibrium.

"You see. You have no intention of telling me why you left your homeland, so why should I tell you why I'm not married," the woman stated.

Joan felt a surge of relief run through her body. *She must think I did something bad there...* she thought.

Thea, now calmer, sat next to her on the rock, taking her hand. "I'm sorry, John. This is hard for me. It has always been a thing of great shame for both me and my family. It caused such agony and distress for us all."

"I meant it when I said my love for you is unconditional."

Thea took a deep breath and looked away at the lake as she started recounting her story. "I was very young and very foolish when it happened. You have no idea how many times I wish I could turn back time and do things differently but I can't, and I will live with the consequences of what I did for the rest of my life..."

She paused for a while and Joan moved her arm around her waist, holding her tightly.

"Not long after my thirteenth birthday, my elder sisters and I went into the city by horse and cart to get supplies from the market. Whilst we were there, we heard that the great warships were back in port and decided to take the long path down to see them. Our parents trusted us when we were together and apart from needing to buy goods, our work for the day was done, so we thought nothing of going off to see the giant vessels.

"When we arrived, the harbour was teeming with giant men who seeing us girls instantly tried to molest us. Terrified, we jumped back in our cart and escaped up the hill. When we reached the top, we noticed a group of three much younger men sitting by the side of the road drinking wine from a cask. Smiling, they called us over to them and my older sisters, who were used to dealing with the advances of men our own age, seemed comfortable in their presence. We spent a while chatting and laughing with them, and they were very pleasant. The did not try to touch us like the older sailors had, so when they asked if we could meet them again the next day, my sisters and I agreed...

"The youngest one, Petros, was not much older than me and had light hair—not as blonde as yours but it was unusual for these parts. He had a smile that made my heart flutter, and I looked forward to seeing him the next day. He did not hail from Athens but from the island of Mykonos. Silas, the young man my elder sister, Callisto, had taken a fancy to, was from Crete. My other sister, Dorkas, favoured the one who was native of Athens.

"So the following day, we met them at the same time and place and went for a walk in the fields. Each day for three days all of us walked together and then, when we stopped, we would sit separately with the boy we liked. Petros would hold my hand as we chatted, and I loved hearing about his life at sea. It was an unspoken rule that each of us sisters would give one another privacy to talk with our men but be near enough to help if we were in trouble. So I never felt vulnerable or at risk. It was fun and exciting. I felt like I was a woman and no longer just a girl.

"After those first few days, Dorkas decided she did not like the Athenian sailor enough to see him any more and stopped coming with us, but Callisto and I carried on meeting Silas and Petros. I could see that Callisto and Silas were falling deeply in love and ten days later when his ship was due to sail they were beside themselves with heartache over having to separate. Silas was so taken with Callisto that he proposed to her and, on her acceptance, went to see my father to officially ask for her hand in marriage. My father was shocked and angry that this man should be so forward. He was deeply concerned that a stranger from nowhere could suddenly ensnare his daughter in such a manner. But my mother, seeing the look of love in both of their eyes, persuaded him to give their permission. It was agreed that they would be wed the next time he was in port, which would be a month later.

"Secretly, Callisto and I arranged to meet Silas and Petros later that night so we could say a final farewell. We sneaked out of the house after dark and met them in the fields where we'd walked during the day. When we arrived, both men swept us up into their arms and kissed us passionately. I had never been kissed like that before and I really liked the way it made me feel. Silas and my sister were completely besotted with one another, and he led her out of sight into the trees. Petros kissed me again and asked if I knew what they were doing. I only had a basic understanding of what men and women did together alone, but I was excited by the fact that they were with one another like that. Petros started kissing me again and soon he was moving us to the ground. I enjoyed the feel of him against me and I started to tingle all over as he rubbed up and down against my thighs. He kissed me again passionately and then suddenly he was pulling up my dress. I did not resist him. It felt so natural to be with him like that and although it hurt, I did not want it to stop... Do you think I am terrible and wanton for liking such a thing, John?"

Joan looked at her compassionately. "Of course not. I know how powerful that need is. Not just for you and me, but I've seen it in others too. How could you help yourself when you were so young and innocent and your sister was doing the very same thing just a short distance away?"

She kissed Thea gently on the cheek and indicated she carry on with her tale, already suspecting what was to come.

"When he had finished, he held me in his arms for a while and said he'd love to see me again next time he was in port. I had wanted him to ask for my hand, as Silas had my sister, but no request came, and I was disappointed. However, I still expected to see him soon and hoped he would ask me then."

Thea stopped again, a look of pain consuming her face. Joan, feeling nothing but sadness, stroked the woman's hair, before saying in a solemn tone, "He never came back, did he?"

"No... Silas came back a month later as promised, but he said that Petros was no longer working on the same ship and he did not know where he was now. Callisto and Silas got married whilst he was here and made plans for her to sail back with him to Crete where his home was. They were so deeply in love and we were all excited for them, even my father, in spite of his initial reservations. The wedding was wonderful and we danced and celebrated all night. Although Petros was not there, and I was upset not to see him, I still thought I might be with him again at some point if his ship came to Athens.

"My sister soon went off to Crete and life went back to normal. But after a few weeks, I noticed that I had not bled for two months, and I started to worry that I might be with child. Then the anxiety became a reality when my belly began to grow and I knew, without doubt, I was in trouble."

There was another long silence as Thea wiped a tear from her eye, but Joan did not feel it fitting to interrupt.

"I had no choice but to tell my parents and, of course, they were disgusted. They called me a 'whore' and every other name one could think of to describe a girl without morals who gives away her chastity to the first man who asks. They would have disowned me if it hadn't been for Dorkas who pleaded on my behalf. Dorkas explained how the men had been so persistent to meet with the three of us, and informed them that Callisto had lost her virginity that night too, instead of protecting her younger sister, as she should have. My parents were deeply shocked by this revelation and could not understand how the hymen was displayed on the bed sheets after their wedding if Callisto had not remained chaste. But Dorkas insisted they must have made it look real even though it wasn't."

"What do you mean about the hymen?" asked Joan, confused.

"Do you not know this tradition?"

"No, I don't understand what you are referring to..."

"When a woman and man come together for the first time, a small piece of skin called the 'hymen' is broken from him entering her, and she bleeds. The day after the wedding, the blood-stained sheets are hung from the bedchamber window to prove to all that she was a virgin and the marriage has been consummated."

Joan found herself uncomfortable with the idea of the spillages of lovemaking being paraded publicly throughout the streets. She had no memory of such a practice from when she lived amongst ordinary people in Frankia. Thea, however, did not seem perturbed by the custom and continued with her story.

"My parents had to try to find a solution to my situation that would not bring shame upon us all. My father's business and our whole livelihood would have been at risk if such a scandal got out. They could not marry me off, because how could I have explained to my new husband about the lack of blood on the sheets? He might even have had me killed for tricking him. So they had to work out a way to save me and themselves at the same time."

"What did they do?"

"They got a message to Callisto begging her to come home urgently, saying I was deeply unwell. When she arrived they explained to her what had happened and asked her to take me back to Crete until my child was born. Taking pity on me, and knowing she should have looked out for me that night, she agreed and before I knew it, I was on a boat to where she now lived. They hid me in her husband's house in the hills. They were happy together and he did not think badly of me for what happened that night—after all, he'd been a part of it himself. The house was large enough and far enough away from the nearest village to hide me, and soon my sister realised that she too was with child. So we agreed that instead of taking the baby to the Orphanotrophia as previously agreed, she would keep it for herself and say that she'd had twins.

"I gave birth just three weeks before she did and the babies were so similar in size and looks that as soon as she had hers, we agreed I would leave and she would love it like her own."

"Did you love it?"

Thea began crying again then. "Yes. And I always will. But I had no choice but to leave him there. It was for his highest good as well as mine and the rest of my family's. He would know Callisto as his mother and me as his aunt from Athens, and that was for the best. If they had taken him to the Orphanotrophia, I would never have forgiven myself, and it would have caused me such an unbearable pain. At least now I know he is loved and with kin…"

"Do you ever see him?"

"Not often. About once a year my sister comes over to visit us with Silas. I have not been back to Crete. It was agreed that I would never make a claim on him as a mother, and if I spent too much time with him, I knew that I wouldn't be able to keep to that promise."

"What is his name?"

"His name is Yiannis…" she stated slowly, looking down at the ground.

Joan held Thea tightly and rocked her gently as she continued to weep. When finished, the woman looked at her worriedly. "You understand now why I could not get married?"

Joan nodded, still holding her close.

"I had reconciled myself to a life alone, and then suddenly you were there…"

"I am so glad I found you," Joan stated, for the first time knowing that was true. Up until this moment, she had wished that they had never met in spite of the amazing feelings of being in love. For her, life would have been so much easier if it had stayed as it was. But now, as she realised that she'd brought Thea as much fulfillment as Thea had her, Joan was only happy that they'd come into one another's lives.

"I am sorry I cannot marry you either, Thea..." she said with a sudden pang of guilt.

"Like you said of yourself before...this is more than I could have hoped for," Thea replied.

CHAPTER 22

In the weeks that followed, Joan became used to her new routine. The solace of Thea's love and their union together had made her life feel almost perfect. The only lack she felt was the presence of Michael. If they still lived together in their little cell, she would be truly happy in every conceivable way.

Now and then she worried that Thea was not content with just a clandestine relationship, but the woman assured her that she was deeply fulfilled and that their union only brought joy into her life.

In their first few weeks together, they were so consumed by their passion that they abandoned Thea's lessons. Eventually, they did find time to teach Thea to read and write, as well as make love. Because of the extra hours they now spent together, Thea mastered the rest of the alphabet in next to no time. Soon, she could spell the names of plants and trees and all that was natural around them. And as the weeks turned into months, she was able to read first sentences, then paragraphs, then even some basic stories. When she was alone in her cell, Joan would rewrite tales of the saints in a way that could easily be read by a beginner. She watched with pride as Thea recounted them confidently and without mistake each time.

Their walks to and from the lake twice a day were steeped in intelligent conversation. Thea was able to give Joan insight into the lives of the ordinary citizens of Athens, along with her views on what needed to be done in order to improve their living conditions. For there were some who slept outdoors without care of family or friend, who lived off scraps of food and had no means to purchase medicines when they were ill. The monasteries refused to serve anyone who was not within God's communion, so there were countless men and women roaming the city struggling to find food and shelter. Joan abhorred this attitude. She believed that Jesus would have made these men and women His first priority, irrespective of their status or respectability. Thea explained that there were many more people living outside the life of the church than it appeared on the surface and that their numbers were steadily increasing. On hearing her love speak so knowledgably about such matters, Joan could now see clearly just why the men of the Council Of Athens had thought her nothing but a naïve and cosseted little boy.

Joan's first trip out proved Thea's point about the numbers. Thea instructed her not to go out alone under any circumstances because she would not be safe. Joan, believing that Thea was exaggerating due to a natural over-protection, ignored this advice. She was also painfully aware that she had no one she could ask to accompany her. She had no real friends apart from Father Takis, and he was far too old to go traipsing around Athens in the boiling heat. Father Nikolis would not be an appropriate choice either, for he was much too busy with his role as Head of Seminary. He was also far too inquisitive. Joan loved him like a second father, but at the same time, she had always kept him at arm's length to protect her guise. If they went out together for hours at a time, he would do nothing but ask her questions about how she was feeling, what she was thinking, and even about her past. So she went alone.

Thea had informed her of a range of places she could visit to see how the outcasts lived—one of them being the southwest foot of the Acropolis, where the derelict Theatre Of Dionysus was situated. Back in the time of the Great Philosophers, this amphitheatre had been one of the focal areas of the city. Literally thousands of men from all across Athens and beyond would gather there to watch performances by groups of men in threes, fours and fives, accompanied by a chorus. Over the centuries before Christ, countless plays, both comic and tragic, were shown there as part of a festival celebrating Dionysus, god of wine and ecstasy. The role of theatre was so important in Greek life, that Aristotle himself had even written a text on the cathartic benefits of watching a tragedy. But since the rise of Christianity in these lands, such festivals to pagan gods had been abandoned and the amphitheatre now stood desolate.

Joan had only ever visited it one time before, with Michael not long after they had come to Athens. It was a structure of both absolute simplicity and absolute genius. Row upon row of stone seating, forming a giant half circle, rose up into the mountain slope, creating enough room to accommodate fifteen thousand men. When they'd explored it together, Joan and Michael had not understood how the people performing in the stone circle at the bottom, could be heard at the very top, so they had experimented. Michael had been particularly interested in this because of course, Amadeus, his great love, was a travelling entertainer. Her friend had wanted to imagine his lover standing there telling tales of the saints to such a massive audience. So Michael had climbed to the top of the empty amphitheatre whilst Joan had walked down to the bottom. Standing where so many ancients had stood before her, Joan told him the story of Pelagia—the saint's tale Amadeus Reichenbach had performed the very first time they saw him—that had given her personal licence to live as a man in order to follow God. Michael and Joan had been astounded that Michael could hear every single word clearly, unaffected by the height and distance between them. It had saddened them both that it was no longer used. After all, there were countless stories in Scripture that could be performed in such a place. How powerful would it be if groups of men came together to enact Biblical tales in a place such as this?

So it was with fond memories that Joan entered the amphitheatre for the second time, nearly five years later, on her special mission to find the outcasts of Athens to see what might be done to aid them in their plight. Tentatively, she walked down through the stone seating to the centre of the performance area and past the shrine to Dionysus. Just as it had been when she'd visited with Michael, no one was in sight and nor could she hear anyone. Then, as Thea had instructed, Joan moved towards the large, crumbling building at the back, called the Skene, that those performing plays had used to help give differentiation of height along with location. The Skene had clearly been majestic in its time, with columns, steps and doors, but now it was crumbling from centuries of neglect, and the ground was littered with giant stones that had fallen away.

It was when Joan reached the back of the Skene that she saw them, living amongst the derelict remains. It was rather like looking for stars on a clear night. First one sees a few and then, when one gazes for long enough, suddenly there are so many it becomes impossible to count. For in amongst the fallen stones of forgotten theatrical splendour, were countless individuals young and old, sitting, lying, crouching and standing. Some alone. Some in groups. Some well-sheltered by the makeshift roofs of their self-built caves; some clearly exposed to the elements, whatever those might be.

As the inhabitants of the derelict Skene noticed the young priest in their midst, heads began popping up everywhere. Suddenly, Joan realised why Thea had warned her not to come alone. These people were not like the well-kempt, civilized colony of lepers, living in careful harmony with the community and the church which served them that she had witnessed whilst visiting Michael. Rather, they were the outcasts, the criminal and the insane. When the braver ones stepped out to peruse her, Joan saw that they were filthy dirty, with wild hair and wearing rags for clothing.

Joan had never witnessed anything like it, and she became afraid. As a group of five women started moving in her direction, cackling and pointing at her with fingernails like talons, she panicked and ran. She sprinted back into the amphitheatre and up through the rows of seats, as fast as her legs could carry her. But the women soon followed, and their cackling, now amplified tenfold, sounded to Joan like peals of satanic laughter. On reaching the exit point two thirds of the way up, she turned and made eye contact with one of the women, who was perhaps ten years older than herself. The disheveled hag was standing in the middle of the Orchestra where the ancients had once performed, gazing up at her. Their eyes remained locked for a moment until the woman's expression turned from a sinister smile to a demonic grin and she started shouting, "You're a girl! You're a girl! You're a girl!"

Joan stood catatonic as the words resounded across the ancient stones, each echo feeling like a fresh slap in the face. Then, to make matters worse, the four other outcast women, still dancing around in the orchestra below, joined in the chanting. All Joan could hear was, "You're a girl! You're a girl! You're a girl! You're a girl! You're a girl." And it felt like the whole of Athens now knew her secret. Realising the abject danger she had put herself in, Joan, bringing her hands to her ears, fled the scene in terror.

She continued running long after the threat was gone, for she needed to process the fear which rushed like waves throughout her entire body. When she finally reached the seminary, all she wanted to do was boil up poppy and valerian tea, and it took her entire might not to succumb to temptation. Instead, she went to the chapel and threw herself at the altar, silently begging her Heavenly Father for protection.

Joan stayed in chapel for so long that she missed dinner, and once Mass was said, all she wanted was to lose herself in Thea. On meeting the woman in the woods she grabbed her by the arm and thrust her against the side of a tree, kissing her passionately. Thea looked a little shocked but did not resist and as Joan started moving again, she matched her frantic pace all the way to the lake. Reaching the protection of their sanctuary, Joan could barely contain her need to possess the woman completely. Thea, clearly enjoying Joan's fervour, spread her legs wide and Joan plunged two fingers deep inside her cunte. Feeling her open up wider than ever before, Joan swiftly added a third finger and then a fourth. Then, suddenly aware that she was consumed by her own desire, Joan stopped, looking into Thea's eyes to check her lover was not being hurt. Thea reached up and touched Joan's cheek. "It's all right, John, I want you to."

On seeing the woman's legs spread further apart again, Joan slid her entire hand inside of the pulsating opening. Thea was saturated and throbbing, and copious liquid began oozing down the sides of Joan's arm. As Thea peaked, she let out a wail so guttural that Joan knew she had reached a deeper part of the woman, previously unbeknownst to her, and they stared at one another, startled by the power of it.

Afterwards, Thea brought Joan close into her. "Are you feeling better now, John?" she whispered softly.

Joan was about to ask how Thea knew that there was anything wrong but then realised that was ridiculous. Instead, she tenderly stroked the woman's hair. "I didn't harm you, did I?"

"No, my love. I am not afraid of you, and your need made me wild. I know you would never hurt me, John."

CHAPTER 23

The next time Joan went out into the city, she took Father Stefanos with her. He was not a talkative individual but his demeanor was gentle rather than aloof. It was the first time Joan had spent any real time with him on her own. Usually, he was working away at some task in the kitchen whilst Father Takis did the chatting. Now, as they walked together through Athens, she was glad to have him by her side. For one thing, he was exceptionally tall. She would not feel as vulnerable and defenceless having him with her as she had when she'd encountered the deranged unfortunates living in the remnants of the Theatre Of Dionysus.

Joan had not told anyone of the incident at the amphitheatre—not even Father Takis. Although he knew her secret, it was not a topic they had discussed again after that day in her cell, and she did not feel comfortable at the prospect of doing so. However, this time, before going out, she did more research about what type of people lived where. There were several locations to choose from and Joan, filled with terror at the thought of ever going back to the derelict amphitheatre, opted that they visit some young people they'd heard lived under the main bridge over the River Ilissos. After much discussion between Father Takis, Father Stefanos and herself, they decided that they would take a basket of bread, two old goatskins filled to the brim with milk and some basic ointments for pains and wounds.

Wanting to be sensible this time, before reaching their destination, Joan decided on a safe approach. "I don't think we should go under the actual bridge," she suggested. "It might lead to getting trapped. I think it would be better if we go to the entrance and state that we've brought food and medicine and allow the occupants to come out to us."

Father Stefanos agreed with this suggestion and when they were a few yards away, Joan shouted their intent. Suddenly over a score of children, most of them boys—rather than young adults as they'd expected—appeared from under the darkness of the ancient bridge. The first ones greedily snatched at the food and ran away with it along the riverbank, and within moments there were children fighting over bread all around them. Neither Joan nor Father Stefanos had any way of controlling the chaos, and Joan had no idea what might happen next.

"Listen!" she found herself shouting. But although a few of the children turned towards her, the others continued on tussling over food and milk, and before she knew it, there was nothing but noise and commotion again. Joan then clapped her hands loudly and Father Stefanos joined in. Finally, after several attempts, the children calmed down, and Joan began to speak. "Are there any adults living here?" she asked.

"I am the oldest," stated a serious looking boy, who appeared to be about thirteen or fourteen years of age.

As she focused her attention on the young man, Joan realised that someone else was hiding behind him, so she craned her neck to see who was there. On doing so, she soon discovered it was a little girl—no older than six years at the most. Straight away she noticed a scattering of fresh bruises along both of the girl's arms and smears of blood staining her legs that were exposed through her badly torn dress.

Joan was filled with alarm, for the tiny child was very badly hurt and obviously needed treatment. She made eye contact with her briefly, but the girl let out scream of panic and buried her face in the boy's tattered tunic. Joan wanted to go straight to her aid, but already knew this would frighten the girl even more, so she took a step back instead.

"How many are there of you?" she asked, trying to keep her composure.

"Most of the time, about twenty—but it varies..." the youth replied, eyeing her with suspicion.

"And why are you not living at the Orphanotrophia?"

"Because we are bad!" laughed a ragged looking boy, aged about ten.

Joan looked across at Father Stefanos. His face was filled with pity. "Does anyone help you?" he asked.

The older boy looked at him fiercely. "Oh yes. Men like *you* help us all the time. They give us coin to buy food...if we bend over!"

Father Stefanos' face dropped, and Joan was overwhelmed with shock as she realised just why the little girl's legs were smeared in blood. No longer able to contain her need to rescue the child, she stepped towards her anxiously, trying to see just how badly she was injured.

"Don't touch her!" barked the boy, jumping back.

Suddenly, the group of children, who were previously scattered, formed a line, and the girl was firmly hidden from view.

"Is that what you two want then? For us to bend over for you now?" the boy asked, with disdain, causing some of the children to giggle but others to shy away further.

Joan could not believe what she was hearing. "No!" she said emphatically. "We are men of God. We only want to give you food and medicine."

The young man became more confident in his stance. Seeing that the others looked up to him, Joan realised if she made a mistake now, they would either collectively attack or run away. Neither of which she wanted.

"In my experience, men of God are the worst of the lot!" he stated aggressively. "Why do you think we choose to live here rather than at the Orphanotrophia with the monks?"

At this, there was a mumble of agreement throughout the entire group and all of them stared at Joan and Father Stefanos accusingly. Finally taking in the magnitude of the situation, Joan had to steady her breathing. She could barely countenance that the assertion was true, but by perusing the terrified and defiant faces before her, she realised that it could be nothing other than the case. Her heart was filled with sorrow, and her worry for the injured little girl being guarded behind the line of children grew tenfold.

Father Stefanos indicated that he thought they should leave but Joan, not wanting another aborted attempt at helping those in need, decided to stand her ground.

"Will you *please* let us help the child you are protecting?" she asked softly.

"How do I know you won't snatch her?" the boy retorted defensively. "You could be carrying a knife."

Joan immediately emptied her pockets and Father Stefanos followed suit, proving to the young man they were unarmed. The youth nodded that he believed them and then turned around to the little girl behind him and whispered something in her ear. The girl moved out enough to see them both, and Joan took one step forward with her hand outstretched, but suddenly, the infant let out a terrorised shriek and hid herself even deeper than before.

"You can see for yourself that she doesn't trust you. And nor do any of the rest of us. Do you think you are the first men to come here promising to help us? How do you think we ended up in this condition except for believing in the kindness of strangers?"

Joan had never felt so helpless or so fearful for another human being. The girl was clearly in need of urgent care but there was nothing she could do. In despair, she picked up a small pot of marigold unguent and held it out, but instead of addressing the young man who was in charge, she now turned her attention to the only other girls in the group who were both about eleven years of age. "As you saw, we bought some remedies with us as well as the bread and milk. Your little friend needs help. This will heal her wounds. Wash her carefully in the river and then rub it in gently anywhere there is blood."

The two girls looked across at their leader with pleading eyes, and Joan could see she had made a breakthrough. She picked up another pot, and removed the cork to show them the contents. "Use this wormwood and helenium ointment to soothe the bruises..." she instructed, before another image of what might have actually happened to the girl engulfed her too much to continue on.

Father Stefanos moved a step closer to Joan, and she realised that he knew how overcome with emotion she was. Thankfully, he turned his attention away from her unto the group, giving her the chance to get a grip on herself whilst he spoke.

"We will come twice a week in the afternoon, around this time," he stated, with a quiet assertiveness. "We will bring food and medicines, like we have today. If you want us to apply ointments or poultices we will do so out here where everyone can witness. Otherwise, if you do not want us to touch you, we will tell you how to do it for each other, just as Father John demonstrated to the girls."

"Why are you doing this without wanting us to bend over?" asked their leader, still cynical.

"Because that's what Jesus would have done," Joan replied, finding her voice once again.

At that, knowing she had gotten as far as she could, she turned without speaking further and moved in the direction of the seminary, with Father Stefanos at her side.

The two priests walked back to their home in absolute silence. Joan was too traumatised by the incident to discuss it straight away, and Father Stefanos who was quiet at the best of times had turned white from shock and remained mute. Not a word was spoken until they reached the herb kitchen and reported back to Father Takis.

Father Takis was less shocked, than they had been. "We once had a boy here who had escaped the Orphanotrophia," he told them. "It took me many months to heal him... The monks who run that place, seem to have become something other than men of God."

"But most of them are children not even grown! I knew it happened to girls and boys who were just coming of age, but not to little ones!" Joan gasped, still horrified as the reality of the situation sank in.

"The little ones can't tell anyone and they can't fight back..." Father Takis explained.

"But how could anyone desire a child? I do not understand?"

"I suspect for some it is about genuine desire and for others it is about power," he stated. "Who can fathom the darkness in the hearts of men?"

Joan found herself vacillating between wanting to break down weeping or smashing every pot in the kitchen against the walls. Father Takis must have seen she was about to crack and put a firm hand on her shoulder. "Father John, you need to take a deep breath. No one will be helped if you do not hold yourself together. Here take some mead and let it relax you."

Obediently, Joan took the tankard he handed her and sipped at it gently, allowing the sweet nectar to soothe her nerves. But like the last time she was traumatised, she was now besieged by thoughts of drinking poppy and valerian tea. She had to fight hard not to look in the direction of where those herbs were stored on the shelves. Father Takis put his hand on her shoulder again, and now feeling a rush of healing flow from his hand into her body, she finally calmed down.

"These children are the ones I believe we should help most of all," she stated firmly. "If we try to serve every community of outcasts, the difference we make will be negligible. But if we aid these infants by giving them regular food and medicine, then perhaps their lives will be transformed for the better."

"Do you agree with Father John?" Father Takis asked, turning to Father Stefanos, who had said almost nothing since they'd returned.

"Yes," he nodded. "I could not sleep again if I thought those children came to harm because I walked away and ignored them."

"Very well. You will need to talk to Father Nikolis and see what he has to say," replied the elderly priest.

Joan, still shocked, nodded her agreement. Then she went directly to the chapel, where she begged God to protect those now in her care.

*

Later, when she discussed what had happened with Thea, God's role in the matter was called into question.

"This is the part of our faith that I have never understood," she stated, solemnly.

"What do you mean, my love?" Joan asked, curious to know her lover's thoughts.

"The suffering of children...I know that when we discussed the issue of evil before, you said you believed having the free will to do good and bad was necessary for us to grow into God's likeness, so we could be capable of having a higher relationship with Him...but I just don't see how that justifies the rape and torture of infants..."

Thea looked at the ground after saying this. Partly, Joan thought because she was thinking of the children and partly because for *her* to say such a thing—in any other context and, indeed, to any other person—could lead to her being severely chastised and possibly even outcast as a heretic.

"It's all right, Thea. I don't mind discussing it like this. You are only talking about what you want to understand properly," Joan replied. "You have to remember that one day, so long as they have been baptised and repented of their sins when they die, they will be in paradise where no suffering will take place again."

"Yes, I know that. But is it worth the price? Even if the children eventually reach paradise, does that really mean it was morally right for God to have created things this way? And what of those children who are not baptised or later do not repent? Do they really deserve the flames of Hell just because they didn't have mother or father to guide them in the ways of Our Lord?"

Joan thought for a moment. Over the years she had been involved in many a ferocious debate regarding the problem of evil and suffering but this was the first time she had heard anyone who believed in God call His morality into question in such an obvious way. Usually the debate centred on refuting arguments that attempted to disprove the existence of God altogether. The most famous version being that of the Greek Philosopher Epicurus who derived the formula:

> *Premise one*: If an all-powerful and perfectly good god exists, then evil does not.
> *Premise two*: There is clearly evil in the world.
> *Conclusion*: Therefore, an all-powerful and perfectly good god does not exist.

Christian theologians had endeavoured to refute this and show both that God did indeed exist yet remained wholly good and omnipotent.

It took a while for Joan to form a counter argument to Thea's point about the sufferings of children, and she knew it was not one that really resolved the issue. "But think of a task that you have had to learn that involved some suffering in order to get it right, such as learning to sew a dress without pricking your finger. Wasn't the feeling of accomplishment when you could finally do so worth the pain getting there?"

Thea nodded and paused before she replied. "Yes, but that's because I already live in a world where pain and suffering are part of the nature of things. I would much rather have not had the pain than have had it. My question is whether God was right to set up the order of things as they are, if the only way those subjected to it could live, was to suffer as a necessary part of it. Why create at all if this was the only way He could do it?"

"Because we humans have the privilege of existing when we might not have done. *And* we also get the chance of achieving a magnificent relationship with God in the end."

"But not everyone does achieve that. What about the ones who go to Hell? They had no choice in being created in the first place and then because of being created and failing to measure up, they end up punished for all eternity."

"Yes, but they had a free choice to turn and embrace God or reject Him, so they have chosen Hell for themselves. God did not send them there…"

"But is 'Love me or go to Hell' a free choice? And if it is a free choice, is the end worth it? All the pain and suffering. So much of it. Did God have to create a world where adults could violate children male and female in order to have enough free will to be in a relationship with Him? Do you think those children would think free will was worth such a price?"

Joan looked at Thea, long and hard. The woman was much more intelligent and sophisticated in her argumentation than Joan had expected, and she felt privileged that she trusted her enough to voice these thoughts, but it also made her worried. "Thea, I am not offended by what you are arguing here, but you must never speak this way with anyone else but me. It would be dangerous."

Thea rolled her eyes with exasperation. "I know that, John. I'm not a fool. I am asking these questions because I know you debate these things in the seminary, and I know you have heard every view on the matter. I trust you to discuss them with me without branding me a heretic for doubting God's justifications. So what do you think?"

Joan took a deep breath. When Thea debated the issue, it felt so much more real than the dialectics she participated in as a daily occurrence within the confines of the seminary walls. For suddenly 'suffering' had a face—the face of a little girl—a girl who hid behind the leader of a group of outcast children, clinging onto his tunic in fear. She could barely think of what that child had already been subjected to at the hands of human free will. "I can only argue that from God's perspective of higher knowledge and understanding, it must be worth it, for God is omnibenevolent and incapable of doing wrong."

Thea did not reply at first but then became even more emphatic. "If I'd have been forced to send my Yiannis to the Orphanotrophia instead of him being brought up by my sister, then this sort of violation may have happened to him. Even if the Beatific Vision of God's glory in Heaven is the bliss that Scripture claims, I would not think it justified my child undergoing that..."

"But your child might, when finally embraced by the unconditional and overflowing love of God..."

"That glorious final outcome is something we can only have *faith* is the case though, Father John."

"Then have faith, for I have experienced such love, and it is more exquisite than anything that can be encountered on earth. It is perfection and satisfaction beyond comprehension. Trust me, Thea, when I tell you that God's love for you, your child, and all of us is real."

"As real as you and me?"

"More so..."

*

That night as she lay in her cell and considered Thea's words more carefully, Joan knew that she had not really given her a satisfactory answer. She felt a little perturbed too. There had always been a niggling thought wanting to form in her mind that she had never allowed to fully arise. Thea had now brought this thought into the light through the questions she had vocalised. Joan had never doubted God's existence and she had never doubted God's love. Her more profound experiences of Him in recent months were simply confirmation of what she had felt viscerally for as long as she could remember—that the Holy Spirit was real and was with her. But the thought had remained half-formed nonetheless. *Why did God need to create human beings? If God was perfect, why did He need to experience the love and also the rejection of what He created? In Scripture, it suggested God had been lonely, but if God is all-powerful and perfect, how could the flaw of loneliness occur within Him? And, as Thea had raised earlier: does the myriad suffering that comes as a necessary consequence of giving human beings freedom to love Him, justify creating them, if the ultimate purpose is merely to stop Him being lonely? Could he not have just created more angels in the Heavens instead?*

It troubled Joan deeply to have these thoughts because her intellect was diametrically opposed to her experience. She was used to arguing about different ideas concerning God, but not God's actual morality. She would feel more comfortable considering the view that God did not exist at all than trying to reconcile herself with believing in a God who ultimately allowed thousands of souls to burn for all eternity just so he would not feel so alone. The overflowing fount of love that had filled her to the brim a thousand times, was suddenly a selfish tyrant. And she did not like it.

But what can I do? she asked herself. *You can work tirelessly to relieve the pain and suffering of His creation, knowing you will never fully understand...* came her own reply.

CHAPTER 24

Persuading Father Nikolis to allow them to concentrate their efforts, along with a considerable amount of resources belonging to the Seminary Of St. Joseph, on feeding and tending the children who lived under the bridge, was not so easy. The seminary head instantly took a broader view. "My concern is that on hearing about such charity, more and more children will run away from the very institution the Church provides to support them and adopt this feral existence instead. It would not only be dangerous for their bodies but, more importantly, for the mortality of their souls."

"Then can we not care for them here at the seminary?" Joan asked.

Father Nikolis looked at her in horror. "Certainly not! This is an academic institution designed to foster the intellect of those who will serve God throughout Christendom. Having wild, heathen children running everywhere will decimate everything we have worked so very hard to create."

"But if we ignore our duty to them, their lives and souls really *would* be in constant peril and *that* would be our fault."

For the first time in all of her years there, Father Nikolis became stern with her. "This is precisely why the Orphanotrophia was built and the monks given the mission to run it. The Church does *not* neglect these bastard children. She gives them a home and a chance of righteousness."

Joan found Father Nikolis' negativity difficult to bear but she had to tread carefully. After all, she had taken a vow of obedience and this seminary was the one place in the world where she felt safe and protected. To lose it, would be to lose everything. She took a deep breath before continuing, "Sorry, Father. I understand that we cannot have them here. But please may we at least help them where they are? Surely we can feed them, if nothing else?"

"Father John," barked Father Nikolis. "We only just sustain ourselves. How on earth can we support a score of hungry children whose numbers might swell by the day? At the very most, you may give them some food twice a week. That was what I originally agreed to when you asked if you could distribute charity across the city. You may take them milk, cheese, honey and olives but no meat. We cannot slaughter any more goats or chickens than we already do, it would bring us to ruin in no time."

"What about more bread?" she asked, already knowing this question was a mistake.

"We have to buy grain, remember, Father John! We cannot purchase more than we already do currently, without endangering our own ability to eat. Enough now, before I change my mind altogether! I would have been far more comfortable with you and Father Stefanos leaving small donations of food and medicine in a range of different places, rather than embarking on this quest. I cannot see how it will lead to the highest good of those children or the seminary. The greatest kindness you could do those young souls is persuade them to return to the Orphanotrophia from which they fled."

"Even if they might be violated?" she snapped angrily, before she could stop herself.

Father Nikolis went so red that Joan thought he might burst, and she realised now she was in serious trouble.

"You have no evidence of that. How *dare* you cast aspersions on the sanctity of those monks because of the tainted accusations of a group feral bastards?"

"I am sorry, Father," Joan whispered, looking at the floor.

"I suggest you leave before I change my mind about sanctioning your mission altogether," he stated flatly.

At this, Joan fell silent and nodded her head in submission to his will.

However, as she walked back to her cell, she realised that she would never feel quite so in awe of her mentor again. He was an excellent theologian and seminary head, but his lack of compassion today appalled her. Then she remembered her thoughts from yesterday. Suddenly for her, 'suffering' had the face of an innocent child. It was no longer merely the subject of an intellectual debate. Had Father Nikolis spent too many years living within the walls of their esteemed institution to now have any sense of the struggle for those men, women and children who existed outside of them? *No wonder the men on the Council of Athens had no respect for me...*

*

The next afternoon, once classes were finished, Joan and Father Stefanos made their second visit to the 'children of the bridge', as they now referred to them.

This time when they arrived, the youngsters were more confident; some even came bounding up to see what food they had bought. As before, the distribution proved impossible to control, leaving some children gorging themselves on cheese whilst others received barely a thing. Both Joan and Father Stefanos tried their best to break up fights but they did not want to touch the children in case it made them more afraid than they already were. Instead, once the food supplies were exhausted and the medicines came out, Joan started talking again to the eldest boy. "You will need to help us keep the children in order if each of them is to benefit from the goods we bring. We cannot afford to feed you every day, and if some of you continue to go hungry, it will be hard to resist offers of money from evil sources."

The boy, who seemed quite intelligent, agreed. "You are right. Thank you for helping us. I will talk to them and help you give out the food next time."

"I am sorry we cannot do more to help you, but we will leave you the baskets we have brought with us today so you can use them to gather fruits and nuts from the trees on the common lands. That way perhaps you will find it easier to keep going in between our visits. Does this river yield many fish?"

"We manage to get some, but we only have one old net and it has almost disintegrated," the boy replied.

"Well that is something we will try to help with as well."

The boy then looked at her suspiciously, like he had during her first visit. "What is it you *really* want from us, Father?"

"Child, please believe me when I say that all I want to do is help you. And please know that were it in my power, I would do far more…"

"You are not like other men," he stated.

Joan flinched for a moment, wondering whether she had somehow given herself away but, from his expression, soon realised this was not the case. "There are many good men in this world. You have just been extremely unfortunate with whom you have encountered so far."

The boy nodded but did not seem convinced.

"What is your name?" she asked him.

"My name is Alkandros, Father."

"And who are you?" she said, stretching round to see the little girl she had worried so much about last time, clinging again to the back of his tunic.

The girl stared up at her but was still too frightened to speak, and Joan, as previously, had to fight the urge not to sweep her up into a protective embrace.

"Her name is Maria," Alkandros stated on the girl's behalf.

Joan reached into the pocket of her robe and pulled out two fresh figs rolled up in a leaf, which she had taken with her for the long walk, and handed them to the girl. "Here you are, Maria," she said softly.

The child's eyes lit up in gratitude, and she opened up her tiny hand. Joan felt a surge of love so strong, she knew that she had been right to insist that this mission was hers.

"Did the medicines we brought help you, Maria?" she asked the girl, who now was half visible.

Both Alkandros and Maria nodded.

"Do you still hurt?"

The child looked up at her protector, and he stroked her head gently.

"She was beaten very badly, Father. She is my sister. She was with me in the Orphanotrophia. When I left last year, I took her with me. She would not have been safe there...as...bad things...had already started... I could not leave her behind. We were doing very well even though we have no home, and she was happy...but then, two nights before you visited last time, she was snatched at knifepoint in the dark. There were three of them and there was nothing we could do to stop them. We found her about half an hour's walk down the riverbank the next morning, and she has not spoken since."

Joan wanted to scream but fought to regain control by taking a deep breath. "Is she bleeding still?" she asked calmly.

Alkandros dropped his head and stared at the ground, whilst his sister hid so far behind him that Joan could no longer see her. "The wounds on her back and arms are healing because of the creams you gave us," he mumbled, awkwardly. "But she is still bleeding from…the top of her legs…The girls have been trying to help her…"

The young man still could not look at Joan, but she was glad that he trusted her enough to at least try to explain. In truth, Joan had no idea how to treat such injuries. After meeting the children last time, she had asked Father Takis if he knew how they might be able to help the girl, if she had indeed been violated as Joan suspected. But even he had not really known what treatment would be appropriate, given his scant knowledge of the female body. And there was nothing in his 'Herbal' that referred to it. However, Joan wanted to instill confidence in the children, so she said what she thought might work best given the circumstances. "Tell the girls to wash Maria in the river twice a day and each time change the cloth they use to stem the bleeding. We brought you soap along with medicines today so you should be able to wash both her and the cloths she uses thoroughly."

"Thank you," muttered the boy, still unable to make eye contact.

Joan looked around for Father Stefanos, to see if he agreed with her instructions, but the priest was now sitting several yards away on the grass, surrounded by a small group of boys, explaining to them what medicines he and Joan had brought and how to use them. As before, they were simple treatments for cuts and bruises, along with willow bark tincture for pain. He told them to store the medicines in the basket out of sunlight and not let them be mixed with anything else.

Then finally, he asked if any of the children had wounds that wanted treating today. At this, there was a sudden change in mood. The boys became nervous and started looking at one another anxiously with none coming forward. Quickly, the fellow priest rose to the ground, leaving the basket where it was.

Joan looked at the group and spoke as reassuringly as she could. "Father Stefanos and I know what has happened to you, and we understand that you are frightened. We want to promise you again that we will *never* harm you in any way. We realise it will take you a long time to believe that. But if any of you do want help, as we said before, we will treat you in the open in front of the others so you know you will be safe when we touch you."

Still none of the boys came forward and Joan knew that it was time to leave before they scared them even more. Together, they bid the children farewell and promised to come back three days later.

*

When Joan reached the lake that evening, she was still reeling from thoughts of little Maria, Alkandros, and all the other children now in her care. She felt so useless not being able to keep them safe. Seeing she was tense, Thea told Joan to sit in front of her. "You are doing all you can for them, John. You mustn't feel guilty," she whispered, holding Joan tightly.

"I just can't stop thinking about them. I feel like what we are going to do for them is pitiful in comparison to what they actually need."

"But you are doing everything you personally can and, ultimately, that is all any of us can do…"

Joan turned to Thea and kissed her on the cheek. "I'm not really doing all I can do. If I were a parish priest, I could let them sleep in the church at night and keep them safe."

"Yet there is no guarantee that you would get a parish here in Athens. Look at what happened to your best friend. He had no choice where he went and ended up three days away from here. If that happened then the children would not have you at all. And besides, where would you find the resources to feed them if you were a parish priest?"

Joan knew Thea was right but it was still hard to accept. She could not bear the thought of Maria left so exposed to danger. *If I were a real man, I would marry Thea, take a parish and adopt that child*, she thought.

"Everything I've achieved up until now seems so insignificant in the face of such suffering. What good does it do the world if I have all this knowledge but don't actually help people with it?"

This time, Thea moved Joan around more forcefully. "You are helping. I'm sure being a teacher does as much good for the world as being a parish priest. You are doing your very best. You must never doubt it."

Joan looked deep into Thea's eyes which overflowed with love, and she kissed her softly. "I love you so much, Thea. I can't begin to tell you."

"You don't need to, John. I feel it all of the time," she replied, placing Joan's hand on her heart.

CHAPTER 25

It took several more visits to the children before the first one stepped forward and allowed them to treat him. He was a ten year old boy called Kyrillos. He had been caught by one of the monks who ran the Orphanotrophia, and dragged back there to live. Terrified at the prospect of what might happen to him again if he remained, Kyrillos had climbed over the high Orphanotrophia wall and broken his wrist on landing.

It was Father Stefanos who reset the bone. The tall, shy priest had a gentle way with the children, and Joan sensed they appreciated his softness. Joan certainly did. She liked having him with her. He was easy to be around, because he said so little and never asked prying questions. On the rare occasion he did speak, though, it moved her.

"My entire being shudders at the thought of what those monks did to those children," he said, as they walked home to the seminary. "How ever hard I try, I find it impossible not to be filled with hate for them. And it horrifies me to know that they continue to rape those infants who are still trapped in their midst."

"I, too, am deeply worried for those still living at the Orphanotrophia," she agreed. "I feel we should move to expose what is happening and put an end to it, but I have no idea how… Where would we start and who would believe us? When I broached the subject with Father Nikolis, he would not hear of it…"

"Is there anyone on the Council Of Athens who might be able to see to it that the monks who do this are removed?"

"I don't think so. How would I even raise it? And from what Alkandros has told me there are several perpetrators not just a few. I can't see how we could bring so many to account. Who is going to believe that so many men of God would collectively commit such atrocities? If the children bear witness, they will be discredited as evil bastards; feral and tainted by nature. And even if somehow we went through with it and succeeded, how would we know that those who replace those evil violators would not do exactly the same thing?

"Then we are as powerless as the children themselves to change anything..." stated Father Stefanos, hopelessly.

"All we can do is pray," she said, in almost a whisper. For the first time in her existence, making that statement sounded somewhat pathetic. However, it was the truth. Joan had spent even longer than usual at the altar beseeching God to protect the infants in her care, particularly little Maria, who still had not spoken since her attack. Joan worked hard to push to the back of her mind the questions about suffering that had arisen when she had first met those whom she now served. Instead, she tried to concentrate on maintaining her relationship with God through being in union with His Holy Spirit. But in spite of still receiving love abundant on each occasion she asked, the niggle about God's goodness remained like an itch left unscratched.

Her anxiety over the children's welfare sometimes even affected her time with Thea. Twice a day Joan still made love to Thea with ferocious passion, allowing herself to become totally lost in their union. But there were occasions when afterwards, she felt guilty about enjoying such personal pleasure. It felt selfish. Thea, of course, was patient and kind. Never judging Joan when her mood was more pensive. Instead, she would stroke Joan's head and soothe her with soft words until she was calm and felt better again.

As the weeks turned to months, in addition to working with the children at the bridge, Joan made it her business to understand the problems in other parts of Athens. Each time they visited the children, she and Father Stefanos would do a detour on their way home to see another part of the city. It did not take Joan long to understand how little she had previously known about the reality of living in Athens as an ordinary citizen. For as well as countless groups of people living in the desecrated remains of resplendent buildings that had their heyday a thousand years before, scattered throughout the city were vagrants, miscreants and whores, all struggling to survive. And, in turn, these outcasts frequently caused distress for the working populace who were subjected to their madness or immorality on a daily basis.

In reality, there was not much she or Father Stefanos could do for the plethora of destitutes they had encountered over the last few months. However, both of them had started subtly increasing the amount of food and medicine they carried in their baskets for the children. They saved this extra fraction to treat whomever they came across during their unauthorised excursion on any given day. Neither of them discussed it openly nor even told Father Takis. It was simply an unspoken agreement between two people who instinctively knew they were doing the right thing.

Gradually, however, the secret of their good works did get out, not at the seminary, but amongst members of the Council Of Athens. After one of the Council meetings, the Chief Magistrate and his assistant approached Joan saying that they had heard of her many kindnesses and wanted to know her opinion about how the city might approach some of the problems she had encountered. To Joan, the answer was obvious and she explained to them her thoughts. Those monasteries and convents in and around the city that did not have a specific mission other than prayer, should start looking after the insane and feeding the homeless. That way, in addition to these outcasts themselves being helped, the general populace would be safer. She was not sure about what would have to change to stop women turning to prostitution, but ultimately, she knew that this too was connected to poverty. So the city needed to make sure that women who found themselves without the protection of a male, were not forced into whoring in order to survive.

The two men were keen on her ideas but cynical about whether the Church would be prepared to do any more. "We pressed for more involvement from the monasteries and convents once before, a few years back, but were told that the holy institutions could barely support themselves and each already had a sanctified mission," stated the Chief Magistrate.

"Does the city have money from taxes it could donate to the monasteries in exchange for them taking in these people?" asked Joan.

"Not much, but if we pushed for it enough and gathered support in advance of the vote, we might be able to make it happen," replied the younger man. "We will need your help though, because the Bishop was totally against it last time. He did not think it fair to make those who had dedicated their lives to prayer be torn away from their vocation and be forced to look after the insane. He thinks we should extend the prison again. The really bad ones are already there anyway as they need to be locked away for their own good as well as that of the city. But is it right to lock up the mad as criminal, especially the ones who are harmless?"

Joan thought about this for a moment. The Bishop had a point. Suddenly thrusting the care of the insane on an established holy order would be unfair. The monks or nuns in question might not have any knowledge or skill that could help the poor souls. And it would cause chaos in terms of their living conditions. But at the same time, if Jesus' words were to be taken seriously, surely were not these the very sorts of things that men and women of God should be making their priority?

"Perhaps the Bishop would be more open to the idea if a new order of monks or nuns were established with this as a specific mission and a specialist building erected for its purpose. When I travelled through Frankia as a boy, there was a hospice for the dying built at the very top of a mountain with a separate building for the nuns to live in away from the area they treated the patients. Perhaps we could create a new mission that is a cross between a monastery and a very pleasant prison?"

Both men looked impressed.

"I have never thought of such a thing, but you are right, it would solve the problem," said the younger one. "The difficulty will be getting the money to build it and the many years that it will take to erect it if we do. It is a fantastic suggestion, though. No wonder they chose you to serve on the Council so young!"

The Chief Magistrate was more confident. "The Orphanotrophia which was built forty years ago was created with a specialist mission and has been a huge success. Monks who feel the call of God to serve feral children make a choice to join that order rather than it being foisted upon them. If the Bishop is given the Orphanotrophia as a comparison with the idea you have suggested, then he might just be swayed."

Joan felt her heart sink to the floor. To hear her suggestion be seen as excellent based on the success of the Orphanotrophia was the worst thing anyone could have said, and she had to feign a coughing fit in order to cover up the shock the Magistrate's comments had caused her. The men waited politely before continuing, having no idea of the distress she was now in. Joan felt truly dreadful, but could not begin to raise the issue of the monks and their abuse of the children in their care. If she did that without the consent of Father Nikolis first, she could be removed from the priesthood for breaking her vow of obedience. So once she had gathered herself together, she respectfully concurred with them instead. The men agreed to ensure that Joan's idea of a creating a specialist mission was raised at the next Council meeting in a month's time and then bid her good day.

As Joan walked down the hill of the Acropolis past the derelict Propylaia and the dilapidated Odeion of Herodes Atticus, she could not be anything other than consumed with her own crumbling faith in humanity. Not only had her hopelessness regarding trying to change conditions for the children in the Orphanotrophia been accentuated in her mind, a whole host of new questions had now arisen. *If a special holy mission was created to look after the confused and the insane, what guarantee was there that it would not attract people who wanted to be there for dark reasons rather than as a spiritual calling?*

Joan remembered how close she had come at thirteen years of age to being violated by a monk at the monastery they'd stayed at in the foothills of the Bavarian Alps. She had been shocked then by the concept that God would allow an unholy man to take holy orders. But Amadeus, being older and wiser, had explained to her that people join religious communities for a multitude of reasons, and there was no guarantee that holiness was one of them.

What now disturbed Joan the most was the thought that many of those monks at the Orphanotrophia had actually joined that order with the malignant intent to violate children—disguised as compassion and calling. They wanted free and easy access to the objects of their desires, and in the eyes of the world, they would have the same status and respect given to a genuine holy man. That such evil could be perpetrated in the name of God distressed her beyond measure. *Why did God allow it?*

There was no way that Joan could think of to resolve the overall problem. If the children in the Orphanotrophia were not fed and watered by the monks, they would not be fed and watered at all. They would end up living like the children of the bridge—submitting to being violated for money in order to survive. The only way Joan could see that the children would have any chance of living without the prospect of constant rape was if only nuns, rather than monks, were allowed to run institutions housing children. And the same would apply if a specialist mission to care for the insane were built. *But what evils lie in the hearts of women?* Joan asked herself. *Could they too create darkness in the name of the light?*

When Joan reached the seminary after the Council meeting, she went straight to the chapel for there was still half an hour before evening meal would be served. She felt polluted from thinking about such wickedness and desperately wanted to commune with God's Holy Spirit. To her distress, however, Benedict was before the altar. She had not been by herself with him for some time, but as always, just when she least needed to see him alone, there he was. The rival priest was lying prostrate and had not noticed her arrive, so

Joan slipped into the back pew and watched him. *Is Benedict evil?* she found herself thinking. *Is he another example of someone who joins a religious order for the wrong reasons?* Watching him lying at the feet of Christ crucified, it was clear to Joan that her enemy had as much faith as she did, if not more. He, to her knowledge, did not harm anyone else at the seminary except for her, and he also had a strong sense of morality. Yet somehow he seemed malignant. His view on what was God's law was so uncompromising and his rigidity so severe that goodness seemed to spill over into evil as a consequence. *But am I good?* came her inner voice. *I have spent a lot of my life praying and believing I am being filled up with the presence of God. I have studied relentlessly to attempt to understand His nature. Now I teach those younger than myself what I have learned and try to help a group of children who without me might still be subjected to unfathomable evil. But am I good? I break my vow of celibacy every single morning and night. Since the age of thirteen, I have been lying to the world about being male. And just because I feel like a male now, does not mean that I am one. I am even lying to the woman I am breaking my vow with about that...Are Benedict and I ultimately the same: two human beings who love God and want to serve Him—neither of us perfect, but with our personal evil manifesting in different ways?*

Joan stared across at the prostrate man one more time and then slipped out unseen by him.

CHAPTER 26

Joan gently caressed the soft skin of Thea's forearm as they lay together in the early morning sunshine.

"Are you excited about tomorrow?" her love asked, smiling.

"I can't wait. It's been nearly a year since I've seen him," Joan replied, grinning back.

"Which means it's been nearly a year since we first made love on this rock!"

Joan turned around and kissed Thea passionately. Her desire for this woman had not diminished over the last twelve months. If anything, it had grown stronger. She could not imagine a life now without the sustenance of them coming together every day. Her existence before then, when she shared a cell with Michael, now seemed nearly as far away as her life back in Frankia. She loved every single moment she shared with this woman and wanted their union to last until the end of her days.

The management of their relationship had been easier in the summer, early autumn, and late spring when the weather was hot and there were longer hours of daylight. Wintertime had been tough but they had dressed warmly and made the most of what they could. For those few months when it had been impossible to get to the lake because it was too dark, they had found instead an area in the woods where the trees were thick and people were unlikely to venture. Being closer to the seminary, they'd had to stifle their moans of lovemaking, but it was enough to sustain them until they could once again get back to their private sanctuary.

Nonetheless, Joan had missed Michael during their year of separation and was eagerly looking forward to his arrival the next day. She had so much to tell him. The last time they'd been together at his parish near Marathon, Joan had been in total crisis about having fallen in love with Thea, and she and Michael had concluded that it was best for her not to act on that love. This, of course, had changed the moment Joan had returned home, but she had not found a way to tell Michael properly. She had tried to inform him between the lines of her frequent letters, but it had been too dangerous to spell it out clearly in writing. He had intimated in his responses that he was glad she had found happiness, but again in a disguised way. So she was excited at the thought of being able to tell him everything in all its glory and for him to properly meet Thea.

"Is there anything else you'd like to do with me before we go to work?" Thea asked cheekily, bringing Joan back to the present.

"Ooh... I'm sure I will think of something," Joan replied, pulling up her lover's dress for the second time that morning.

*

Later, when she had finished teaching, she and Father Stefanos made their way down to the River Ilissos to take food to the children as they did every

Tuesday afternoon. The homeless waifs trusted both of them now and whenever the two priests appeared, they would run up excitedly greeting them with smiles. Joan and Father Stefanos had even started teaching a few who wanted to learn how to read and write. It was only a short lesson each Tuesday and Friday, but the children loved it, and Joan felt that, if anything, this in the long term might help them more than the food they brought.

Joan had talked a lot with Alkandros the natural leader of the group. He was a compassionate, kind and intelligent young man, fiercely protective of all the children in his care. At nearly fifteen years of age, Joan was sure that Father Nikolis would let him join the seminary, with a bit of persuasion from herself and Father Stefanos. But the boy would not hear of it. His commitment was to the well-being of his sister, and he could not countenance leaving her in the hands of others, whether it was her friends at the bridge or back at the Orphanotrophia.

As they arrived today, Joan smiled at Maria fondly and the girl smiled back, pleased to see her. In the nine months they had been serving the children, Maria had never spoken to her, and Alkandros claimed she had not said a word since the day he had found her violated by the men who had snatched her. But the child trusted her now. She no longer hid behind her brother's tunic, and she beamed at Joan with delight every time she came to visit. Maria looked a lot better now too. One of the practical things that Joan had been able to do for the female children was clothe them. This was thanks to Thea, who had wanted to play her part in aiding the unfortunate infants. She had donated a handful of old dresses that she and her sisters had outgrown which had not been turned into other garments or used for cleaning cloths. Thea had managed to sew several large patchwork blankets out of scraps of material too and she'd even made some pillows. Father Stefanos had never questioned where Joan had sourced these items but, as always, had given his silent approval of her for doing so.

Joan and Father Stefanos, with the help of Alkandros, gave out the food to the twenty-five waifs, currently living under the bridge. The children were now much better at waiting and sharing fairly, and Joan and Father Stefanos had been able to source various items that ensured the children had means of gathering and storing sufficient food between their visits. Not long after they'd first started aiding them, Joan had gone down to the harbour and asked groups of fishermen to donate any old nets that they no longer had use for. She and Father Stefanos had spent hours repairing them the best they could so the children could use them for fishing in the river. They had also gradually slipped out older cooking pots from both the herb and food kitchens at the seminary, unbeknownst to anyone but each other. In fact, both of them had become experts in silent theft. The children now had enough objects suitable for cooking with and eating from in a civilized fashion. Every time Joan saw something at the seminary with a small crack or chip, she would snaffle it for this purpose.

Once the food was given out and they had helped with some minor cuts and bruises, Joan sat down on the parched grass of the riverbank and started the children's lesson. She was so glad that she had been successful in teaching Thea to read for it gave her confidence in doing the same for these infants. So far, they only had five quills, so the dozen children who were learning needed to be patient and take it in turns to form their letters. Joan could still see that each child was progressing, however gradually, from her instruction. Even Maria was joining in. The tiny child did not repeat the names of the letters along with the others, but she did form each one in ink on the tattered scraps of parchment Joan provided. Today, they were working on the letter 'upsilon', and Maria mastered it almost immediately. When the child beamed up at her, Joan's heart once again overflowed with love and sorrow. As if sensing Joan's emotions, Maria still excited from her success, jumped up from where she was sitting and kissed Joan on the cheek. Witnessing such happiness, the other children spontaneously got up too and before Joan knew it, each of them was hugging her and saying thank you. Joan felt so filled up with emotion that she had to control herself from clutching each child to her breast.

Is this what it feels like to be a mother or a father? she found herself asking. She no longer knew what sex she was and which of her emotions counted as male or female in the eyes of the others. However, she did know that she loved these children deeply and wanted to fiercely protect them from all danger, particularly Maria.

Her own mother had never shown her much affection but her father had been deeply loving until their relationship broke down in her final few months of living at home in Frankia. She remembered how he had taught any child in the village who wanted to read and write, believing it was his duty to God. And how naturally caring he had been of all the youngsters in the village. *I am my father's child...I wish he could see me now*, she thought. She became sad then. She did not think of him now as often as she used to, but in moments like this, she wondered whether if he knew who she was and what she had done, he would be proud of her in spite of what the Church might say. That she would never know, pained her.

Feeling melancholic, Joan looked across at Maria. *I am blessed. At least I was with my family until I was thirteen. I can't begin to imagine what it is like for her*, she thought. Alkandros had told Joan their story a few months ago. Their father had been a baker, and they had lived in a busy quarter of the city and had a good life. Then fire had broken out killing both of their parents and their five other siblings. Alkandros had saved Maria from the flames but could not get to the others. It had happened when he was twelve and she was four years old. After the fire, they had been taken in by the Orphanotrophia, but within a few weeks Alkandros had been raped by one of the monks. He put up with being violated for nearly a year by the same man, and was aware that other Brothers in the order were also targeting boys, but to his knowledge his sister, being a girl, was safe. Then, one day he found her in tears and she told him that a monk had touched her and made her hurt. Realising what she meant, he had escaped with her during the night. He knew that there were children living under the bridge because when they were alive, his parents had always forbidden him from going down to the river, saying they were dangerous and wild. So after they'd fled, he'd taken Maria there and they'd been living there for several months by the time Joan and Father Stefanos had come.

Alkandros had managed to keep Maria safe, apart from the terrible night when she had been snatched at knifepoint, but he, like many of the others, had sold himself on many occasions so he could get enough food for them to survive.

Joan still wished that there were a way she could take a parish, marry Thea and adopt them both. But it was impossible. She could not marry Thea, because then Thea would expect them to make love in a way that would bring about a child and that would mean she would find out 'John' was not a real man, which would be the end of everything. All she could do was keep helping Alkandros and Maria as she did at the moment and pray that one day they would find a proper home and not have to spend the rest of their lives selling themselves in order to survive. Indeed this was Joan's prayer for all of the children whom she served—those now and those she knew would come in the future.

CHAPTER 27

When Michael arrived the next day, Joan was ecstatic. It took all her self-discipline not to jump on him in delight, but he had arrived in the hall during dinner hour so she gave him a brief embrace instead. He looked extremely pleased to see her too, and she knew that he was just as keen for them to be alone straightaway. However, he had to respond to the attention of a sea of old friends before they were able to have the personal reunion they both craved.

After Evening Mass, Joan walked with Michael towards the woods where she had arranged to meet Thea as usual. There was not time enough to recount all of the events from the past year, but she was able explain to him how she and Thea were now in an established relationship, and how Thea allowed herself to be made love to in ways that would avoid her becoming with child. Michael, as always, was hugely supportive and also keen to meet Thea properly, for she had only just started working at the seminary when he had left for his parish.

Once they were out of sight, the pair of them stopped and gave one another a proper hug.

"I have missed you, Pickle. I can't begin to tell you how much."

"And me you. Not a day goes past when I don't wish you were still here, sharing a cell with me."

"I miss that too," he whispered, looking at her, softly.

Joan looked at her friend, feeling sorry to the core. "Are you still feeling lonely there?"

Michael nodded. "I can't stand it, John. It's getting more and more difficult. I don't have any real friends. Not a single one. Everybody is very pleasant, but they are all married with families. I miss living in a community. I miss being with you."

She hugged him again, this time for longer, and soon she felt him growing hard against her. Joan's heart sank. He had been lonely for a long time and had come here with the expectation of relieving that loneliness. "I'm sorry, Michael. I can hug you and chat with you for hours, but I cannot do what we used to do when we were alone now I am with Thea. It would feel like I was committing adultery."

Her friend did not disguise the disappointment in his face and Joan felt guilty that she was unable to help him. Michael was not meant for celibacy. He needed human touch and intimacy, just like she did. It was not natural for him to be cut off from such warmth. She took his hand in hers and stared softly into his sad blue eyes. "We can cuddle a little though," she reassured him.

At this he seemed more relieved, and as they continued walking together she put her arm around his waist, so he'd feel comforted straight away. Then, once they'd met Thea and had all greeted one another enthusiastically, Joan walked in the middle of them both, linking her arms with theirs. To Joan's delight, Michael and Thea had an instant rapport. Michael was keen to get to know Thea straight away, asking her countless questions about her life at the seminary and her family. Joan could tell that Thea liked him immensely for she had a spring in her step and smiled effortlessly as she responded to him.

Michael was amazed by the lake. He could not believe that he had lived near it for so long without knowing of its existence. Joan had asked Thea if she wouldn't mind if Michael joined them for their evening time over the five days he would be staying, and she had been more than happy let him come along. Once the three had settled together on a large rock, dangling their legs over the edge of the water, Thea asked Michael all about his parish and his work with the lepers. He told her about his attempts to improve on the medicines that gave relief to those afflicted but how frustrating it was that no one had discovered a cure. He also talked of the many funerals he had conducted since living there and how his existence now was steeped in nothing but relentless suffering and death. He was living a useful life serving others but not a sufficiently loving or fulfilled enough one for him to be able to cope with the abject misery he witnessed on a daily basis.

Joan felt guilty again for being the *real* reason that Michael had not stayed with Amadeus, his true love, all those years ago. Michael would have been happy with that life on the road in spite of its risks. Now Joan was older and more aware of the way the world worked, she also knew that Amadeus and Michael could have found some way to stay safe together living the life of travelling players. Amadeus would have more than learned his lesson about not giving away the status of their relationship and was a clever enough performer to know how to make it look like he was interested in the female sex. He could have easily taught Michael how to do the same in order to protect himself. Now that Joan had experienced true love for herself, she knew if she had not needed Michael to look after her back then, the men would never have parted and Michael would not be in the situation he was in now.

After their time chatting with Thea, Michael and Joan remained in the woodland for a while so they could have some more privacy. He had been given a guest cell in the main sleeping block, and she wanted to make the most of her time with him before going off to bed.

"Thea is wonderful," Michael said to her. "You don't know how fortunate you are to have found a love like that…"

"Yes, I do," she replied, hugging him. "I'm so sorry you are lonely, Michael. I wish you could live with me here again."

"That's one of the reasons for my visit. I hope to persuade Father Nikolis to give me a job back here at the seminary. Will you help me convince him, Pickle?"

"Of course. I want so much for you to happy and my life would be absolutely complete if you were here too. I know Father Takis and Father Stefanos would love to have you back with them as well. They have both missed you terribly. Father Stefanos doesn't talk much, as you know, but whenever I mention you, he always says how well you worked on the farm and in the kitchen."

"I'd love to work alongside them. But in truth, I'd take even the lowliest job just to live here again. I can't begin to tell you how hard it is for me being away from you all. This is my true home."

Joan saw that Michael was fighting back tears so she held him tightly in her arms and stroked his back. He gripped on to her trembling, and she was filled to the brim with sorrow. As he remained there, being rocked gently in her arms, Joan asked God's Spirit to be with him, and gradually, she felt healing energy begin flowing through her.

Please let him come back to live with us, Dear Lord, she prayed silently.

*

For the second time since joining the seminary, Joan was appalled by Father Nikolis' attitude. When Michael had asked Father Nikolis this morning if he could come back there to work, the seminary head had flatly refused. Michael told Joan that he had beseeched and begged, explaining to Father Nikolis how lonely he was and how he had no proper friends. However, in spite of being sympathetic, Father Nikolis had asserted that he believed Michael was in the correct place and had to accept that the priest's lot was a lonely one by nature.

On hearing this, Joan spoke to Father Takis, who also believed Michael needed to come home to the seminary, and together they went to see Father Nikolis to plead Michael's case.

"If every priest who struggled with his calling gave up his position when times got tough, then God's work would never be done!" Father Nikolis argued.

"But Father Michael might not have gone through with his vows last year if he'd known he would be given a parish rather than remaining here with us. He thought he would spend the rest of his days working in the herb kitchen," explained Joan, emphatically.

"No seminarian is ever promised a role in the community here. If we kept on every young man who had made a valuable contribution or proved popular with students and staff, barely a priest would be dispatched."

Father Takis intervened then. "Father Nikolis, we understand that, but both Father John and I know Father Michael very well, and we can see that he is suffering from terrible melancholia because of the position he is in. He is not suited to live a life of such isolation."

"Then he should relinquish his vow of celibacy and take a wife. It is not the most ideal solution, and of course, the Bishop will frown upon it greatly, but it would solve the problem."

Father Takis briefly exchanged a look with Joan that made her realise that he knew that Michael would never marry a woman. But instead of bringing the issue to the fore, which would be dangerous, the old man tried to sidestep matters. "Father Michael, could do that, yes, but would it not be better to simply transfer him back here where he will be happy than put him through the shame of having to relinquish such an important vow? There is more than enough work for him on the farm we are terribly understaffed, as you know."

"No. I will not hear of it. The parish of St. Lazarus needs a priest with skills in medicine. There is no one here apart from you two and Father Stefanos who has sufficient knowledge of herbs to take on that role. Besides, you are all far too established and important here to be sent away."

Joan, unable to contain herself, tried one last approach. "Could we not train someone to go in his place? What about Zacharias who joined us from Thebes after the ransacking? He's been working on the farm since he arrived and is due to be ordained next spring. I am sure that Father Takis would be able to teach him enough in that time to be ready to serve the lepers."

Father Nikolis looked at her, frowning. "Father John. As you know, I have nothing but respect for both your acute mind and your compassionate spirit. But it is not for you to decide the fate of other holy men. That is the role that has been bestowed upon me under the direct supervision of the Bishop. It is simply not fitting for you to make such suggestions."

On hearing this, Joan's gaze dropped to the floor and she had to bite her tongue. If she said any more, she would only make things worse. But the Seminary Head now fell even further down in her estimation than he had when he'd refused to give his full support to her mission with the Children of the Bridge.

She felt sad that she had come to see him so differently, and it made her think back to her own father, whom she had also thought so highly of, only to be disappointed in him in the end. *Is this the same for all men—even the good ones—that eventually their flaws will become so apparent that they seem much less than before?* she asked herself.

*

Michael was beside himself with the outcome. "I can't go back there, John. I can't stand the loneliness. If Father Nikolis won't let me stay here, I am going back to Frankia to find Amadeus," he cried as they sat together by the lake.

"But how on earth will you find him? He could be anywhere…" Joan stated, worriedly.

"I can ask from village to village as I go. Someone will have seen him somewhere, I am sure!"

"Where will you sleep? How will you afford travel? I have no coin, and there is no way Father Nikolis will give you any. You would starve."

"I could throw myself on the mercy of each monastery I pass along the way. Ask for bed and food in exchange for labouring at whatever they need."

"Michael, I don't want to make things worse by not supporting you, but how will you make it through those Alps without a horse and wagon? It is too far to walk, and even at this time of year you would be in terrible danger from the elements."

Michael began trembling then and Joan put her arm around his shoulders as he wept. Thea, who had remained silent whilst they'd walked from the trees to the lake, took Michael's hand. Joan had explained to her about Michael and Amadeus long ago, and she did not think that their love was wrong. "Perhaps I could help you by saving up some coin over the next year and you could go then. That way, you will be able to purchase a horse and saddle when you get to Frankia."

Michael calmed a little at this. "Would you really do that for me?" he asked, shakily.

Joan and Thea exchanged a look of agreement. "Yes. It will take me a while, but if I am careful I could gradually put aside enough. And I am sure that John, nearer the time, could stock you up with enough food to last on the boat and your first few days on the road."

Michael hugged them both, thanking them profusely. Joan looked across at Thea again and mouthed a personal 'thank you' to her. The woman had come up with a solution that had given Michael at least some hope for a happier future. Joan was also flooded with relief. She was worried about him going off with no plan other than to find his lost love. At least this way there was time to think through all the permutations of how it might work and what Michael could do if things did not turn out as he hoped. She had not wanted to voice her deepest fear about him going on such a quest—that Amadeus Reichenbach might not even be alive anymore. It had been five and half years since they'd left him waving goodbye at the harbour in Venice. Anything could have happened to him since then. Her other fear was that Michael might find Amadeus but then Amadeus might not want him. The man could easily have found love again with someone else since they were together last. Joan was glad she had not been forced into suggesting either possibility when her friend was already in such distress. Thea had saved the day by creating more time.

For the rest of that evening Michael was happier. He had hope now that one day his life could be joyous again. Joan remained with him in the woods until it was way past nightfall, chatting and holding him tightly. He talked almost constantly about seeing Amadeus again and together they reminisced of the amazing man who had been a mentor to her and a lover to him. Joan vowed to herself that every day from now on she would pray that if Amadeus was still alive and if it was for their highest good, that the two men would be reunited one day because she could see that this was the only way her friend was ever going to find absolute peace and fulfillment again.

Her relief spilled over the next morning when she met with Thea for their usual time together. Grateful to the woman for finding a way to calm down Michael, and having missed their lovemaking the night before, Joan literally ravished her—first with her fingers and then with her tongue.

"Will you really save your money for Michael?" she asked, afterwards, when Thea was lying sated in her arms.

Thea nodded and smiled. "Yes. And I will be able to help him get a good horse here in Athens that he can take over with him on the boat. With my father being a blacksmith, I could get one far cheaper than he could."

"But why would you do that for someone who you hardly know?"

"Because you love him, and I love you." Thea stated, matter of factly.

Joan smiled and took the woman's chin in her hand. "You, my love, are the most magnificent being I have ever met!"

*

By the time Michael accompanied Joan and Father Stefanos on a visit to the Children of the Bridge, he was far more buoyant. Joan had spent a lot of time holding him and comforting him over the past few days, and she had already promised that she would try to visit him at his parish during the winter. The hope of being able to change his situation within a year made all the difference to his spirit.

Joan was still cross with Father Nikolis though. It was blatantly obvious to those who loved Michael that he was in trouble and needed the comfort of friends. Father Takis had even tried speaking to the seminary head again on his own, but Father Nikolis would not be moved on the matter.

It was good to see Michael smile a little when they reached the bridge and some of the boys came running up to them. In general, the children were more reticent than they had been in recent weeks, still worried about any stranger that visited their haven. But, because Joan reassured them that Michael was her friend, eventually they relaxed. When he explained he worked at a leper colony, some of the children were fascinated.

"Is it true that they have horns?" asked one of them, in all seriousness.

"Do they really dance with the Devil at night?" asked another.

Michael, having a natural way with children, laughed and teased them before finally telling them they were wrong.

Maria liked him so much that when he said goodbye to them she hugged him. Joan had a tear in her eye. The little girl she loved so much could see how good her friend was. *Love knows love. Love begets love and love drives out darkness* she thought.

On their way back, he talked a lot about how great the work was that she and Father Stefanos were doing, and how much he wished he could be a part of it. Joan loved sharing her world with Michael again and decided that she would come up with a fresh plan to persuade Father Nikolis that it was right to let him move back there. She would also pray. She always had Michael's health and well being at the top of her mental list of prayers but now she would be more specific. She would ask her Heavenly Father to bring him home until the time was right for him to be with Amadeus again.

"Do you think you will stay with Thea for the rest of your life?" Michael asked her, once they were alone again.

Joan did not have to think for long to answer that. "Yes. I love her more than my own self. I could not countenance living without her now. As far as I am concerned, she is my wife and so only death shall part us."

"I am so glad you found someone. I was worried you would not cope when I left. That you would find it too hard. God has given you such a special gift. You know that, don't you?"

"Yes," Joan nodded. "I am blessed beyond all measure."

*

The morning that he was due to leave, Joan took Michael to the lake instead of meeting Thea, so they could talk and be alone together one last time. Most of it was spent weeping, for they were both devastated at the separation. In addition to her sadness, Joan was still deeply worried about the state of her friend's mind in spite of the glimmer of hope he now had for the future.

Father Takis, as always, had helped as much as he could and had shown him how to make a very strong tincture of hypericum perforatum and given him a clump to take back to plant in his herb garden. He said it would help Michael stave off the melancholia and that it also had mystical powers of protection, which is why it was also known as St. John's Wort. In Father Takis' Herbal it explained that Christians had named this mystical plant after John The Baptist, having noticed that the yellow petals looked like a halo. When it was picked it literally 'bled' a red liquid that looked like spilled blood and the flowers themselves usually came to bloom around 24th June, which was the Saint's birthday.

Joan hoped with all her heart that the tincture would help and decided that she would implore St John himself to intercede on Michael's behalf for him to be happy again.

She would miss Michael for selfish reasons too. Although Thea fulfilled her emotionally, the woman did not know her secret and Joan had not talked much about her past, even though they had been making love for over a year. Michael was still the only person with whom she could truly relax and who knew her real story from the beginning until now. He was the only one who understood what her life in Frankia had been like, who had known her family and had known her as a girl as well as a boy. It was strange really, because when they had lived together in their shared cell, they had barely mentioned their life back home. The odd passing remark or memory would slip into conversation but they never actually discussed it as a topic in its own right. But during this visit, they had talked about it in great detail. The main question on both of their minds was whether their parents and siblings were still alive. For neither of them had made any contact since the day they had run away. The truth was, they would unlikely ever know the answer, because even if they wanted to take the risk now that so much time had passed, getting a message to the north of Frankia would cost a fortune and there was no certainty that it would even get there and even less that they would receive a reply. Joan hoped that all of her family was well and happy, although it was only her father who she longed to see again. Michael did not miss either of his parents very much because they had treated him with such hatred after the incident with the monk. His mother and father had only let him remain on the farm so that they could find a way of sending him off that would not give rise to a scandal, and he had been forced to sleep in the barn until his departure to the seminary. However, Michael did miss his siblings and yearned to know how they had faired in the years he had been absent.

During their final hours together, Michael raised the question regarding Amadeus that a few days before Joan had avoided discussing so as not to distress him further. "I don't even know if Amadeus is still alive..." he stated in almost a whisper. "...Sometimes I believe I still feel him with me, but it is such a weak sensation compared to how it was when we first separated, that it's hard to know whether it is real or just a memory."

Joan held his hand. "I have no idea, Michael, and it is one of the reasons why I think you should be cautious about planning to go back to Frankia to look for him. I worry that you could leave here only to find that he is gone, and you'd be stranded even further away from me and Father Takis than you already are."

"I know...I have thought that too. But I have to plan for a brighter future. I cannot live out the rest of my life on that mountainside alone."

"Well, we will prepare for it as we agreed and pray that if it is right, Our Lord will open up the way for you."

CHAPTER 28

It was a few weeks after Michael had returned to Marathon that it happened. Joan knew as soon as she reached the bridge that something was wrong because only two children, Milo and Vassillios, were present, and they appeared totally distraught.

"What is it?" Joan questioned them, anxiously.

"It's Maria. We can't find her anywhere. She was snatched again two nights ago by the same men who came last year," Milo replied, trembling.

Joan felt a rush of fear so consuming that it made her dizzy, and she had to take several deep breaths before responding. She looked at Father Stefanos who had turned white. He was as afraid for the child's safety as she was.

"Where are the others?" he asked.

"They are out looking for her in groups of four. We stayed behind in case she finds her way back," explained Vassillios, who looked down as he spoke, trying to hide tears of distress.

"Do you know which direction the men took her?"

"Yes," Milos said, pointing towards the bank of the river leading south.

Joan looked across at Father Stefanos who nodded his concurrence with her thoughts. They left the food baskets with the children, but took with them some pieces of fresh cloth and vinegar in case Maria had wounds that needed cleaning straight away.

For the first quarter of an hour walking along the riverbank, they saw no one and neither of them said a word. Joan scoured the area from left to right searching for the slightest glimpse of anything out of the ordinary. Then, every so often, she would stop altogether and look behind, in case she spotted something from the opposite view point.

Eventually, they saw Kryllios and three of the other boys moving in their direction through the fields that lay between the city and the river, and they went over to meet them. This small group of children had been hunting all day yesterday and today, but had not found a trace of Maria anywhere. Seeing how tired and hungry they were, Joan sent them back in the direction of the bridge so they could replenish themselves, and told them to take rest as they had not slept. When they had gone, she and Father Stefanos forged ahead as before but with every step, Joan's sense of foreboding increased.

It was over two hours before they spotted a much larger group of children in the distance. Joan did not need to stare at them for long to know that they were in distress, and suddenly she found herself sprinting towards them, with Father Stefanos keeping pace alongside her. By the time they were halfway there, all Joan could hear was screaming and crying, and she already knew that Maria was dead.

It was not hard to work out what had happened when she examined the girl, and Joan made no attempt to disguise or hold back the tears which streamed down her cheeks as a result of her findings. It was clear that the child had been violated by more than one person then strangled and dumped in the river, only to wash up further down. Joan felt her heart literally breaking inside of her chest, and she could barely contain herself.

Alkandros, Maria's devoted brother, was kneeling on the ground next to the body and rocking with silent tears unable to look at anyone. The others stood together in clusters, holding one another and crying. Father Stefanos had turned away from them all, but Joan could see from the shudders in his back that he was weeping too.

Joan simply picked up the dead child and held her to her breast, burying her face in Maria's hair. "My poor, poor, baby girl," she whispered, as tears continued pouring. "I should have adopted you. I should never have let you out of my sight. My poor, sweet child. I cannot believe they did this to you. I'm so sorry I did not protect you. I will never forgive myself for not saving you from this."

She remained like that, cradling the dead girl in her arms for several minutes, until she realised that only she and Father Stefanos could do what was now necessary for both Maria and the grieving children. Gently, Joan placed the child back on the ground, covering up her body as much as she could with the torn, wet dress, and crossing the girls hands over her chest.

"We need to inform the Chief Magistrate so he can dispatch the City Guards to track down these heinous transgressors. Once they have been here to see exactly what happened, we will take her to the seminary and bury her there, if that sits well with you, Alkandros." she stated, remembering that the distraught young man should approve of her suggestion before she went ahead with it.

The young man just nodded. He was too broken to speak. However, she was glad that he'd consented to let his sister be buried at the seminary. Maria needed to be laid to rest in consecrated ground to ensure her entrance to Paradise, but Joan could not possibly allow her to be buried in the cemetery at the Orphanotrophia, given the child had been violated there as well, before escaping to the bridge with her brother.

Joan was not sure whether Father Nikolis would respond positively to her wishes, but she was already determined that she would not take 'no' for an answer. She had let this child down in life. She would not do the same thing in death.

"How are we going to get the body back to the seminary?" asked Father Stefanos, who had not spoken until now.

Joan thought for moment. "When I see the Chief Magistrate, I will ask him to provide us with suitable transportation. The City Guards should come straight away, because they will want to see exactly what happened to her and ask the children to describe the men they need to hunt down. Hopefully, they will bring the body up to the seminary once they are done."

"Are you able to organise it on your own? I am hopeless with words, as you know, and I would prefer to stay here and look after the children."

Joan thought for a moment. "Yes. You stay with Alkandros and any of the children who think they can describe the perpetrators accurately to the City Guards. The rest should go home to the bridge and tell the others what has happened... But first we need to pray."

Joan asked the children to gather around Maria's corpse and together they said the Lord's Prayer. Joan also said the Prayer for the Dead just in case Father Nikolis refused her request to have the burial at the seminary. "Eternal rest grant unto her, O Lord, and let perpetual light shine upon her. May the soul of the faithful departed, through the mercy of God, rest in peace. Amen."

Then, Joan left Father Stefanos, Alkandros, the two girls and small group of boys together to watch over the body whilst she walked towards the city and the other children went back to the bridge.

*

Joan led the Funeral Mass herself. She had never performed this rite before but she could not countenance anyone else, even Father Stefanos, taking the service.

It had not been that hard to persuade Father Nikolis to allow the funeral to happen at the Seminary Chapel and for Maria to be buried in the small cemetery which lay tucked behind it. For Maria was not a 'bastard child' born outside of Holy Matrimony. She had been baptised and brought up in a good family before they were killed in the fire. The child was also under the age of seven which meant she was really too young to have committed any grievous sins with mal intent that would destine her for hell—she was, in effect, an 'innocent'.

However, Joan liked to think that the real reason why Father Nikolis had allowed the funeral to take place at the Seminary of St. Joseph was because he'd finally realised that the decision he'd made about not letting the children be sheltered amongst them had directly impacted on their lives; and for one of them, this decision had led to the most diabolical consequences.

Last night, Maria's body had been brought up to the chapel in a cart driven by a City Guard, as Joan had requested of the Chief Magistrate. Joan had been too overwhelmed with grief to do anything but give cursory details of Maria's circumstances before death and then how she had been snatched, raped and murdered. The Chief Magistrate had been thoroughly appalled by such a savage act of evil and had assured Joan that he would do everything in his power to track down the culprits. Whether in reality he would have any success in tackling the matter, she did not know, but there had to be something he could do to address the fact that a group of men roamed the city and violated children at their whim.

She had not made it to her usual liaison with Thea, but during the Wake attended by all the children, Father Stefanos, Father Takis and Father Nikolis, Joan had slipped out to use the latrines and under cover of darkness had also sneaked across to Thea's cottage.

She'd stayed only a few moments—just enough for the woman to know what had happened and understand her absence that evening. Thea had been devastated for her and Maria, but Joan had not allowed herself to remain because Thea's tenderness would result in her breaking down completely. She knew she needed to keep going for the sake of the children and also, even in such horrific circumstances, she had to maintain some kind of guise of masculinity.

Now, as she they sang the final Psalms before the body was interred, Joan was struggling not to fall apart altogether. For all she could think of was the innocent face of the child whom she'd loved so much smiling up at her in trust, followed by the hideous image of the demonic evil done to her in the last few hours of her short life. And Joan knew that from that day on she would forever be haunted by that vision.

For the first time in her existence, Joan felt absolute hatred. Not just passing hate, as she had experienced for Albrecht, the monk who had nearly violated her when they had stopped at the monastery during the journey through Frankia. And not just the flashes of hatred she occasionally felt for Benedict when he goaded her and made her question her own goodness. But real hate. A hate that consumed her. She had no idea whether she would ever forgive these men in spite of it being fundamental to her faith to do so. She certainly knew she would never want to.

Even worse, and altogether more disturbing, was that she was now overwhelmed by an all-encompassing anger with God. From the day she had met Maria, nearly a year ago, she had prayed for the child morning and night. She had petitioned the Deity for the girl's protection and asked that Maria might find a home full of love and solace. Yet the infant had been raped, beaten and murdered instead. How could a God of love allow this?

So as Joan performed each element of the girl's final rite of passage, she did so in order for the child to rest in peace but felt no connection to the Heavenly Father whatsoever. She conducted the entire ceremony from start to finish not knowing whether she would ever believe that God was good again. And the question that Thea had asked so poignantly a year before this atrocity had taken place, now resounded over and over in Joan's mind: *No matter how beautiful and blissful Paradise might be in the end, was the suffering of this small child worth it to get there?* And the answer kept coming back: *No.*

Once the final handful of soil had been scattered over the tiny coffin, Father Nikolis and Father Takis left Joan and Father Stefanos with the grieving children in the cemetery. Each of them was totally exhausted, both from the long hours of searching for the missing girl and then staying up all night for the Wake. Father Nikolis had permitted the children to stay at the seminary for the rest of the day so long as they were not left unattended. If they wanted to sleep there for a few hours, Joan and Father Stefanos would have to accompany the children to the Great Hall where, as it was a Saturday and there were no lectures, they could lie on the floor. However, the children themselves were reticent to go off and sleep in an unfamiliar place, and instead sat in clusters near Maria's graveside, unable to bring themselves to move. The only person still standing was Alkandros who stared down at his sister's grave. After a while, Joan rose from where she'd been kneeling comforting a group of crying little ones and went to the young man's side.

"Do you want to stay here with us and join the seminary, Alkandros?" she asked softly.

The boy turned to her angrily. "I no longer believe in God!" he snapped.

Joan stared at him hopelessly. How could she possibly convince him of the existence of a Deity, when she was no longer even sure whether that Deity was even worthy of worship? "I have no idea why God would let this happen, Alkandros. All I know is that He does exist, and Maria is with Him now and will be suffering no more," she said weakly.

The boy turned his gaze back to his sister's grave. "I will never believe in God again. Because if God existed, He would not have stripped me of every single member of my family, first by fire and then by rape and murder. I am going to join a warship and get as far away from this city as I can. I never want to see this place again."

At that, the boy turned and began walking away. Joan felt moved to stop him, but before she could, Father Stefanos put a hand on her shoulder. "Let him go, Father John. What life could he have if he returned to the bridge? This is his only hope."

Joan had managed to hold back tears since her outpouring whilst cradling the dead infant in her arms the day before, but now they simply streamed down her cheeks in spite of herself.

"I will take the children back down to the bridge," Father Stefanos whispered, gently. "You need to sleep, you are exhausted."

Joan looked at him through blurry eyes. "Yes, Father. Thank you," she replied.

She bid each of the children goodbye, promising to visit them on Tuesday as usual, and then made her way to her cell. However, when she reached the empty herb kitchen, so overwhelming was her sorrow, she could not help but begin boiling poppy and valerian tea.

CHAPTER 29

Joan did not understand why she was being shaken and began lashing her arms violently at whoever was doing it. She could hear a warped voice and see a dark figure through her hazy vision but could not make out who it was.

"Wake up, John! Wake up, John. Please!" was the phrase Joan finally deciphered. She tried with all her might to force her eyes to stay open but they simply would not, at least not until she was suddenly jolted awake by a bucket of water being poured over her head.

"What's going on?" she shouted leerily, now just able to make out that she was with Father Takis in her cell. Joan looked around anxiously not understanding why the person who was supposed to be her protector had assaulted her with water.

"You've been asleep a whole day and night, and I could not wake you up, however much I shook you. You've been on the poppy and valerian tea again, haven't you? I saw the remnants in the pan you left out!"

Overwhelming sorrow welled up inside of her as memories of the past few days flooded back, and Joan let out a howl. Father Takis, now looking sympathetic sat on the bed and took her in his arms. "I'm so sorry, John," he whispered, as he rocked her whilst she wept.

"Why?" she asked him, unable to contain herself as the horror of what happened to the little girl overtook her completely.

"I don't know," he answered, still holding her. "I simply do not know."

"But I prayed for her especially..." Joan wailed, incapable of gaining control.

"All we can hope for is that she is in God's care now..." the elderly priest said solemnly.

"Aargh," came her voice, no longer able to make words.

"Here," said Father Takis, handing her a toalia so she could dry her face and hair. "You will need to wash yourself thoroughly and change your sheets too," he stated flatly.

Joan looked down and saw that as well as being saturated from the water in the bucket, her bed was sodden with urine. Immediately she was totally ashamed and she could not meet Father Takis' eye.

"Fret not, John," he continued. "I understand why it happened. But we need to talk seriously about you taking the tea again without permission..."

Joan still did not look at him. "I just could not stand the pain any longer..." she whispered.

"I know, John. But I told you before. It is dangerous to make it for yourself unsupervised, and it is also addictive. You should have come to me to help you, rather than take matters into your own hands. I have been deeply worried about you. I have been coming in every half hour, and you really have been impossible to wake. You do realise you could have died from drinking tea that was too strong, don't you?"

Joan nodded. "I am sorry…"

"I do not wish to be cruel to you, but unless you promise me in the name of Jesus Christ Himself that you will never touch either of those herbs again without my consent, I will have to stop you working in the kitchen and you will lose your single cell as a result."

Joan was suddenly filled with fear. That Father Takis had given her this cell and was helping protect her secret was essential to her. It was what she relied on in order to thrive undetected and without fear. She forced herself to make eye contact. "I really am sorry, Father Takis. I do swear in the name of Our Lord Jesus Christ that I will never touch that tea or those herbs again unless you give them to me."

Father Takis looked at her sternly, examining her face to ensure she was telling the truth. "Very well," he stated, eventually.

Joan hung her head in both exhaustion and shame. "I don't know what to do with myself now."

"You need to grieve and you need to drink nettle tea and plenty of water. I will ask Father Nikolis to excuse you from duties for a few days. He is very concerned about both you and Father Stefanos. He knows how much this will have hurt the two of you."

Joan now remembered that she was not the only one who had cared for the child. "How is Father Stefanos coping?" she asked.

Father Takis looked sad. "He has neither spoken nor eaten since he returned from taking the children back to the bridge, nor has he come out of his cell."

Joan nodded. "He loved her too. She was innocent and did not deserve this. She wasn't even seven years old. There is no sense in such evil being allowed to flourish, left unchecked by God…"

Father Takis said no more and simply handed her a tankard of nettle tea that he must have brought in with him along with the bucket of water. Joan sipped at it gratefully. "Thank you for watching over me."

"You are special, John. I will never understand the ways of Our Lord, but I know you are marked out in a manner that I have never seen before. God's light shines through you. You must never doubt that. Now, drink, clean yourself up, and then get some fresh air."

At that, the elderly priest turned and went out through the heavy oak door, shutting it firmly behind him.

As soon as she was certain he was out of earshot, Joan buried her face in her pillow and howled again for the murdered child that she had loved so very much.

*

When she finally saw Thea that evening, the woman embraced her immediately, offering soothing words of love. Then silently they walked to the lake holding hands. Thea was very forgiving about Joan's unexplained absence. She understood that Joan had been exhausted from both the shock and the fact that she had missed an entire night's sleep. Joan did not tell her about having taken the poppy and valerian tea for she was too ashamed of herself and she also did not want the woman to worry. Besides, Father Takis' threat had such serious consequences, that Joan knew it would be extremely unlikely that she would succumb to temptation again, no matter how traumatic her circumstances.

On reaching their hidden sanctuary, Joan buried her head in Thea's breast. She did not cry, but nonetheless allowed herself to be rocked gently in the woman's arms. Joan did not have to tell Thea how she was feeling, for her love understood without need of explanation.

They stayed up together late into the night, far past darkness, and Joan only returned to her cell because she knew that Father Takis would worry considerably if he discovered she was not there. Joan would have liked nothing more than to fall asleep wrapped around the woman she loved with all of her heart and the only source of genuine comfort she had.

When finally she climbed into her bed she was engulfed by sorrow yet again. Joan had not been to chapel that day, nor had she been able to bring herself to pray. As she lay there in the dark, she thought of poor Alkandros, perhaps by now already at sea, and wondered whether he would ever find even a modicum of happiness. His life had already brought nothing but pain and misery. Suddenly God seemed so very cruel and His purpose so malignant, that Joan could not understand how she had ever thought Him perfect. *Sometimes I wonder whether the Manichaens were right, and rather than there being one God who created all things, that instead there are two forces—one good and one evil doing battle for all eternity,* she thought, instantly feeling guilty at seeing the appeal of a religion that had almost been wiped out because of asserting this appalling heresy. *It makes much more sense though...if this good and loving Spirit I experience is separate to that which is evil, and it battles against such darkness yet cannot always win...But if this were true, then God is not God and everything I have learned and studied for and embraced my whole life is a sham...Didn't St. Augustine himself reject Manichaeism before embracing Christianity as the true path?*

Feeling another rush of shame for even contemplating believing in something so heretical, Joan quickly turned her thoughts back to Maria. "I am so sorry, Maria," she whispered out loud. "Please forgive me for not protecting you."

*

After three days of rest, Joan knew that no matter how ambivalent she felt about the Deity, the only way she was going to be able to continue on with her existence at the seminary, would be to begin teaching again and to study harder than ever before. She would, of course, continue to help with the children living at the bridge but equally, she would now refocus on her role as a scholar. Perhaps through more study and contemplation, she could begin to make sense of why the Lord had allowed such an atrocity to take place.

Generally, although they had not known the child, her colleagues and students were sympathetic to her—each offering condolences and prayers. Joan still did not socialise with the staff except when absolutely necessary but in this instance she was grateful for their support and kind wishes. Even Benedict, although not forthcoming with words, gave sympathy in his own way, for he did not goad her or rile her into debate during the public lectures for nearly two months after Maria's death. Then, of course, his jealousy outgrew his compassion and once again he began finding flaws in each of her arguments and making cutting remarks on the rare occasions he was alone with her.

Father Stefanos was inconsolable and Father Takis started treating him with St. John's Wort like he had done Michael but even that gave little results at first. It took him several weeks to perform his duties except for visiting the children twice a week as he always had. During their walks to and from the bridge he did not say a word and Joan did not try to force him to. It was heartbreaking for both of them going there twice a week and remembering so vividly the beautiful young soul who had been savaged and killed so brutally.

Joan also missed Alkandros. The children were less trusting and more nervous without his protection and even their reading lessons soon ground to a halt. More often than not, Joan and Father Stefanos would simply leave the food and medicines for the children to sort out themselves and stay no longer than a few minutes. Everything had changed forever.

Joan was now spending far more time in the library than in the herb kitchen or the chapel, where she only did the minimum required of her. Studying proved sweet solace, and as a result of the extra time absorbed in texts and grappling with philosophical issues, her teaching improved immensely. She became more confident than ever and was able to engage effectively even with the most challenging questions from both seminarians and visitors. Within a few months, people were attending her Friday Lectures in the hundreds, and when she walked through Athens on her way to see the children, or attend a Council meeting, she was regularly stopped by an ardent fan of her rhetoric. Joan fell in love with learning again and absorbed herself in scholarly pursuits in a way that she hadn't done since before becoming a priest and meeting Thea.

However, she did not blot out Maria's death completely and each day, before attending evening Mass, she stopped for a while at the child's grave and tended it with love. Joan knew she would never forgive herself for not adopting Maria or at least trying to find her a home with someone who could have given her the love and protection she'd deserved. And whereas in the library and in the classroom, the teachings of Iraeneus on the need for evil in order to grow into God's likeness made sense and the price seemed worth it, at the graveside of the violated child they did not, and the concept of cosmic dualism—that two eternal forces one good and one evil existed in constant battle—gained ground in her mind. For in reality, only this made sense of the prevalence of so very much evil in this world.

*

In reality, it took Joan nearly a year to recover from the shock of Maria's murder and reach a place where she was able to reconcile her faith in Christianity with the mystery of our deepest sufferings. In the end, it was by meditating on the image of the Suffering God Himself—the part of God, Christ Jesus, who took on flesh and as a result was whipped, beaten and crucified—that made her regain confidence that God had no other way to bring about His higher purpose. God had subjected part of Himself to abominable, unjustified suffering along with us and for us. Now, rather than prostrating before the altar with her eyes closed as she used to, each day Joan knelt staring at the nails in Jesus' hands, the wound in His side and the blood dripping down His face from the crown of thorns. And as time went on, she found peace in God once again and was able to lift her hands to receive the Holy Spirit.

Thea also did much to mend Joan's wounded being. Joan could not make love to Thea for several weeks after Maria was killed. Such unadulterated pleasure seemed inappropriate to her in the face of what had happened. Thea, never once complained. Instead, each morning and evening they would hold one another tightly, Thea stroking her hair and rubbing her back, asking for nothing. Then, one day, Joan found her hand moving to Thea's breast and their lovemaking recommenced, gently at first and eventually with passion again.

Joan continued to attend the monthly gatherings of the Council of Athens. She was as well versed in the affairs of the city as any man present and, as one who wanted to make things better through practical means rather than mere talk, when she did open her mouth, she was now listened to. The members of the Council knew what she did for the children, along with the small acts of charity she performed for other homeless communities within the city. She had gained the Councilmen's respect and she was glad of that. Although she despaired at whether anything major would change for the better given the range of opposing views on every subject, she was pleased when little things that made such a huge difference came about because she had personally pressed for them. One of her most comforting achievements was to get a City Guard posted by the bridge over the River Ilissos to ensure that none of the children would ever be snatched in the darkness again.

Joan's confidence when amongst the powerful men of the city was also boosted by the fact that she had gradually come to look like those with whom she served. During the two years she had been a member of the Council, she had continued taking the tincture of tribulus, as prescribed by Father Takis, and had kept to a punishing routine of exercise in her cell in spite of her long period of grief. Her muscle bulk had doubled, and she no longer appeared like a weak and feeble boy. Although she had cut back on her time learning the herbs in favour of more academic study, she still worked on the farm each evening and made herself do the heaviest work she could find. Her moustache had grown thicker again from consistently applying the rosemary oil, and she even had some light down on her chin. In addition to this, she diligently practiced walking and sitting with the posture of the army generals who sat alongside the men of God and Law. Joan now had a masculine presence that could not be doubted.

CHAPTER 30

It was not long after the anniversary of Maria's death that Joan went to visit Michael for the second time at his parish. Thea had kept to her word and started saving coin so that Michael would be able to buy a horse and other supplies in order to return to Frankia and find his lost love, Amadeus Reichenbach. However, a few months after his last visit, Michael had written to say that he was now being helped once a week by one of the monks from the monastery in Marathon, who was also a specialist in herbs. There had been an increase in the number of lepers living in the colony, and Michael had written to the monastery requesting assistance with their care. As a result, Brother Barak had been sent out to help him for one day each week. Michael did not make it explicit that they had formed a union, but over the course of three letters he had stated that the monk had become a good friend; that they had many common interests, and that he no longer felt so lonely. Given that he had not appeared at the seminary anxious to leave, a year after Thea's promise to help as expected, Joan had assumed that even if the two men weren't lovers, the monk had made Michael feel positive enough to stay where he was for the time being at least.

It was hard leaving Thea for two weeks, but Joan was glad to have the opportunity to see her best friend. She had told Michael about the murder of little Maria in her letters, but she longed to talk to him about it in person and discuss with him the crisis it had caused her faith and where she was now with her thoughts in relation to God and suffering.

When she arrived at the Church Of St. Lazarus, Michael greeted her with open arms, and they embraced one another for several minutes.

"I've missed you terribly," she said, taking both his hands in hers, as they pulled apart.

"And me you. I wanted so much to come to you in your suffering, but the Bishop forbade me leave here," Michael stated despairingly, shaking his head as he spoke. "Sometimes it is the vow of obedience that runs hardest against the grain. I am so very, very sorry I could not be with you. You must have been devastated beyond measure."

"I was broken," she whispered, remembering the full strength of the horror.

For the next hour, Joan proceeded to tell Michael everything that had happened from the girl's disappearance to her burial in the seminary graveyard.

"Did the City Guards catch the perpetrators?" he asked solemnly.

"No," replied Joan, flatly. "The descriptions given by the children could have fitted a hundred men. She was taken at night and they were wearing hooded cloaks. The guards had no chance of finding them."

"So evil went and remains unchecked. No wonder your faith was so rocked."

It was then that Joan was brave enough to expand upon the doubts she'd had with regards to God's goodness. He was the only man of God with whom she would ever feel comfortable having this kind of frank discussion, and she was anxious to know his thoughts on the subject.

"Do you think it is worth it?" she asked him.

"Yes. But not for the right reasons..." he replied.

"What do you mean?"

"I have never been as sure of God's presence as you have, John. Sometimes I believe I have felt Him, but largely my faith has just been that—faith. So I do not have your sense of what that bliss might be like at the end of the day. But I do think it was worth being born and living this life in spite of its suffering, because I have had you as my friend, and I got to meet Amadeus and be loved by him..."

Joan looked at her friend and nodded. For those lucky enough to experience it, perhaps it was worth it for the love that could be shared. However, she knew that this still begged the question for those who were not lucky enough to have a best friend or a true love in their life.

They went into the kitchen and prepared a stew for their evening meal, and Michael began telling her all about Brother Barak. The monk had started working there about four months after Michael visited the seminary last year when he had been in such a melancholic state. Michael had found a little improvement in his emotions since taking the St. John's Wort but had still been planning to leave the priesthood and go back to Frankia in search of his love. However, when Brother Barak joined him, they got on well straight away and within a few visits became firm friends. Their mutual interest in the herbs and their genuine pity for the lepers which came without making a judgement that they were 'cursed', meant that the two men had found it easy to talk to one another. Barak was only a year younger than Michael and had joined the monastery specifically because he wanted to learn the way of the herbs and help the sick.

One night, after a few weeks into learning about one another, Barak had stayed later than planned, and Michael had invited him to remain there until morning rather than ride home in the dark. Although they were becoming good friends, Michael had been very careful not to touch the monk or be suggestive in any way, lest he end up in trouble like he had done as a young man back in Frankia. The consequences of his making that kind of a mistake as a man would be far greater than as sixteen year old, and he could not risk it—in spite of his growing attraction towards his friend. That night, Michael had made up a bed for Barak on the floor of his tiny quarters attached to the back of the main chapel building. Not long after blowing out the candles, Barak had whispered through the darkness, "Do you ever feel lonely, Michael?" And Michael had replied, "Yes. I sometimes wish I had someone to hold at night." At which point, Barak had tentatively reached up and put his hand on Michael's arm. Michael had responded by turning from his back to his side and reaching over and laying his hand over Barak's. Then after a few minutes, he had gently and bravely begun stroking the monk's arm. At this, Barak had joined Michael on the bed and had begun kissing him passionately and then, within moments, had entered him and they'd made love. Michael was not shy about talking with Joan of what it was like to find himself first being taken by Barak and then penetrating the man in return, for she had pleasured him on countless occasions when they'd shared a cell and she understood his needs. In addition, Michael knew that Joan made love to Thea twice a day, and she had not been reticent herself in describing to him the many ways she had discovered of pleasuring the woman when they had discussed it during his last visit.

Since this first encounter, each week when Barak visited Michael's parish, the first thing they would do was make love, and then after a day spent creating medicines and tending the lepers, they would join again before the monk rode back to his monastery. Barak rarely stayed over, as they did not want to arouse suspicion about their relationship. Just knowing that he had this union once a week with a person for whom he had such tender feelings had transformed Michael's life from one of bleak despair to one with purpose and joy.

"Do you love him?" Joan asked, when he had finished describing their time together.

Michael nodded. "Yes. Not in the impassioned way I loved Amadeus, but in a gentle way. I love spending time with him, and I love his touch."

"Has he ever been in love before?"

"Yes, he loved a friend in his village, but he did not dare pursue it and then when the boy got married, he joined the monastery, broken-hearted and decided to devote his life to medicine instead of love.

For several years he pleasured one of the older monks, who sensed that he needed the touch of men, but he was never in love with him. That monk died not long before Barak started working here. He tells me he loves me every time he sees me and that I have made him happy too."

*

A few days later, Joan met Brother Barak for herself. He was a short man with soft round features, black hair and dark brown eyes. He was not strikingly handsome like Amadeus Reichenbach, but he had a pleasant face and a gentle spirit. Joan was relieved that Michael had found the comfort of human touch and the sense of peace that came with that. She could not imagine living without the solace of Thea in her arms, and knowing that Michael needed human presence even more than she did, Joan had been terrified until now that he might end up in total despair and never recover.

Seeing him buoyant and joyful once again, made her own heart light. She could see that Barak loved him too and as the three of them created medicines together, she enjoyed watching their natural rapport. In order to allow the men to make love with one another, Joan had taken some time in the chapel so they could be alone. She was glad that Michael did not feel he had to hide his love from her, and they were able to have their special time in spite of her presence.

She did, however, experience a small twinge of jealousy about their freedom to be inside of one another. She would love to be with Thea like that, and she wondered whether Thea longed for it too in spite of how diligently Joan worked to give her every kind of pleasure. Yet Thea never touched Joan's phallus with her hand; she only pressed herself against it through Joan's clothing. So Joan had faith that the woman must be satisfied, or else she would have given into temptation by now and tried to get Joan to enter her in spite of the risk of ending up with child.

After the men had shared their love, Michael called Joan back to the kitchen where they ate a simple meal of bread and cheese before Barak returned to the monastery. Barak did not know Joan had been born a female and, after he had gone, Michael told her that the monk had been curious as to whether he and Joan had been in a relationship. Michael had assured him that they were just friends, but Barak had found it difficult to believe that Michael would have been able to resist such a handsome man with whom he had such a close friendship. Joan giggled a little. She never really thought of herself in terms of her looks. She was satisfied that when she saw her reflection it was a male face that looked back rather than a female one. Thea often told her she was handsome, but she had no sense of that being something that other people might think as well. She was flattered. "Did you manage to persuade him in the end that we were not in love?"

"Yes. He wasn't angry just a little worried."

"I am glad you reassured him."

"Do you miss what we do?" he asked softly.

Joan looked at him carefully, unsure about why he would ask. "Do you mean do I miss touching you or do I miss touching a man?"

"Both..."

"I miss our closeness, and I am glad that we have snuggled together in your bed whilst I have been here. I have also missed holding your phallus and pretending it was mine. But I do not feel the need to be with a man. I never think of wanting a phallus inside of me. More than anything, I wish the one that I have was real so I could be inside of Thea and also so I would not have to guard my life so secretly in order to live as a scholar and priest. This time up here has made me realise how much effort I put into living every day so I remain undetected. Hidden away from the eyes of the world here with you, the only person in my life who knows all my secrets, makes me feel light and featherlike. I see clearly that I live every day in a state of constant tension, and it feels good to finally relax."

Michael smiled at her sympathetically. "Have you ever regretted your decision to adopt this life? Do you ever long to live as a woman and have children?"

Joan felt sadness then as she remembered Maria's sweet little face smiling up at her in trust. "I never for one moment have regretted becoming a man, but if I could have married Thea and adopted Maria and her brother as my own kin, I would have done so. That I am certain of."

*

Joan thoroughly enjoyed her visit with Michael and as she had done the last time she'd been there two years previously, she worked tirelessly alongside him to create a stockpile of medicines for both the lepers and the parish at large. When they tended the lepers, she was not as frightened as before and, like him, was keen to understand more about their condition and how it might be aided through innovative concoctions of herbs.

She loved being with her friend, but missed Thea immensely, and when her time at his parish was over, she was looking forward to going home to the woman. She would always feel bereft at Michael's absence in her everyday life but knowing he was happier now made it easier to separate from him this time. So long as he had Barak then his life in the mountains would be one that he could bear.

Nevertheless, when it came time to climb in the cart on her final morning, it was not without shedding tears that she left him behind. "I love you so much, my beautiful friend," she said, sorrowfully.

"And I love you the same, Pickle," he replied using his favourite term of endearment towards her. "I will visit you in Athens this time next year, I promise."

CHAPTER 31

On seeing Thea for the first time after returning from her visit to Michael, Joan literally devoured the woman. Thea was also hungry for Joan's touch and, even after an hour of being pleasured with fingers and tongue, she asked for yet more. She simply did not want Joan to stop. Nor did Joan. She had literally ached for the feel and taste of her lover whilst away, and it gave her nothing but unadulterated joy to make Thea shudder and moan time after time.

"When we meet tonight, I want you to do that all over again," Thea giggled, as they gathered themselves together to start their working day.

"That would be my pleasure," Joan replied, pulling her in for another kiss. "I can think of several other things I want to do to you in addition."

Thea smiled cheekily. "Are you sure you can't fit one of them in now?"

Joan knew it would make her late for the Friday Public Lecture in the Great Hall, but she just could not resist. She pulled up Thea's dress again and plunged her fingers into the woman's wetness and this time as well as penetrating her from the front, she gently pushed a finger inside her anus too. At first, Thea looked at her in shock but then, as her body accepted Joan inside of her, her expression changed from one of distress to one of deep and greedy desire. It had not occurred to Joan to try entering her lover in this way before, but thoughts of how Michael and Barak made love had made her wonder whether a woman might also feel pleasure from it, and clearly she could. Thea's groans of satisfaction were deep and primal, and rather than shutting her eyes as she was taken, her gaze bored deep into Joan's right up until her crescendo when she finally lost control and threw back her head screaming.

Afterwards, Thea was so overwhelmed that her legs were shaking and she could not stand. Joan, not caring anymore how late she would be for her obligations, held her lover tightly until she was recovered enough to walk.

"Are you sated now, my love?" she asked, with a sly grin.

Thea pushed her in jest, laughing. "No! It didn't work. You need more practice."

At this Joan picked her up playfully and spun her around. "You have become altogether far too cheeky, young lady!"

"Then perhaps you'd better spank me later as well..." Thea replied, as Joan put her down.

For once Joan was speechless but then as she imagined exposing Thea's buttocks across her lap and playfully slapping the rounded cheeks with her hand, she found herself smirking. "Yes. I can see the only way is to punish you. You are a very naughty girl."

"You'll have to catch me first," Thea cried, racing up the path.

Joan, full of delight, sprinted after her lover and on reaching her, grabbed her roughly and took her by the mouth.

"Yes. You are a very naughty girl indeed," she stated, as she let the woman go again.

Thea nodded, with a smile which also had a serious edge and Joan knew that this moment, along with the way she had penetrated her earlier, marked a new phase in their lovemaking.

When they bid each other goodbye at their usual spot in the trees, Joan watched the waggle of Thea's buttocks as she walked away down the path. She thought of what Michael was able to do to Barak and imagined how wonderful it would be to thrust herself into Thea from behind as well as from the front. There were not many things that she felt that she missed out on in her life, and she knew that she made Thea happy, but sometimes her own longings were unbearable. Thea looked back, giving Joan one last wave before disappearing altogether. Joan then found herself going back into a thicker area of trees where she rubbed her phallus ferociously with her right hand whilst pleasuring the tiny mound inside her flesh with the left, all the time imagining entering Thea from behind.

She reached the Public Lecture just as Benedict had begun speaking, so slipped in and sat at the back. However, noticing her return, several of the visitors turned around and greeted her enthusiastically, and Father Nikolis had to request silence in the hall. This made things worse because the men at the front then looked toward the back to see what had caused the commotion, and before she knew it, the whole room was clapping in celebration of her return.

Joan's gaze met Benedict's for just a short moment, but it was enough to see he was consumed with anger and his hatred of her had just rekindled tenfold. Her spirits sank. He had not seriously goaded her since Maria's murder but instead simply avoided her as much as she avoided him except during her lectures where he challenged her as a matter of course. But this, she knew, would be too much for him to bear. Especially since she had already heard from Father Nikolis when she reached home last night that the numbers attending the Public Lectures in her absence had more than halved.

It took several minutes for the noise in the hall to calm down and the men to turn their attention back to Benedict's carefully prepared words. As always, the subject the serious young priest lectured on was totally in line with Church orthodoxy and in itself should not have sounded so hideous but, unfortunately, it did. His focus related to the idea of the inherent sinfulness of man—a topic that he had discussed many times before from different angles. Today, he was discussing how St. Augustine had realised that his life as a sexual being was not compatible with his Christian faith, and on renouncing Manichaeism and embracing the form of Christianity endorsed by the Emperors of Rome, Augustine had also broken up with both of his concubines.

There was nothing unusual in Benedict's claim that St. Augustine endorsed the view of St. Paul that it is better to be celibate and concentrate on God than marry. But Benedict failed to note that St. Paul had also believed that Jesus would return in *his* own lifetime and that the end of the world was nigh, making the evangelisation of all around a matter of utmost urgency. Thus, if a man had strength to devote himself wholly to God and the salvation of both Gentile and Jew, then he should do so. However, St. Paul had included the caveat that someone who did not have the strength to contain his urges should marry, so he could express those urges in a sanctified union, without falling into sin.

What made St. Augustine's teachings more severe, and in essence more negative, was that he thought the act of copulation itself was indicative of the corrupt nature of man for it was part of God's punishment for the Fall of Adam and Eve as recounted in Genesis. Augustine believed that, even in the confines of marriage, such a union between man and woman should only take place with intention of procreation. The sainted scholar believed that the bearing of children could be God's only purpose for allowing copulation at all. Although Augustine admitted that marriage served to aid men in confining their urges, he discouraged men from seeking any pleasure or joy from it.

However, St. Augustine's views on this matter were not espoused by everyone within Christendom. Many felt that it was unrealistic that a man should not enjoy union with his wife and did not believe the pleasures of marriage were sinful. In today's lecture, Benedict sided with St. Augustine's view, arguing that it was an ungodly pleasure and therefore wrong. This was not an astute manoeuvre for a priest who wanted to gain popularity with a crowd, for of the scores of men present from the city, only a handful were unmarried. As her rival lectured on the matter, Joan noted that the audience of men shuffled in their seats, looking at their feet or fiddling with their hands. Joan found herself thinking *Only a man that has never known the joy of woman could stand up there and preach something so utterly ridiculous.* The whole session was painful to witness, and the only people clapping in genuine praise at the end were the other lecturers and students of the seminary; the men of the city were less than half-hearted in their response.

What made matters worse was that when it was Joan's turn to speak, having slipped in late, she had to walk up the centre aisle from the back of the hall to the front, and as she did so the crowd began cheering with excitement. Once again, Benedict was white with humiliation and rage.

Joan, unbeknownst to her when she had prepared the lecture during her last few days with Michael at his parish, had written about the beauty of human love as God's gift to all of us. Inspired by Michael's belief that experiencing the joy of loving friends and falling in love with a lover made the many sufferings of this world worthwhile, her lecture was a celebration.

The men of Athens hung on to her every word, and as she read 1 Corinthians 13 to close her session they were transfixed by her.

Though I speak with the tongues of
men and of angels, and have not

love, I am become as sounding brass, or a tinkling cymbal. And though I have the gift of prophecy, and understand all mysteries, and all knowledge; and though I have all faith, so that I could remove mountains, and have not love, I am nothing. And though I bestow all my goods to feed the poor, and though I give my body to be burned, and have not love, it profiteth me nothing. Love suffereth long, and is kind; love envieth not; love vaunteth not itself, is not puffed up, Doth not behave itself unseemly, seeketh not her own, is not easily provoked, thinketh no evil; Rejoiceth not in iniquity, but rejoiceth in the truth; Beareth all things, believeth all things, hopeth all things, endureth all things. Love never faileth: but whether there be prophecies, they shall fail; whether there be tongues, they shall cease; whether there be knowledge, it shall vanish away. For we know in part, and we prophesy in part. But when that which is perfect is come, then that which is in part shall be done away. When I was a child, I spake as a child, I understood as a child, I thought as a child: but when I became a man, I put away childish things. For now we see through a glass, darkly; but then face to face: now I know in part; but then shall I know even as also I am known. And now abideth faith, hope, love, these three; but the greatest of these is love.

On finishing, the resounding applause bounced off the walls, and men rose to their feet and went over to shake her hand. As Joan looked to her left, she saw Benedict not white now, but purple, glaring at her one last time before turning and disappearing out of the hall.

*

It was a few days later that Benedict reaped his revenge. Joan knew it would come because his humiliation had been so crippling during the lecture and that there would be no way he could stop himself. As a result, she had been extra vigilant. Although she knew she could defeat him in a violent attack as she had two years previously when she had broken his nose, she still worried that he could catch her unawares, thus gaining the upper hand. What he did instead, was infinitely more flagitious and malevolent.

As Joan made her usual visit to the murdered child's place of rest, she knew something was wrong immediately for she could not see the wings of the cherub that guarded the top of the tombstone. As she neared, she realised that the entire grave had been smashed to pieces. Joan did not need to seek proof or witnesses to know it was Benedict who had done this. There was no one else in the entire world who would want to. If it had been an act of mindless destruction from a gang of wayward youths, or the work of a madman, then other graves would have been targeted as well and the damage done to it not so severe. Maria's grave had not been grandiose or conspicuous—just a small cherub carved and mounted on the headstone. Only someone who particularly wanted to visit it, would even notice its existence. It had been simple compared with the elaborate statues of saints and seraphs scattered throughout the rest of cemetery. Yet, it was the only statue to have been damaged, and it had been repeatedly assaulted with a heavy object until shattered beyond repair.

Joan was completely devastated—not just by the material ruination, but by the defilement of the dead girl's memory as well. It would have been cleaner for Benedict to attack her with a knife than desecrate the grave of a violated and murdered child. It was a level of cruelty that she had not believed possible, even of him.

She allowed herself to cry, not loudly in a way that would be heard from someone passing, but enough for the absolute horror and wretchedness she felt at the heinous act to be expressed. She refused to look up and around, for she knew that somewhere from a hidden vantage point, Benedict would be watching her devastation and revelling in it.

Joan remained there throughout evening Mass, unable to quash the misery she felt for both herself and the memory of the child she had loved so very deeply. When the service had finished, she went to see Father Nikolis to inform him of her discovery, but she was not in a position to accuse Benedict for there was absolutely no evidence that it was he.

As expected, Father Nikolis' hypothesis was one involving the Children of the Bridge themselves. Saying the only scenario that made sense was that one of them who had disliked Maria had destroyed the grave out of spite. There was no way Joan could accuse a fellow priest of such a crime. Such sacrilege was unthinkable for an ordained man, and it would be the darkness of Joan's own heart that would be called into question. *That's why he did it,* Joan thought. *He knew he could not damage me through physical attack, and he knew that even though he might argue that he would never win a theological debate or sway the crowd in his favour, so he attacked what I most cared about instead.*

Joan felt sick to the stomach. *How is it that such darkness can masquerade as light?*

CHAPTER 32

Joan did not give Benedict any indication that she knew it was he who had committed the malevolent act of desecrating Maria's grave. She did not want to give him the satisfaction of acknowledging his power to destroy that which she held most precious.

After reporting the incident to Father Nikolis, the only person she'd mentioned it to, apart from Thea, was Father Stefanos. Joan had not known how to explain to him what had happened, and on seeing it, tears had streamed down his cheeks, once again. He had not pressed her for an explanation only stated, "Is there no end to the horrors that one small child can be subjected to? How is it that such evil can be perpetrated against an innocent in death as well as life?" Then, he had gone back to his cell and remained there for two days before returning to his duties.

Thea had been totally irate on Joan's behalf, as well as being horrified by the vile action in itself. Over the time they had been together, Joan had talked a little about Benedict's hatred and jealousy towards her, but generally avoided it, not wanting it to pollute their beautiful time together. But in this instance, she had been so wounded by the attack she had needed to tell her lover exactly what had happened and why. Thea had held and soothed her, reassuring Joan that none of this was of her own making. She'd also argued that Joan should not lessen her achievements in order to fend off more attacks, for this was exactly what Benedict wanted, and doing so really would mean that evil was victorious.

On the surface, things soon returned to normal after Benedict's abhorrent act of destruction. Joan continued on with her duties, the headstone was replaced, this time with no cherub but with just a small engraved slab, and Joan went there every evening before Mass in order to pay her respects as she always had done. However, since the attack, Joan had been extra careful with anything that was important or sacred to her. She now made sure that parchments containing lectures she was working on were hidden in her cell which she double checked was locked, and she did not leave anything of personal value in her classroom or at her desk in the library in case Benedict were to deface or steal it. She was also even more elaborate in her varied routes to and from the spot in the woods where she met Thea each morning and night.

Joan did make one large change that she hoped, in time, would prevent further outpourings of Benedict's resentment. She could not allow the possibility of another event to so clearly demonstrate the crowd's preference for her over him, as this would only cause more attacks on her personage. Because she was in charge of timetabling the Public Lectures, Joan decided to change their structure so that she and Benedict would speak on alternate weeks, instead of both speaking every week in the same session along with those others inclined to give talks.

Father Nikolis was not pleased with this decision because the crowds 'Father John' drew not only brought prestige to the Seminary Of St Joseph but also large donations to the upkeep of the building which needed work. Joan argued that in the end it would be better because she would be able to lecture for longer and answer more questions before they ran out of time, so potential visitors from further afield would be more inclined to make a special journey to see her, but Father Nikolis was not really convinced.

Within a few weeks, it was clear that Joan's solution had not cured the problem of Benedict's lack of popularity compared to hers. It simply illuminated it in a different manner. Benedict was no longer upstaged by her in front of a giant crowd, but instead, the number of audience was reduced by more than a half on the weeks when he was the main speaker. To make matters worse, because her lectures now had to be longer and in more depth, Joan put extra time and effort into their preparation, which resulted in a sharpening of her knowledge along with her confidence and charisma. As a consequence, her fame and popularity grew to the point where there were not enough chairs for men to sit in on the weeks when she lectured. Yet during Benedict's weeks the rows at the back of the hall were largely empty.

During the eight years Joan had been living at the seminary, she had become an expert in avoiding being alone with Benedict in her day to day life, and as a result of this increase in her popularity, she honed her avoidance skills even further. He had no reason to visit the herb kitchen or the farm, and it would be too conspicuous for him to do so. The classrooms and corridors were always bustling with students and staff at times when they were both present, as were the dining hall, the chapel and the library. At most, he managed to whisper the occasional abusive remark in her ear when they were caught up in a crowd.

Joan also spent more time outside of the institution, dealing with matters of the city. A few weeks after Benedict's destruction of Maria's grave, the Council Of Athens passed a motion that a special mission should be created to care for those in the city who were mad or confused. As Joan had envisioned, it would be a cross between a hospice and a jail, where those being looked after would have a safe, clean place to live out their lives but would be locked away from the general populace. The nuns who would run it would have their own quarters away from where the insane themselves lived, so they could participate in the other aspects of leading a sacred life uninterrupted by the inmates. Joan still worried about the motives of those who might join such a mission, but because it would be a women's institution rather than a men's, she chose to believe that it would do more good than harm. The chance of the inmates being violated would be significantly reduced since women, in general, seemed less prone to violence. And she had to trust that not all who claimed to have a vocation with the vulnerable were disguising mal intent.

The Bishop of Athens had been against the idea at first, but he liked Joan and as a result, she had persuaded him of its merits. As well as the dreadful incident with Maria, over the last decade whilst the

Bishop had been in office, there had been several random murders without any obvious motives, and it had often been speculated that the perpetrators could as easily be mad as bad. And although those living in the ruins of the Theatre Of Dionysus were generally too afraid to enter the populated areas of the city by day lest they were attacked by stone or shovel, it was suspected that they were largely responsible for thefts that took place at night. This mission to lock them away with compassion, felt kind and Christian to the alternative of letting them rot in an underground dungeon or locking them up in a 'Fool's Tower' and feeding them on pig swill as was the practice in some other cities. Each inmate would have his or her own cell with a barred but large window so it was not dark like a prison, a comfortable bed and stone latrine leading directly to a running sewer underneath. The doors of the cells would be made of iron bars rather than solid wood, which as well as being more secure, gave prisoners the opportunity to see out into the corridor and chat to those in the cells opposite if they chose, and at the same time enabled the nuns to see in and not be greeted by anything unexpected when they entered. The inmates would be given clean food and fresh water, and if they became physically ill, their ailments would be treated with care.

The cost of the building was massive, but Joan had persuaded the Council that it was worth the price for the greater benefits it would bring to the city, particularly in lowering the crime rate. Once the decision to go ahead had been passed, the Council had even asked Joan to meet regularly with the architect to base his design of the complex on the rough sketches she had put together in order to clarify her vision during discussions. The architect was inspired by Joan's concept and the only ideas he added, other than his own artistry, were to build the external walls much higher, followed by an outer ring of sharp rocks to make jumping from them lethal, so that escape would be practically impossible and even trying undesirable. He also asserted that if the internal grounds were large enough for inmates to enjoy a satisfying walk, it would minimise their wish to be free.

Joan felt proud of her achievement and could now see that when used in a way that served others, her intelligence and status as an academic was as much a moral gift as an intellectual one. She knew, however, that if she had not continued to visit those in need throughout the city and learned of its people and their problems, she would never have gained such sway in practical matters, in spite of the power of her brain and the popularity of her lectures. Now, at just twenty-one years of age, Joan was one of the Council Of Athens' most influential participants.

CHAPTER 33

It had been nearly a year since Joan had visited Michael for the second time at his parish, and she was excited that he would be coming to visit her at the seminary again in less than two weeks time. She was particularly looking forward to showing him the new mission being built to house the insane which was now under construction in an area just east of the old city walls. Michael's letters had remained sparse in detail but she could tell from their tone that he was still much happier with his life serving the leper colony now that Brother Barak was by his side. Joan thought of him often and missed him in her day to day life, but was used to it now and did not worry so much about him.

Mostly, Joan was enjoying her life again, in spite of Michael's continued absence, Benedict's hatred and the crisis of faith she had undergone after Maria's murder. Whenever she doubted the reason for the sufferings of the world, she would meditate before the figure of Christ Crucified and know that hers was a suffering God too. She kept faith that in the afterlife she would understand why it was indeed necessary for evil to prevail at times unhindered. Joan also endeavored to be filled to the brim with the Holy Spirit each day, for when she failed to make this a priority, both fear and doubt crept into almost every area of her life and so much joy was lost.

Joan only led Evening Mass once a fortnight, but when she did, several of the participants stayed behind to receive the Holy Spirit through her laying on of hands. She found that many of the boys and men asked for physical healing along with spiritual renewal, and she received increasing numbers of reports that they had been made well from her touch. This worried her, because she did not believe that the healing came from her. She was but a conduit for God's Spirit, and anyone with sufficient knowledge and faith could perform the same function if they practiced being filled up by the Holy Spirit every day as she did. It was not she who healed people—it was God and God alone. It was for this reason that she did not encourage those who came to her public lectures to stay behind and ask for healing there. Instead, she insisted that they request it of her after Mass and reminded them that Father Nikolis along with many of the other priests could perform it just as easily. However, still the requests came and the number she blessed increased each time she took the service, until it became obvious yet again that she was accumulating followers.

This last year, her relationship with Thea had grown deeper than ever and connecting with the woman twice a day was as necessary to her as being filled up by God's spirit. On the rare occasion they missed their time together, she felt severed and without direction. Their lovemaking had also not diminished in its frequency or power. Sometimes it was soft and gentle, expressive of their deep love and appreciation of one another and at other times, it was ferociously passionate or playful depending on their mood. It did not matter to Joan which manifestation occurred so long as they were together and in love. God was the air that she breathed, Thea was the water she drank and her studies were the food that she ate. All were vital and integral to her survival.

Thea could now read as well as a first year seminarian, and Joan regularly brought her books from the library about the Greek Philosophers and Greek History, which she reveled in learning. Each day as they walked to and from the middle of the woods to the lake, they would discuss what she was reading and sometimes argue about it either seriously or in jest. Joan loved hearing Thea's views on all that she read, and she always trusted that the woman would be totally honest about her thoughts. Joan also found it helpful to be able to talk about theological issues with someone who did not have a rigid idea of the boundaries of acceptable belief. Even at this seminary, which discussed a broad range of views, students and staff were careful not to say anything that could lead them into being seen as unfaithful or a heretic. Alternate ideas to the doctrine of Rome were discussed thoroughly but with the expectation that Roman Christianity always won the debate. The only ideas where it was seen as acceptable for students and staff to hold a range of differing opinions were ones that were ongoing sources of discussion within the faith itself.

As Joan walked to the woods to meet Thea that evening, she found herself tingling, as always, at the prospect of what was to come. It had been a warm day, and she had been out in the city for most of the afternoon, feeding the children at the bridge and then tending a homeless man with a wounded leg. She looked forward to losing herself in the arms of passion now that her duties to those in need were done.

As always, when they reached their secret sanctuary nestled in the rocks, Joan was eager to strip Thea straight away. Being late summer the weather was still hot, and Joan regretted that they could not jump naked into the enticing aquamarine lake to play and make love together there too. However, she would not let such a small loss ruin her evening and as she opened Thea's legs and took her with her mouth she felt nothing but pure, unadulterated pleasure. Joan expertly and greedily explored Thea's cunte with her tongue before focusing on the nub that lay at the centre and massaging it rhythmically in circles, which always made the woman moan with delight. Joan enjoyed transporting Thea to the high plateau of pleasure that lay tantalizingly close to full climax—but not quite. Thea loved to be teased like this and could go on for almost an hour sighing, moaning and demanding Joan never stop. Liquid poured into Joan's mouth and she drank greedily, basking in the pleasure she was giving. Then, when she sensed that the woman was able to take no more, she inserted two fingers deep inside of her and began thrusting, her tongue changing from gentle circles to harder movements up and down. Thea began screaming as she always did, and Joan was overwhelmed with joy as the woman became louder and louder. But suddenly the scream turned to one of horror, and Thea violently pushed her away looking terrified.

"What is it, Thea?" Joan cried. "Have I hurt you?"

Thea was no longer looking at Joan but instead anxiously reaching for her dress. It was then that Joan heard a cough. Still disorientated from the sudden change in Thea's behaviour, she looked around to try to understand what was going on, and that was when the full horror of her situation hit her. Father Nikolis was staring down at her looking aghast, with Benedict standing a step back to his left, smirking triumphantly for having caught her in such a compromising position. Mortified at being discovered, Joan instinctively wiped her mouth with her sleeve to hide what she had been doing, only to reveal it further by the wet patch left on the garment. She turned purple from shame and did not know where to look.

"I am sorry you had to witness this filthy affair, Father Nikolis," spoke Benedict sternly, hiding his glee as he stepped parallel with the seminary head. "But you said you would not believe it unless you saw it with your own eyes, and now you have. I was shocked by it myself, as you know, and simply could not let it pass, given this man is a leader amongst us and should be beyond reproach."

Father Nikolis nodded his agreement. "Thank you, Father Benedict. You were right to inform me... Father John, I suggest you gather yourself together. I will see you in my office before sundown. As for you, young woman," he said, looking at Thea in disgust. "I suggest you return to your cottage and start packing your things to leave."

Thea, who had moved further back into the rocks, nodded but did not look him in the eye. Joan stood there, heart pounding in her chest, terrified at what would happen next. *Will I be disrobed and cast out? Will I be sent away to tend a leper colony in the middle of nowhere—even worse than the one where Michael lives?* The situation was horrific.

At this, Father Nikolis turned on his heel, followed by Benedict, who was trying hard to look appalled even though he clearly wanted to laugh from victory. Joan gazed after them in open-mouthed shock.

Once they were out of sight, Thea put a hand on Joan's arm, but Joan pushed her away violently. "Get off me, woman!" she shouted angrily, jumping backwards at the same time to increase the distance between them.

Thea looked totally aghast at Joan's reaction and rubbed her arm from where she'd shoved her. Joan knew she should apologise but was now so out of control that instead she raced off in the direction of the seminary to beg Father Nikolis to let her remain a priest.

When she entered Father Nikolis' office a few minutes later, he did not rise from his chair and stared at her sternly before speaking. "Father John. I need not inform you that you have become ensnared by sin."

Joan could not maintain eye contact and looked down at the floor, ashamed. In spite of his faults, she still loved and respected this man, and seeing that he'd lost his respect for her, wounded her to the core.

"Yet, at the same time," he continued, "it does not surprise me that one with your extraordinary intellectual energy and talent would not have a masculine urge to match. The Devil is a woman and never hesitates to tempt us, and I can see that you have fallen into her clutches."

Joan was so affronted by the sentiment that she could not contain herself. "Thea is not a tool of Lucifer, Father Nikolis, and I won't have that charge made against her. Or her job put at risk! This is entirely my fault and none of it hers. If anything, it was I who was used by the Devil. For I was the one who took a vow of celibacy that I was then unable to keep and ended up seducing her. None of this was of her making."

"Father John! Do you think you are the first of my staff to break his vow of celibacy? I have seen the ways of women bewitch more than one man of God, and each of them has said it was not her fault. It's all part of Satan's temptation of us to use women to beguile us and make us stray from God's path."

Joan still appalled, struggled to keep her breath, before finally finding words. "I beg of you, Father Nikolis. Please do not punish her. I am the one to blame. She is *not* a tool of Satan. It is I—I have caused this. I will accept any punishment you see fit for me, but I cannot stand by and let you ruin her life because of my sins."

Father Nikolis did not respond at first but instead looked her up and down trying to work out, she supposed, whether she was telling the truth or just being protective of her paramour.

"Do you want to continue on as a priest, Father John?" he finally asked, solemnly.

"But of course, Father!" she almost shouted, shocked that he'd even ask that.

"Then you have two choices: either you must relinquish your vow of celibacy and marry this girl immediately and take a parish or give her up altogether and she will be dismissed from her position as washerwoman. I will not allow you to remain teaching here if she is present. You cannot carry on like this in sin, and if she stays, you will only become ensnared again which will endanger your mortal soul and bring shame upon the entire seminary."

Joan looked at him anxiously, still distressed at the position she was in and even more fearful for Thea. "I will marry her then, Father," she said flat voice, lowering her eyes to the ground again.

"There is also a third option," he then stated, which made Joan look up at him once more.

"I was going to wait until tomorrow before I told you this, but perhaps you should know now as it may help you with your decision... Rome has gotten wind of your fine reputation. They have asked for you to become Head of the Greek School there."

For the second time that evening, Joan stared at him open mouthed, until finally she repeated, "Rome?"

"Yes, Father John. Rome. You would mingle with the greatest theological minds in Christendom— including the Pope himself."

"And they want me?"

"Yes."

"When?"

"Immediately."

Joan could not believe what she was hearing. To become the head of the Greek School in Rome was an honour she had not even hoped she might attain. It was one of the most prestigious academic positions in the Empire and more than one Head of School had gone on to be made a Cardinal. Suddenly a whole world she had never considered had been offered her on a plate; just at the point when she'd thought she might lose everything. She looked across at Father Nikolis who still appeared stern and disappointed.

"And would I be able to go as a married priest or is it a celibate institution like this one?"

"As far as I know, there is no expectation of you being celibate, but the majority of the staff at the school will be. And as you know, the chances of you being given the full respect you deserve and rising yet higher than that post, will be very slim indeed if you marry."

"By when do I need to make a decision?" she asked, already knowing what she wanted to do.

"Think it over for the next two days and then come to me with your decision. But do not let yourself be swayed again by sin whilst you deliberate. I will allow the washerwoman to stay if you leave to take the position."

"Yes, Father."

Joan nodded in obedience one more time and then left the room trying to contain her surprise.

When she reached the bottom of the stairwell, Benedict was waiting for her with another smirk of satisfaction on his face. On seeing his expression she could do nothing but burst out laughing, and he looked like she had slapped him hard across both cheeks as a result.

CHAPTER 34

"I am *not* going to Rome, John and that's final!" stated Thea, for the third time during their conversation.

It was the following morning and they were at their usual place by the lake but with no intention of making love. Thea had been furious with Joan for pushing her last night and even angrier at the way Joan had run off. It had taken many apologies for the woman to calm down and Joan felt terrible that she had hurt her love both physically and emotionally.

"But I do not understand why you won't come with me, Thea. I can relinquish my vow and we could be married. We could start a new life together there as man and wife."

"The level of your audacity is truly astounding!" snapped Thea angrily.

"I'm not being audacious. I love you and I want us to be happy together…"

"And exactly what am *I* supposed to do in Rome, whilst you're swanning around with Cardinals and the Pope? I'll be stuck inside alone with no one to talk to and nowhere to go. I can't even speak the language."

"But we will be in the Greek School, Thea. Of course you'll have people to talk to. And you'll have me with you day and night. Besides, I could teach you Latin in no time at all."

"I barely see you *here*, as it is. I know you. Once you get there, they'll all want a piece of you, and you'll love every moment of it. I'd be lucky if I saw you for an hour a day. At least here I have my job and my family to keep me occupied. In Rome I would have no one and nothing!"

"But I'm sure you'll make friends with other women at the school."

"Do you even know if there *are* any other women at the school? What if all the other priests made a vow of celibacy like you did? What if I'm the only one there? I'll go mad."

"But I love you and I'd miss you... We could start a family of our own, then you wouldn't be lonely..."

The slap across her face was a hard one, and Joan gasped, stunned by the action.

"How *dare* you?" barked Thea angrily.

"What?" asked Joan, alarm rising within her.

"How dare you insult me like this?"

"Thea, what do you mean? Why am I insulting you?"

"Do you really have such contempt for my intelligence that you think I don't know?"

Joan did not want to embrace what she feared was coming and resisted it with all of her mind. "Know what?" she almost whispered.

Thea began shouting even louder and gesticulating angrily. "You are astonishing! You really think I'm stupid, don't you?"

"Thea, what's the matter with you? You know I don't think that. You're the most intelligent woman I've ever met…"

"Yes. 'The most intelligent *woman*!'" she mimicked, in an ironic tone.

Joan's head began pounding. *No, surely she hasn't worked it out…?*

"Am I even more intelligent than you then?"

"What are you talking about? I'm not a…" But it was useless, there was no point denying it, she could tell from Thea's face that the woman had no doubt whatsoever. "I…When…How on earth did you know?"

At this, Thea threw her head back and laughed, making Joan feel ridiculous and totally exposed.

"You really are the most arrogant human being I have ever met! How could you possibly have believed all this time that I did not know?"

"But how? We never… Could you not feel…?"

"Could I not feel what?" Thea spoke disdainfully. "The lump you keep in your underwear to convince the world that you're a man. John—or whatever your real name is—you have kissed and touched me in every way possible for three years. Did it never occur to you that the softness of your lips and the smell of your skin might just give you away?"

"But I have a moustache—surely that would have been enough?"

"So have most of my aunties! It would take more than a few blonde hairs on your upper lip to convince me you are male."

Joan did not know what to say. She felt humiliated and like a child. She looked at Thea despairingly. Thea continued to stare at her crossly for a moment but then suddenly her expression softened. "Besides, no man, however devoted to God, would give so much pleasure and ask for so little in return. You are woman through and through, John, whether you want to be or not!"

At this Joan felt totally defeated and collapsed to the ground and buried her head in her hands, stifling the tears that inevitably came from the assault. Within moments, Thea's arms were wrapped around her, rocking her as she cried.

"I'm sorry, Thea. I…"

"Shh…I love you my beautiful woman-man. Now tell me everything from the very beginning."

*

For the next few hours Joan told Thea her story from start to finish in every detail. Each decision she had made and why, was recounted, as were the good times and the bad. Thea listened with little interruption, only occasionally asking questions for clarity. When she was finished telling her story, Joan looked at her and asked, "Do you think it was wrong of me?"

"No!" said Thea, with conviction. "I loved you before I knew why you had chosen this and now I know your story, I love you even more. What you have done is not wrong. You have sacrificed almost everything for a life of devotion to God. How could that be sinful?"

"But still you won't come with me to Rome?"

"No, because if I do, I would be isolated and lonely and grow to resent you. Our love would be spoiled, and I will not do that to us."

"Then let's get married here, and I'll take a parish as near to your home as they will let me."

"No, because then you will not be happy in your work and you will begin to resent me. Go to Rome, John, and be a great scholar. It is what you were born for."

"But I cannot live without you!"

"Yes, you can and you will. You will always have my love, and I know I will always have yours."

"But how will you cope here all alone?"

"I will have my memories, my family and my job."

"Can we make love again before I go?"

"Yes, but not here. Tonight I want you to come to my cottage and spend the night. I think I should make love in a bed at least once in my life…"

*

Joan did not fear being spotted going to Thea's cottage, as the worst had already indeed happened. Nonetheless she was careful not to flaunt it and kept to the shadows.

Once the door was shut, Thea who must have been aching to touch her for so very long, tore Joan's robes from her body. Joan, scared of displaying her womanhood, tried to fight it at first, but Thea would not relent, working the knot of Joan's binding and unwinding it without delay. Then she stood gazing at

Joan's bare breasts. Joan stared down at them too. She only took off the binding to wash and even then tried to avoid looking at them lest she acknowledge they were really hers. She felt totally exposed, and it was terrifying.

Then Thea's attention turned to Joan's braies, and she pulled them down to reveal the phallus that remained there held expertly by the leather harness that had been carefully stitched by Amadeus Reichenbach so many years before. Thea gasped and then giggled before untying it and throwing it onto a chair. Joan didn't know whether her rush of alarm came from her further exposure or the fact that Thea had shown such disrespect for the very thing that made her feel like a man. But there was not much time to react, for Thea was hungry and took Joan's mouth with her own and then expertly manoeuvred them to the bed where she pushed Joan down and proceeded to explore every inch of her body with her hands.

"You are beautiful," Thea whispered, before taking a breast in her mouth. Joan felt herself going crimson and then a wave of sheer pleasure rushed through her as Thea sucked tightly at her nipple. "Oh, my Lord!" she exclaimed, relinquishing the last of her control. Thea must have sensed that this was her moment and plunged her fingers inside Joan who was already soaked with desire. The penetration was deep and powerful and Joan knew it had broken her hymen. Yet, although there was some pain, the pleasure outweighed it ten times over, and she found herself pushing harder into Thea's fingers each time they thrust, until she felt like she was flying.

She had only ever pleasured herself externally whilst holding onto her phallus. It had been enough until now, but to be given such pleasure deep within was a gift of such unbridled ecstasy, that she did not know how she would exist without it any longer.

"This is what you've given me, my love. So many times. So unselfishly," whispered Thea, as Joan travelled upwards to even greater planes of fulfilment. "You have no idea how I've longed to return this pleasure."

Joan opened her eyes and looked deep into Thea's. "Thank you!" she cried, as her body finally exploded and her legs flooded from the release.

Thea held her and soothed her like a child whilst she shuddered with aftershocks. She had never felt so vulnerable yet so totally loved. Joan knew now that no matter what lay ahead, their souls would never be parted and all she needed to do was think of this moment and she would find Thea still with her.

They remained like that for over an hour, until Thea got up to fetch them some mead. As she sipped the sweet liquid, Joan found her desire rising again and sensing it, Thea removed the tankard from her hand. "Fetch your binding and camisia!" she instructed.

"But why? I thought I was staying all night."

"You are but there's something else I feel you need to do now you've finally acknowledged you are a woman."

"What?" asked Joan, feeling fear rise within her again.

Thea reached across and picked up the phallus still lying on the chair where she'd thrown it, and smiled. "Acknowledge that you are a man!"

Terrified but on fire, Joan allowed herself to be pulled from the bed whilst Thea re-bound her breasts. Then she found herself stepping into the harness, which Thea pulled tight to her buttocks. As soon as Joan saw the phallus sticking out from her erect, she was overwhelmed by a primal monster that took control of her and made her shudder with desire.

"Yes. That's it. Let him through," Thea urged, turning back towards the bed. With this permission, Joan let herself become fully John in every way she wanted to be and pushed Thea violently back to the sheets. Thea spread her legs obediently and looked deeply into his eyes. "Now take me, John. Take me deep and take me hard."

John thrust his phallus deep into Thea's saturated cunte and found himself pounding her ferociously, becoming faster and harder with each blow, spurred on by Thea's cries for more. He was flooded with raw male energy rushing through his veins and he pumped her mercilessly, feeling intoxicated with power as she screamed with climax beneath him and then went limp. He stayed inside her and pinned her body completely with his own, showing that she belonged to him and him alone. Thea reached up and kissed him tenderly on the lips, then ran her finger over the light moustache as she had so many times before. "Whenever you waver and cannot find the strength to go on with your quest, think of this and know that you are not just pretending, John."

When they finally pulled apart, John looked down at his saturated phallus and smiled at the delights it had brought them both. Thea took it and massaged it gently. John felt himself tingling again and the energy came quickly racing back. He moved to rejoin her but she shook her head "No, John. There's something else I want to give you." He had no idea what was coming next and nearly bolted when Thea started to kiss the shaft of his phallus. Then suddenly he felt Thea's thumb searching below where the leather ballokes met his body. The moment Thea found the small mound which made him female, she also engulfed his phallus with her mouth and he became all things at once, not male not female but a complete fusion of both and something far beyond that again. He climaxed within moments, and Thea smiled cheekily, knowing exactly what she had achieved. John was Joan, and Joan was John and had never felt so complete.

But it was not long before Thea had more plans for them. Expertly, she undid the harness and pulled the phallus away from view. "Now let me make you feel like a woman again," she said in a tone that was more of a command than a request.

The moment Thea's mouth made contact with her wetness, Joan felt herself become totally female. She turned soft and yielding and found herself opening her legs up wide and welcoming. Thea's tongue expertly massaged her centre and Joan experienced climax after climax like relentless waves crashing onto the shore. A never ending sea of pleasure belonged to her and she wept with gratitude for her lover who knew what she needed more than she did herself. For the first time in her life Joan cherished being a woman, knowing that she may never have such privilege again…

END OF PART 2.

Thank you very much for reading *The Legend Of Pope Joan, Part 2. Athens*. If you enjoyed this novel, please tell your friends and/or share your thoughts and reactions via Amazon, Goodreads and your social networks.

Feel free to contact me with questions or comments about my work at: daxrachel@yahoo.co.uk. And please do visit my website: www.racheldax.com.

ALSO BY RACHEL DAX

The Legend Of Pope Joan, Part 3. Rome (DUE Autumn 2014)
Having caught the attention of Pope Leo IV, Joan moves to Rome where she is appointed as his Chief Advisor. Her knowledge of medicine along with her practical care of citizens both rich and poor, soon make her one of the most popular figures in the city. On Pope Leo's death, she finds herself in contention with two powerful enemies over who should inherit the Papal Throne. Ultimately, however, it is love that proves to be the most dangerous force in her life.

After The Night (2010)
After The Night is a sweeping lesbian love story set in a British prison in 1960. When Nurse Leah Webster begins her first job at a prison hospital, little does she know that her world will be turned upside down by falling in love with Chief Officer Jean MacFarlane. But

the course of lesbian love does not always run smoothly and together Leah and Jean have to fight homophobia both within and without the prison walls.

CPSIA information can be obtained at www.ICGtesting.com
Printed in the USA
LVOW10s1630150315

430631LV00031B/1768/P